THE COWBOY WAY

THE COWBOY WAY

THE COWBOY WAY

ELMER KELTON

THORNDIKE PRESS
A part of Gale, a Cengage Company

Copyright © 2020 by Elmer Stephen Kelton Estate.
Thorndike Press, a part of Gale, a Cengage Company.

**LIBRARY OF CONGRESS CIP DATA ON FILE.
CATALOGUING IN PUBLICATION FOR THIS BOOK
IS AVAILABLE FROM THE LIBRARY OF CONGRESS.**

ISBN-13: 978-1-4328-8692-9 (hardcover alk. paper)

Published in 2021 by arrangement with Forge

Printed in Mexico
Print Number: 01   Print Year: 2021

COPYRIGHT ACKNOWLEDGMENTS

"Hewey and the Wagon Cook" originally published in *American West: Twenty New Stories from the Western Writers of America,* Forge, 2001

"Fighting for the Brand" originally published in *Texas Rangers,* September 1956, Vol. 64, No. 1

"Coward" originally published in *Ranch Romances,* January 1, 1954, Vol. 182, No. 4

"The Black Sheep" originally published in *Everywoman's,* October 1956

"A Bad Cow Market" originally published in *The Best of the West,* Doubleday, 1986

"Duster" originally published in *Farm Journal and Country Gentleman,* April 1956

"No Music for Fiddle Feet" originally published in *Ranch Romances,* August 3, 1951, Vol. 166, No. 3

"The Debt of Hardy Buckelew" originally

published in *Frontiers West,* Doubleday, 1959

"The Burial of Letty Strayhorn" originally published in *New Trails,* Doubleday, 1994

"Horse Well" originally published as "Showdown at Horse Well" in *Ranch Romances,* February 1, 1952, Vol. 170, No. 1

"Continuity" originally published in *Louis L'Amour Western Magazine,* September 1995, Vol. 2, No. 5

"Yellow Devil" originally published in *Hound Dogs and Others,* Dodd, Mead and Company, 1958

"Dry Winter" originally published in *Ranch Romances,* May 8, 1953, Vol. 178, No. 3

"The Reluctant Shepherd" originally published in *Roundup!,* La Frontera, June 2010

"That 7X Bull" originally published as "The 7X Bull" in *Texas Rangers,* July 1954, Vol. 55, No. 2

"Man on the Wagon Tongue" originally published in *They Won Their Spurs,* Ace Books, 1962

CONTENTS

CONTENTS

Hewey and the Wagon Cook

Chuckwagon cooks were expected to be contrary. It was part of their image, their defense mechanism against upstart young cowpunchers who might challenge their authority to rule their Dutch-oven kingdoms fifty or so feet in all directions from the chuckbox. Woe unto the thoughtless cowboy who rode his horse within that perimeter and kicked up dust in the "kitchen."

The custom was so deeply ingrained that not even the owner of a ranch would easily violate this divine right of kings.

Even so, there were bounds, and Hewey Calloway was convinced that Doughbelly Jackson had stepped over the line. He considered Doughbelly a despot. Worse than that, Doughbelly was not even a very good cook. He never washed his hands until *after* he finished kneading dough for the biscuits, and he often failed to pick the rocks out of his beans before he cooked them. Some of the hands said they could live with that because the rocks were occasionally softer than Doughbelly's beans anyway, and certainly softer than his biscuits.

What stuck worst in Hewey's craw, though, was Doughbelly's unnatural fondness for canned tomatoes. They went into just about everything he cooked except the coffee.

"If it wasn't for them tomatoes, he couldn't cook a lick," Hewey complained to fellow puncher Grady Welch. "If ol' C. C. Tarpley had to eat after Doughbelly for three or four days runnin', he'd fire him."

C. C. Tarpley's West Texas ranch holdings were spread for a considerable distance on both sides of the Pecos River, from the sandhills to the greasewood hardlands. They were so large that he had to keep two wagons and two roundup crews on the range at one time. Grady pointed out, "He knows. That's why he spends most all his time with the other wagon. Reason he hired Doughbelly is that he can get him for ten dollars a month cheaper than any other cook workin' out of Midland. Old C. C. is frugal."

Frugal did not seem a strong enough word. Hewey said, "Tight, is what I'd call it."

Doughbelly was by all odds the worst belly-robber it had been Hewey's misfortune to know, and Hewey had been punching cattle on one outfit or another since he was thirteen or fourteen. He had had his thirtieth birthday last February, though it was four or five days afterward that he first thought about it. It didn't matter; Doughbelly wouldn't have baked him a cake anyway. The lazy reprobate couldn't even make a decent cobbler pie if he had a washtub full of dried apples. Not that Old C. C. was likely to buy any such apples in the first place. C. C. was, as Hewey said, tight.

Grady was limping, the result of being thrown twice from a jug-headed young bronc. He said, "You ought to feel a little sympathy for Doughbelly. He ain't got a ridin' job like us."

"He gets paid more than we do."

Grady rubbed a skinned hand across a dark bruise and lacerations on the left side of his face, a present from two cows that had knocked him down and trampled him. "But he don't have near as much fun as us."

"I just think he ought to earn his extra pay, that's all."

Grady warned, "Was I you, I'd be careful what I said where Doughbelly could hear

11

me. Ringy as he is, he might throw his apron at you and tell you to do the cookin' yourself."

It wasn't that Hewey couldn't cook. He had done his share of line-camp batching, one place and another. He could throw together some pretty nice fixings, even if he said so himself. He just didn't fancy wrestling pots and pans. It was not a job a man could do a-horseback. Hewey had hired on to cowboy.

He appreciated payday like any cowpuncher, though money was not his first consideration. He had once quit a forty-dollar-a-month job to take one that paid just thirty. The difference was that the lower-paying outfit had a cook who could make red beans taste like ambrosia. A paycheck might not last more than a few hours in town, or anyway a long night, but good chuck was to be enjoyed day after day.

Hewey was tempted to draw his time and put a lot of miles between him and Doughbelly Jackson, but he was bound to the Two C's by an old cowboy ethic, an unwritten rule. It was that you don't quit an outfit in the middle of the works and leave it shorthanded. That would increase the burden of labor on friends like Grady Welch. He and Grady had known each other since they were shirttail buttons, working their way up from horse jingler to top hand. They had made a trip up the trail to Kansas together once, and they had shared the same cell in jail after a trail-end celebration that got a little too loud for the locals.

Grady was a good old boy, and it wouldn't be fair to ride off and leave him to pick up the slack. Hewey had made up his mind to stick until the works were done or he died of tomato poisoning, whichever came first.

It was the canned tomatoes that caused Doughbelly's first real blowup. Hewey found them mixed in the beans once too often and casually remarked that someday he was going to buy himself a couple of tomatoes and start riding, and he would keep riding until he reached a place where somebody asked him what to call that fruit he was carrying on his saddle.

"That's where I'll spend the rest of my days, where nobody knows what a tomato is," he said.

For some reason Hewey couldn't quite understand, Doughbelly seemed to take umbrage at that remark. He ranted at length about ignorant cowboys who didn't know fine cuisine when they tasted it. He proceeded to burn both the biscuits and the beans for the next three days. Another thing

Hewey didn't quite understand was that the rest of the cowboys seemed to blame him instead of Doughbelly.

Even Grady Welch, good compadre that he was, stayed a little cool toward Hewey until Doughbelly got back into a fair-to-middling humor.

After three days of culinary torture, those tomatoes didn't taste so bad to the rest of the hands. For Hewey, though, they had not improved a bit.

Like most outfits, the Two C's had two wagons for each camp. The chuckwagon was the most important, for it had the chuckbox from which the cook operated, and it carried most of the foodstuffs like the flour and coffee, lard and sugar, and whatever canned goods the ranch owner would consent to pay for. The second, known as the hoodlum wagon, carried cowboy bedrolls, the branding irons and other necessities. It also had a dried cowhide, known as a cooney, slung beneath its bed for collection of good dry firewood wherever it might be found along the way between camps.

Like most of the cowhands, cow boss Matthew Mullins was a little down on Hewey for getting the cook upset and causing three days' meals to be spoiled. So when it came time to move camp to the Red Mill pasture, he singled Hewey out for the least desirable job the outfit offered: helping Doughbelly load up, then driving the hoodlum wagon. Hewey bristled a little, though on reflection he decided it had been worth it all to dig Doughbelly in his well-padded ribs about those cussed tomatoes.

The rest of the hands left camp, driving the remuda in front of them. Doughbelly retired to his blankets, spread in the thin shade of a large and aged mesquite tree, to take himself a little siesta before he and Hewey hitched the teams. A little peeved at being left with all the dirty work, Hewey loaded the utensils and pitched the cowboys' bedrolls up into the hoodlum wagon. He could hear Doughbelly still snoring. He decided to steal a few minutes' shut-eye himself beneath one of the wagons.

The cowhide cooney sagged low beneath the hoodlum wagon, so Hewey crawled under the chuckwagon. His lingering resentment would not let him sleep. He lay staring up at the bottom of the wagon bed. Dry weather had shrunk the boards enough that there was a little space between them. He could see the rims of several cans.

Gradually it dawned on him that those cans held the tomatoes he had come to hate so much. And with that realization came a notion so deliciously wicked that he began laughing to himself. He took a jackknife from his pocket and opened the largest blade, testing the point of it on his thumb.

Hewey did not have much in the way of worldly possessions, but he took care of what he had. He had always been particular about keeping his knife sharp as a razor. A man never knew when he might find something that needed cutting. He poked the blade between the boards, made contact with the bottom of a can, then drove the knife upward.

The can resisted, and Hewey was afraid if he pushed any harder he might break the blade. He climbed out from beneath the wagon and quietly opened the chuckbox. From a drawer he extracted Doughbelly's heavy butcher knife and carried it back underneath. He slipped it between the boards, then pushed hard.

The sound of rending metal was loud, and he feared it might be enough to awaken Doughbelly. He paused to listen. He still heard the cook's snoring. He began moving around beneath the wagon, avoiding the streaming tomato juice as he punched can after can. When one stream turned out to be molasses, he decided he had finished the tomatoes, at least all he could reach. He wiped the blade on dry grass, then on his trousers, and put the knife back into the chuckbox.

Whistling a happy church tune he had learned at a brush-arbor camp meeting, he went about harnessing the two teams.

Doughbelly rolled his bedding, grousing all the while about some people being too joyful for their own good. Concerned that the cook might notice the leaking tomatoes and the molasses, Hewey hitched the team to the wagon for him while Doughbelly went off behind the bushes and took care of other business. He had both wagons ready to go when the cook came back.

He had to fight himself to keep from grinning like a cat stealing cream. Doughbelly stared suspiciously at him before climbing up onto the seat of the chuckwagon. "Don't you lag behind and make me have to wait for you to open the gates."

Opening gates for the wagon cook was almost as lowly a job as chopping wood and helping him wash the cookware, but today Hewey did not mind. "I'll stick close behind you."

For a while, following in the chuckwagon's tracks, Hewey could see thin lines of glistening wetness where the tomato juice and molasses strung along in the grass. The lines stopped when the cans had emptied.

Hewey rejoiced, and sang all the church songs he could remember.

As he walked past the chuckwagon to open a wire gate for Doughbelly, the cook commented, "I never knowed you was a religious sort."

"Sing a glad song and the angels sing with you."

Hewey knew there would sooner or later be hell to pay, but he had never been inclined to worry much about future consequences if what he did felt right at the time.

He helped Doughbelly set up camp, unhitching the teams, pitching the bedrolls to the ground, digging a fire pit and chopping up dry mesquite. Doughbelly mostly stood around with ham-sized hands on his hips and giving unnecessary directions. The cowboys came straggling in after putting the remuda in a large fenced trap for the night. They were to brand calves here tomorrow, then move camp again in the afternoon. Hewey had never been able to keep a secret from Grady Welch. They had spent so much time working together that Grady seemed able to read his mind. He gave Hewey a quizzical look and said, "You been up to somethin'."

Hewey put on the most innocent air he

could muster. "I'm ashamed of you. Never saw anybody with such a suspicious mind."

"If you've done somethin' to cause us three more days of burned biscuits, the boys'll run you plumb out of camp."

The camp was thirty miles from Upton City, and even that was not much of a town.

"All I done was dull ol' Cookie's butcher knife a little."

Doughbelly started fixing supper. Hewey tried to watch him from the corner of his eye without being obvious. He held his breath while the cook reached over the sideboards and lifted out a can.

Doughbelly's mouth dropped open. He gave the can a shake and exclaimed, "That thievin' grocery store has swindled the company."

He flung the can aside and fetched another, with the same result. This time he felt wetness on his hand and turned the can over. His eyes widened as he saw the hole punched in the bottom. "How in Billy Hell . . ."

He whipped his gaze to Hewey. He seemed to sense instantly that Hewey Calloway was the agent of his distress. He drew back his arm and hurled the can at Hewey's head. Hewey ducked, then turned and began to pull away as Doughbelly picked up a chunk

19

of firewood and ran at him.

"Damn you, Hewey, I don't know how you done it, but I know you done it."

The other cowboys moved quickly out of the way as Hewey broke into a run through bear grass and sand. The soft-bellied cook heaved along in his wake, waving the heavy stick of firewood and shouting words that would cause every church in Midland to bar him for life.

Cow boss Matthew Mullins rode up in time to see the cook stumble in a patch of shinnery and flop on his stomach. Like Doughbelly, he instantly blamed Hewey for whatever had gone wrong. "Hewey Calloway, what shenanigan have you run this time?"

Any show of innocence would be lost on Mullins. Hewey did not even try. "I just saved us from havin' to eat all them canned tomatoes."

"You probably kept us from eatin' *anything*. It'll be a week before he cooks chuck fit to put in our mouths."

"He ain't *cooked anything yet* that was fit to eat."

Mullins motioned for Hewey to remain where he was, a fit distance from the chuckwagon, while the boss went over to try to soothe the cook's wounded dignity. Watching from afar, Hewey could not hear the words, but he could see the violent motions Doughbelly was making with his hands, and he imagined he could even see the red that flushed the cook's face.

By the slump in Mullins's shoulders, Hewey discerned that the pleadings had come to naught. Doughbelly stalked over to the chuckwagon and dragged his bedroll through the sand, far away from those belonging to the rest of the crew. His angry voice would have carried a quarter mile.

"By God," he declared, "I quit!"

Mullins trailed after him, pleading. If he had been a dog, his tail would have been between his legs. "But you can't quit in the middle of the works. There's supper to be fixed and hands to be fed."

Doughbelly dropped his bedroll fifty feet from the wagon and plopped his broad butt down upon it. "They can feed theirselves or do without. I quit!"

Hewey had roped many a runaway cow and dragged her back into the roundup, bawling and fighting her head. He knew the signs of a sull when he saw them, and he saw them now in Doughbelly.

Mullins stared at the cook for a minute, but it was obvious he had run out of argument. He turned and approached Hewey

21

with a firm stride that said it was a good thing he did not have a rope in his hand. His voice crackled. "Hewey, you've raised hell and shoved a chunk under it."

Hewey felt a little like laughing, but he knew better than to show it. "I didn't do nothin', and anyway the old scudder had it comin'."

"You know he'll sit out there and sulk like a baby. He won't cook a lick of supper."

"I've heard a lot worse news than that."

"You ain't heard the worst yet. Since he won't cook, you're goin' to."

"I ain't paid to cook."

"You'll cook or you'll start out walkin'. It's thirty miles to Upton City and farther than that to Midland. Which'll it be?"

Thirty miles, carrying saddle and bedroll . . . For a cowboy, used to saddling a horse rather than walk a hundred yards, that was worse than being sentenced to sixty days in jail. He looked at Doughbelly. "Maybe if I went and apologized to him . . ." He did not finish, because he had rather walk than apologize for doing what every man in the outfit would like to have done.

Mullins said, "You're either cookin' or walkin'."

Hewey swallowed. "Damn, but this is a hard outfit to work for." But he turned toward the chuckwagon. "I've never cooked for anybody except myself, hardly."

"Nothin' to it. You just fix what you'd fix for yourself and multiply it by twelve. And it had better be fit to eat."

"At least there won't be no tomatoes in it."

Hewey had always taken pride in two distinctions: He had never picked cotton, and he had never herded sheep. He had not considered the possibility that he might someday cook at a wagon or he might have added that as a third item on the list. Now he would never be able to.

He grumbled to himself as he sliced the beef and made biscuit dough and set the coffeepot over the fire. He glared at the distant form of Doughbelly Jackson squatted on his bedroll, his back turned toward the wagon. He figured hunger would probably put the old scoundrel in a better frame of mind when supper was ready, and he would come back into camp as if nothing had happened. But he had not reckoned on how obstinate a wagon cook could be when he got a sure-enough case of the rings.

At last Hewey hollered, "Chuck," and the cowboys filed by the chuckbox for their utensils, then visited the pots and Dutch ovens. He fully expected to hear some complaints when they bit into his biscuits, but nobody had any adverse comments. They were probably all afraid the cooking chore might fall on them if they said anything.

Grady Welch tore a high-rise biscuit in two and took a healthy bite. His eyes registered momentary surprise. "Kind of salty," he said, then quickly added, "and that's just the way I like them."

Hewey looked toward Doughbelly. He still sat where he had been for more than an hour, his back turned. Matthew Mullins edged up to Hewey. "Seein' as you're the one caused all this, maybe you ought to take him somethin' to eat."

"The only thing wrong with him is his head. Ain't nothin' wrong with his legs."

"At least take him a cup of coffee."

Hewey thought a little about that thirty-mile walk and poured steaming black coffee into a tin cup. Each leg felt as if it weighed a hundred pounds as he made his reluctant way out to the bedroll where Doughbelly had chosen to make his stand, sitting down. He extended the cup toward the cook. "Here. Boss said you'd ought to take some nourishment." To his surprise, Doughbelly accepted the cup. He stared up at Hewey, his eyes smoldering like barbecue coals, then tossed the coffee out into the grass. He pitched the cup at Hewey. "Go to hell!"

"I feel like I'm already halfway there." Hewey's foot itched. He was sorely tempted to place it where it might do the most good, but he managed to put down his baser instincts. He picked up the cup. "Then sit here and pout. You're missin' a damned good supper."

Hewey knew it wasn't all that good, but he guessed Doughbelly would sober up if he thought somebody else might have taken his place and be doing a better job.

That turned out to be another bad guess. Doughbelly never came to supper. At dark he rolled out his bedding and turned in. Hewey sat in lantern light and picked rocks out of the beans he would slow-cook through the night.

Mullins came up and lifted Doughbelly's alarm clock from the chuckbox. "You'd better put this by your bed tonight. If he don't get up at four o'clock in the mornin', it'll be your place to crawl out and fix breakfast."

Hewey felt that he could probably throw the clock fifty feet and strike Doughbelly squarely on the head. He took pleasure in the fantasy but said only, "If I have to."

As Mullins walked away, Grady sidled up. "He's bound to get hungry and come in."

25

Hewey glumly shook his head. "He could live off of his own lard for two weeks."

Hewey lay half awake a long time, then drifted off into a dream in which he fought his way out from a huge vat of clinging biscuit dough, only to fall into an even bigger can of tomatoes. The ringing of the alarm saved him from drowning in the juice. He arose and pulled on his trousers and boots, then punched up the banked coals and coaxed the fire back into full life. He kept watching for Doughbelly to come into camp, but the cook remained far beyond the firelight.

After a time Hewey shook the kid horse jingler out of a deep sleep and sent him off to bring in the remuda so the cowboys could catch out their mounts after breakfast. He entertained a wild notion of intercepting the horses and turning them in such a way that they would run over the cook's bed, but he had to dismiss the idea. The laws against murder made no special dispensation for wagon cooks.

The cowboys saddled up, a couple of broncs pitching, working off the friskiness brought on by the fresh morning air. Grady Welch had to grab the saddle horn to stay aboard. Pride gave way to practicality; he was still aching from the last time when he didn't claw leather. Hewey had to stand beside the chuckbox and watch the cowboys ride out from camp without him. He felt low enough to walk beneath the wagon without bending over.

Doughbelly rolled his blankets, then sat there just as he had done yesterday, shoulders hunched and back turned. Hewey went out to a pile of well-dried wood a Two C's swamper had cut last winter for this campsite. He began chopping it into short lengths for the cookfire.

He heard the rattle of a lid and turned in time to see Doughbelly at the Dutch ovens, filling a plate. Hewey hurled a chunk of wood at him. Doughbelly retreated to his bedroll and sat there eating. Angrily Hewey dumped the leftover breakfast onto the ground and raked it into the sand with a pot hook to be sure Doughbelly could not come back for a second helping. He hid a couple of biscuits for the kid horse jingler, who would come in hungry about midmorning.

Hewey was resigned to cooking the noon meal, for Doughbelly showed no sign that he was ready to come to terms. He peeled spuds and ground fresh coffee and sliced steaks from half a beef that had been wrapped in a tarp and hung up in the nearby windmill tower to keep it from the flies and larger varmints.

From afar he glumly watched horsemen bring the cattle into the pens, cut the calves off from their mothers, and start branding them. He belonged out there with the rest of the hands, not here confined to a few feet on either side of the chuckbox. He had been in jails where he felt freer.

Doughbelly still sat where he had been since suppertime, ignoring everything that went on around him.

The hands came in for dinner, then went back to complete the branding. Finished, they brought the irons and put them in the hoodlum wagon. Mullins told Hewey, "The boys'll drive the horses to the next camp so the jingler will be free to drive the hoodlum wagon for you."

By that Hewey knew he was still stuck with the cooking job. He jerked his head toward Doughbelly. "What about him?"

Mullins shrugged. "He's your problem." He mounted a dun horse and rode off.

The kid helped Hewey finish loading the two wagons and hitch the teams. Hewey checked to be sure he had secured the chuckbox lid so it would not drop if a wheel hit a bad bump.

At last Doughbelly stood up. He stretched

28

himself, taking his time, then picked up his bedroll and carried it to the hoodlum wagon. He pitched it up on top of the other hands' bedding.

An old spiritual tune ran though Hewey's mind, and he began to sing. "Just a closer walk with Thee . . ." He climbed up on the hoodlum wagon, past the surprised kid, and threw Doughbelly's bedroll back onto the ground.

Doughbelly sputtered. "Hey, what're you doin'?"

Hewey pointed in the direction of Upton City. "It ain't but thirty miles. It you step lively you might make it by tomorrow night."

He returned to the chuckwagon and took his place on the seat, then flipped the reins. The team surged against the harness. He sang, "As I walk, let me walk close to Thee."

Doughbelly trotted alongside, his pudgy face red, his eyes wide in alarm. "You can't just leave me here."

"You ain't workin' for this outfit. You quit yesterday."

"Hewey . . ." Doughbelly's voice trailed off. He trotted back to where his bedroll lay. He lifted it up onto his shoulder and came running. Hewey was surprised to see that a man with that big a belly on him could run so fast. He had never seen the cook move like that before.

Hewey put the team into a long trot, one that Doughbelly could not match. The kid followed Hewey's cue and set the hoodlum wagon to moving too fast for the cook to catch.

Hewey had to give the man credit; he tried. Doughbelly pushed himself hard, but he could not help falling back. At last he stumbled, and the bed came undone, tarp and blankets rolling out upon the grass. Doughbelly sank to the ground, a picture of hopelessness.

Hewey let the team go a little farther, then hauled up on the lines. He signaled the kid to circle around him and go on. Then he sat and waited. Doughbelly gathered his blankets in a haphazard manner, picking up the rope that had held them but not taking time to tie it. He came on, puffing like a T&P locomotive. By the time he finally reached the wagon he was so winded he could hardly speak. Sweat cut muddy trails through the dust on his ruddy face. "Please, Hewey, ain't you goin' to let me throw my beddin' up there?"

Hewey gave him the most solemn expression. "If you ain't cookin', you ain't ridin'."

"I'm cookin'."

"What about them damned tomatoes?"

"Never really liked them much myself."

Hewey moved over to the left side of the wagon seat and held out the reins. "Long's you're workin' for this outfit again, you'd just as well do the drivin'. I'm goin' to sit back and take my rest."

Supper that night was the best meal Hewey had eaten since Christmas.

FIGHTING FOR THE BRAND

You hear a lot of talk nowadays about loyalty and what it means. Old-time cowboys knew what it meant. The loyalty they had to the brand they worked for has seldom been equaled, before or since. Sometimes they loved the outfit; sometimes they didn't. But as long as they rode its horses and ate its grub and drew its pay, they were loyal. Even when that meant risking their lives for it. Even when it meant taking up a gun against a friend.

Up in the Texas Panhandle, old-timers still talk about the day Shag Fristo and Curly Jim came riding into Dry Fork, pockets empty and the seats of their pants shiny and thin from rubbing a saddle so long.

They were cousins, but it didn't show.

Curly was the short one, his shoulders as thick and broad as an ax handle is long. And he was always grinning, even the few times he ever got mad. The boys said he slept grinning. Riding into Dry Fork, he was sing-ing to himself. Not pretty, but loud enough that he couldn't hear his stomach growling at him.

Shag Fristo was the one folks always looked back at a second time. He was uncommonly tall, his shoulders a little slumped, the way those old cowboys often got. His hands were as big as a saddle blanket. His rusty red hair bristled out over his ears, the reason people called him Shag. He was scowling that day because he was thirsty and hungry. That always made him restless, and restlessness usually put him in a frame of mind for a fight. He hadn't had a fight for the better part of a month.

That fight had had far-reaching implica-tions, however, and was the reason Shag and Curly Jim were riding the chuckline, look-ing for work. They'd been playing a peace-ful game of poker down in the Pecos country when the house man had decided he didn't like the cut of Shag's clothes, or maybe the lack of cut of his hair, and Shag had decided he didn't like the cut of the deck. The disagreement had wound up with the sa-loonkeeper looking for somebody to help him build the saloon back, and the sheriff looking for Shag.

Shag's scowl deepened as he reined his

sorrel horse toward the twin set of wagon ruts that passed for a street in Dry Fork. There were two rows of sunbaked adobes, with a few new lumber houses sitting up on blocks so high off the ground they made Shag think of a barefooted fat woman hoisting her skirts to wade a puddle of water.

Shag pulled out a lonesome-looking silver dollar. "Last steer from a mighty herd," he said. "Do we eat it or drink it?"

"Flip it," said Curly.

"Heads for whisky, tails for beef." Shag flipped it, caught it in his hand and slapped it down on his thick red wrist so hard the dust flew. He swore under his breath. Tails.

In the little box-and-strip eating place they hungrily inspected the quarter of good red beef hanging up there, then laid their silver dollar on the counter and took chili.

Cornering the last spoonful, Curly asked the slump-shouldered cook, "You know any outfit that needs a couple of good hands? Shag here can ride and rope anything that's got hair on it, and I'm better than he is."

Just a chuckwagon cook moved to town, the cafe man nodded his bald head. "Matter of fact, I do. Old Man Jesse Wheat out at the Flying W was in this mornin', lookin' for a cowboy."

Curly stood up, wiping the chili from his

chin. "Let's go, Shag."

The cook held up his dough-crusted hand. "Just a minute there. I said *a* cowboy. When Jesse Wheat says *one,* he means one. Kind of set in his ways, he is."

Thoughtfully Curly and Shag eyed each other. Curly looked at the few cents change and said with regret, "We better do it, cousin. Maybe it won't be for long."

Shag picked up a coin and flipped it.

"Heads I take it, tails you do." It was tails again.

So Curly rode out for the Flying W, but not before he had dug deep into his war bag and pulled out his most prized possession, a pair of silver-mounted spurs. He had won them roping steers against another roper of some reputation down in South Texas. He had never once contaminated them with horse sweat.

"If you don't find you a job pretty quick," he told Shag, "you're liable to need these. Somebody ought to pay a right smart for them."

So it was that Shag Fristo and Curly Jim got tallied out to different brands. It was the first time in years the cousins had been more than rock-chunking distance apart.

Shag took the change from the dollar and went down to the wagon yard. A friendly little game of poker got started on a saddle blanket. By suppertime Shag had won enough to buy chili for several days, along with prairie hay for his sorrel horse.

Next day he was sitting in the shade of the livery barn, thinking of buying that saddle blanket and a deck of cards and setting up in business for himself. A buckboard came rattling into town, its dust winding down past the wagon yard and drifting up to the doctor's house.

Two men followed it on horseback. One of them shot a quick, hard glance at Shag. He was a little old wrinkled-up man with bristly gray whiskers as stiff as barbed wire and eyes that looked like the business ends of two .45 cartridges.

"That there's Skinner Hamilton," the hostler informed Shag, pointing the stem of a pipe that would knock down a grown dog. "Owns the Rafter H, and is as ornery as a wildcat with the hives. Him and Old Man Jesse Wheat, they're like a couple of fightin' roosters. Been feudin' so long they probably don't neither one of them remember what started it."

"Wheat?" Shag frowned. That was the man Curly Jim had gone to work for.

The hostler nodded. "They're both old bachelors. Stands to reason a woman caused

36

the bust-up. And here of late it's broke out kind of mean. Been a little old squatter outfit between their ranches for years. This squatter, he had the best hole of water in fifty miles of here. A little while back he quit. Left the country.

"Some folks say Jesse and Skinner squeezed him out. I reckon that's more idle talk than solid information, but anyhow the minute the squatter's wagon and his cattle went out of sight over the hill, them two had their cowpunchers pushin' cattle in behind them. They been playin' tug-of-war ever since. Jesse's men hold the water a few days and don't let nothin' drink there but Flying W cattle. Then Skinner's bunch shows up and runs them off, and they chase out everything but Rafter H stuff.

"Folks call it the banty rooster feud. It'd be comical if they wasn't gettin' so serious. Liable to be a killin' out there yet, you watch what I tell you."

About then the two men Shag had won the money from came back with a fresh stake. In considerably less time than it had taken him to win it, he lost the whole wad. So Skinner Hamilton struck him at the right moment.

The old man stood there and looked Shag up and down like he was a horse or a plow mule. "Man tells me you're lookin' for work."

Shag nodded. The old man looked at him harder, as if about to chew him up and spit him out. "You're not one of them newfangled cowboys that wants to quit soon's it's dark and expects to laze around all day Sunday, are you?"

Shag solemnly assured him he worked twenty-six hours a day, forty days a month.

The old man chewed his tobacco and kept looking him up and down. "One more thing, then." He motioned Shag into the livery barn and pointed at a stack of hundred-pound grain bags. "See how hard you can hit that top sack."

Shag put his shoulder into it and hit the sack so hard it tumbled off. The stitching broke, spilling grain on the dirt floor.

Skinner's whiskered jaw worked the tobacco faster. "You'll do." He turned to a man who had ridden in with him, a medium-tall cowboy with a cut and bruised face and one eye a shade blue. "This here's my foreman, Peeler Milholland."

Shag shook Milholland's hand. "Pleased to meet you."

Milholland just nodded. Shag looked into his eye — the one that wasn't swollen shut — and thought he could see sympathy

38

there. Or perhaps it was just pain.

At the ranch that night, Shag studied the faces of the cowboys over his plate of beef and frijoles. Every man looked as if he had stumbled and fallen into a meat grinder — black eyes, skinned noses, blue-bruised cheekbones.

After supper Skinner Hamilton called him out beneath the cool branches of a huge old cottonwood tree. The old man tried to sit down on his heels with Shag's easy grace. Halfway down he caught himself and straightened up, swearing, his gnarled old hand pushing against his hip to get the kink out.

"Reckon you heard in town about that connivin' old cow thief they call Jesse Wheat?"

"A little bit," Shag admitted.

"You know he's tryin' to take away a waterhole that's mine by rights? Tryin' to starve my poor old cows to death, rob me of fifty years' rightful gatherin'?"

Shag said he'd heard a little mention of it.

Skinner's wizened face clouded up. "He's as mean as a rattlesnake. Cunnin' as a fox. Greedy as an old boar."

With what little tact he had, Shag said, "Man told me you-all used to be friends, a long time ago."

39

Skinner violently shook his gray head. "I was too young to know any better." A glow came into the lead-gray eyes. "You know what the old chickensnake done last night? I had five men down at the waterhole, mindin' their own business, just seein' to it that my cows got all they wanted to drink. That old warthog come a-chargin' in with thirty gunslingers — twenty, anyway — and beat one of my boys up so bad I had to haul him to town."

Skinner pointed a crooked forefinger at Shag. "But you're a man that can put him in his place. Use them fists a little bit, and old Jesse won't dare to come back, ever."

From what Shag had heard, old Jesse *would* come back. In fact, it'd probably tickle him to death to try.

But Shag didn't say so. Especially since he hadn't drawn any pay yet.

The cowboys groaned when Peeler Milholland passed on Skinner's orders to load their guns and saddle their broncs. "Even whisky never was as habit formin' as this," one limping cowpuncher complained.

But not one of them failed to go along, or even hesitated more than long enough to stretch his sore limbs. They rode at a stiff trot, not joshing each other or spinning windies to pass away the miles the way cowboys usually do. Weariness lay heavily on every man's shoulders, but a dogged persistence kept them going. As for Shag, the prospect of a little fight didn't bother him. His fist was itching a little.

He grinned as a thought struck him. What if Curly Jim was there? It would be a laugh if Shag got to boot him in the britches. It would be something Shag could hooraw him about someday when they were working together again.

Shag sensed the temper of the cowboys changing as they approached the waterhole. Any resentment, any reluctance seemed to fade. Now, no matter what, they were Rafter H men, and there was pride in that fact.

Skinner Hamilton raised his knotty fist and said, "We'll give old Jesse somethin' to rattle what teeth he's got left! We'll show him what's the top outfit in this here country."

It was like a shot of whisky starting a man's blood to pumping again.

Times, maybe, these punchers got mad enough at Skinner Hamilton to spit in his bloodshot eye. But now they were with him all the way.

Not far from the waterhole they reined up for a hasty war parley, hardly able to see each other in the dim light of the quarter moon.

"They're bound to have a guard out," Milholland said.

"Well, now," Shag volunteered, "I'm the new man around here. How about me doin' the missionary work?"

He was elected. He hung his jingling spurs over the saddle horn so as not to disturb any Flying W men who might have retired early and needed their rest. He handed the reins to somebody and set out afoot.

The waterhole was bright silver under the thin wood shaving of a moon. Cattle were bedded down not far from its banks. Up at the head of it, Shag had been told, a little spring bubbled water enough to keep the hole full but not enough to start a running stream.

Presently he spotted the guard. A match flared, and a freshly rolled cigarette glowed. Shag rubbed his knuckles.

He moved around behind the man and tapped him on the shoulder. When the guard looked back, there was a quick, solid thud and the cigarette went sailing. Shag rubbed his smarting knuckles again. The skin was torn, maybe bleeding a little.

He hadn't felt so good in weeks.

He looked down at the groggy man, and

his mouth dropped open. It was all he could do to keep from laughing out loud.

Curly Jim would never hear the last of this.

Still laughing inside, Shag walked on up to the campfire. Only five men here. He squalled like a panther and headed for the first man who jumped up.

By the time the rest of the Rafter H got there, they didn't have much to do.

When Skinner Hamilton strutted around later, crowing about what "we" had done, something went sour in Shag's stomach. Damned old pelican hadn't bruised a knuckle.

And suddenly Shag wondered if the old rancher ever had. He was mighty good at exercising his jaw. But had he ever done a lick of real fighting himself against this Jesse Wheat he hated so all-fired much?

Skinner delegated Shag and four others to stay on and let the Rafter H cattle come up to water. He suggested that they kind of drift the Flying W stock away a little piece, say ten or fifteen miles.

Only a pile of charred poles showed where the squatter's shack had been. It had fallen victim in the first tussle over this waterhole. Now a well-stocked chuckbox was set up in the open shade of the cottonwoods. Scattered about on the ground was the bedding the Flying W's had left in their obliging retreat. Shag wondered how often the chuckbox and the bedding had already changed hands.

It came close to changing hands that afternoon. Out pushing away Wheat's cattle, Shag saw the Flying W's coming. He and the other Hamilton cowhands got back to the waterhole first. They were sitting there diligently rubbing their guns to a high polish when the eight riders came up.

Curly Jim wasn't with them, Shag noted with amusement. Probably soaking his aching jaw in a wet cloth somewhere.

Shag had never seen Jesse Wheat, but he knew him now on sight. Wheat was about the same cut of man as Skinner Hamilton, two years older than the Canadian River, and wrinkled up like a peach seed. His beard was a shade shorter but just as gray as Skinner's and just as scraggly. He had the same kind of piercing eyes, and the same fierce pride was shining in them.

Old Man Wheat frowned at the guns in the punchers' hands. "You fellers don't need them things. We didn't come here to fight. We just come to ask you to move along peaceable."

The old man had more gall than a bull yearling. Shag stood up to his full six-feet-

44

five and laughed in Jesse Wheat's face.

The rancher's eyes snapped. "You're the one," he accused. "You're the one hurt my poor boys last night." Then the eyes stopped snapping. The same calculating look came into them that had been in Skinner's when Shag had knocked the grain bag down with his fist.

"You know, cowboy," he said confidentially, "that's a sorry greasy-sack outfit you're a-runnin' with. You'll die ragged and in disgrace, workin' for an old turkey buzzard like Skinner Hamilton. Why don't you come on the ride for me?"

Shag shook his head. "Skinner Hamilton's buyin' my grub and payin' my wages. I reckon I'll stay."

Wheat shrugged. "Your funeral, then. All right, boys. Take 'em!"

The Flying W's jumped down and came swarming. In about two minutes it was over with, and Shag had *two* sets of skinned knuckles.

Old Man Jesse Wheat sat in his saddle, blinking in disbelief at his cowboys piled up like cordwood.

"Now you've *really* split your britches," he raged, when his Adam's apple quit bobbing. "The Flyin' W will cut you down to size. You watch."

45

Helping Wheat's battered cowboys back into their saddles, Shag got the notion they weren't quite so enthusiastic.

But they'd try again. That was the cowboy way. They'd try as often as Jesse Wheat said to, as long as they stayed on his payroll. They might finally draw their pay and leave, but they'd never let up as long as they worked for him.

They didn't let up. They came again that night, and the next night. They came with guns and tried to scare off the Rafter H men by sending bullets whining high over their heads. But Shag Fristo stood solid as a rock wall and aimed his gun a little lower.

Skinner Hamilton listened to the telling of it, a malevolent grin splitting his whiskery face. "Old Jesse'll bust a blood vessel," he said gleefully.

But Peeler Milholland, the foreman, was less than gleeful. "First time it's ever come to shootin'. Anything can happen now."

Shag tried to ease him. "Aw, it wasn't much. Nobody got shot at. Just a few cartridges got burnt up."

"But what about the next time?" Peeler demanded, flicking a quick, half-angry look at old Skinner dancing around as if he had just raked in the whole pot from a high-stakes table. "Somebody's liable to get killed, and there ain't enough water in Texas to be worth that."

If Skinner Hamilton heard him, he showed no sign of it.

The next time was not long in coming. It was that night. There was little warning, just all of a sudden a clatter of hoofs and the yells of the Flying W men sweeping down like demons after a three-day drunk. Scattered all around the waterhole, Skinner Hamilton's cattle jumped to their feet and broke into a run. The Flying W's fired their guns into the air.

The Rafter H horses stampeded in terror, all but one hobbled in camp. He reared and threshed and threw himself to the ground, fighting the rawhide thongs that bound his forefeet.

Nothing is more useless than a cowboy left afoot. Shag grabbed a rope and ran after the threshing horse as it struggled to its feet and tried to run away in an awkward three-legged gait. He swung the loop, made his catch, and whipped the end of the rope around his hip, digging his high heels into the ground. The panicked horse turned back, fighting the rope.

Then, from out of the darkness, a rider bore down on him, firing into the air, trying

47

to make the horse break away.

In a flush of fury, Shag pulled out his own pistol and aimed over the cowboy's head, hoping to booger him away. He fired once . . . twice. Then, as he squeezed the trigger again, the horse made a hard lunge. The gun jerked down.

The thud of the bullet was thunder loud to Shag. The man cried out and tumbled from his saddle.

Cold fear hit Shag a belly blow. He ran to the fallen rider. "Lord of mercy, man," he cried, "I didn't mean —"

He turned the man over, and all the strength dropped out of him. Curly Jim!

Eyes burning, Shag felt for the wound and found it, low in the shoulder. He pulled his hand away, warm and sticky.

"Curly . . ." His voice broke. "I swear to God, I wouldn't of shot you for the world."

The shooting and yelling had stopped. Friend and foe, they all gathered around and stood, dull from shock, looking at Shag Fristo and Curly Jim.

"We got to get him to town," Shag said.

He and a Flying W man stanched the bleeding and wrapped the wound. There was no wagon, so they caught Curly's horse and put him back on it. Shag threw his own rig on the horse with which he had been struggling. With the Flying W man to help him, he headed for town, holding Curly in the saddle.

One of the Rafter H cowboys ran to catch up with him. "Old Skinner ain't goin' to like this. What can I tell him?"

Shag's voice ripped like barbed wire. "Tell him to go to hell!"

The doctor never was going to get through in there, it seemed like. Shag had drunk so much coffee his stomach sloshed when he moved. But he was boiling up another pot of it, his red-webbed eyes on the door behind which the doctor worked. The Flying W man sat patiently watching him. He knew about the kinship between Shag and Curly Jim.

He suggested, "Why don't you set down a spell and get some shut-eye? I'll wake you up when the doc comes out."

Shag walked wearily to the window and looked out into the new day. This was all his fault. Remorse clung to him, heavy as lead.

"I won't be able to sleep till I know if Curly's goin' to make it." He lowered his red head. "If he don't . . ." He did not speak the thought aloud, but if Curly died, Shag was liable to kill a couple of iron-headed old ranchers.

The cowboy nodded sympathetically and joined Shag at looking out the window. "I'm scared, Shag," he confessed. "This business has come to a head, I'm thinkin'. Liable to be a hell of a fight out at that waterhole today."

Shag's face was hard and grim. He doubled his big fists. Hadn't those stiff-necked old warhorses had enough?

The door hinges creaked, and the doctor stepped in. He was not exactly smiling, but his eyes bespoke confidence. "Your friend is made out of rawhide and barbed wire. He'll make it."

On his way back to the waterhole, Shag rode hard and steadily, irritably touching spurs to his horse any time the animal lagged or pulled to one side or the other. Shag's eyes were bloodred from loss of sleep, and they burned as if they had sand in them. He hadn't eaten any breakfast, so hunger was working on him. All in all, he was in no humor for church.

Mostly his mind was on Curly Jim. Curly had every right never to speak to him again. But the first thing Curly had done when he had opened his eyes was to grin and call him a name that could only be considered profane.

That was more than being kin. That was friendship.

Even before Shag got to the waterhole he could see that the Flying W puncher had been right. There, on the west, the whole Flying W was lined up on either side of Old Jesse Wheat. On the east, every man from the Rafter H even to the cook was siding old Skinner Hamilton. There was enough artillery in the outfit to reopen the Civil War.

Shag noted with a scowl that only two men in the whole bunch were not packing iron — Skinner Hamilton and Jesse Wheat.

The two wrinkled old ranchers hunched on their horses, hurling threats and barbed language in each other's direction. Skinner cut his angry eyes at Shag. "Where the hell you been?"

Shag growled some kind of answer.

"High time you got back!" Skinner grumbled. "We're fixin' to have us a showdown here, for once and for all. We need every gun we got."

Something was simmering inside of Shag like chili on a hot stove. He pointed his red-stubbled chin at Skinner's hip. "I don't see yours."

Skinner's face flamed. He wasn't used to being spoken to this way. Not by anybody but Jesse Wheat.

51

"I got a good mind to fire you, Fristo."

"You ain't *got* any mind, and you can't fire me. I done quit." He reached down and came up with his pistol. He motioned at Skinner. "Git down."

Skinner's mouth dropped open. "You've gone crazy, that's what."

"Probably. But I said git down. And you too, Jesse Wheat."

Dumbfounded, the two oldsters looked to their men for help. Shag made a sweeping motion with the gun. "All you fellers move around here in front of me, to where I can see you. First man reaches for a gun is apt to get his toes shot off."

Nobody wanted to get burned, so everybody stood off and looked at him. He went on, "These two old buzzards been wantin' a showdown, and I think it's time they had one. It ought to've been done twenty or thirty years ago." He turned to Hamilton and Wheat. "This time you two are goin' to fight it out yourselves instead of lettin' your cowpunchers beat their brains out for you. Hit him, Skinner!"

The old man hesitated. Shag pulled back the hammer. It clicked loudly enough to be heard across the county line.

Skinner swung his fist weakly and gave Wheat a tap.

"Harder! Make it a good one."

The second one made both men grunt.

"That's more like it. Now, Wheat, you hit him back."

Wheat did.

"Go on and fight now, both of you. Get it out of your damned systems for once and for all."

Looking apprehensively at Shag, the two ranchers went at each other like two tired old bulls, half the time swinging so wildly they didn't even connect. When it looked as though they might stop, Shag motioned with the gun again.

"Keep it up. You ain't half started yet."

So they fought and wrestled, rolling over and over in the dirt, losing their hats, tearing buttons from their shirts. Neither could hit hard enough to break the shell on an egg. Shag stood over them menacingly. Each time it looked as though they might give up, he gently nuzzled one or the other in the ribs with the barrel of the pistol.

Their fierce dignity gone, the two old ranchers were an almost ludicrous sight. One by one, the cowboys began to grin.

It went on and on until finally both men tottered in the mud at the edge of the waterhole, dirty and disheveled, their clothes hanging, sweat streaking the dust on their faces. Skinner gave Wheat one final tap and fell on his face in the water. Wheat sat down with a muddy splash.

Skinner rolled over and wiped the water from his face, leaving a broad track of mud. Both men were heaving for breath. For a long time they sat in the water and stared at each other. They were a sorry-looking spectacle, the both of them. They looked as if they knew it.

Jesse Wheat said finally, "Skinner, you look like hell."

Skinner rubbed another smear of mud across his face. "You ain't no mornin' glory yourself."

Shag Fristo towered over the two men, his lips tight against his teeth. "Now then," he said brittlely, "there's water enough here for both of you, and you're goin' to share it. If ever I hear of you two old terrapins raisin' hell with each other again, I'll come back and rub them two gray heads together till by Judas you can smell the hair burn!"

Stiffly he walked back to his horse.

Jesse Wheat followed him with his eyes. "Skinner," he said, "maybe you'd let a man like that get away, but I'll be dogged if I will. If you ain't takin' him back to your ranch, I'm takin' him to mine."

"You keep your hands off of him, Jesse

Wheat. Fristo's *my* man." He waved his arm wildly at Shag. "Shag Fristo, you come back here!"

Shag took his time about it, but he came.

Skinner said, "Looky here, Shag, I been lookin' for a man like you for twenty years. You ain't fired."

"I know it. I quit."

"You can't quit. I'll raise your wages. Forty dollars a month. There ain't no better in the country than that. And nothin' but gentle horses, either."

There wasn't a really gentle horse in the whole remuda, except the ones Skinner kept for himself. Shag scratched his rust-colored head, then started to walk away from the group of men.

Jesse Wheat spoke up. "Wait now. We'll *both* hire you, me and Skinner. We'll need us a line cabin up here anyhow, and a rider to keep our cattle from gettin' all mixed up. I figure you'll be fair to both of us. We'll split your wages."

Shag chewed his lip and looked up at the cotton-puff clouds in the Texas sky. The fire and fight went out of him.

"Well, now, I might do that. But a line cabin's a two-man job. And it just so happens that I know a good man. . . ."

COWARD

His hands tense on the leather lines, Dick Fladness flicked a quick, searching glance at the two women who shared the tight buckboard seat with him.

"Brownwood just ahead," he said.

He might as well have said nothing, for the women sat in dusty, tight-lipped silence, their eyes brittle on the scattering of frame buildings that spread out across the open prairie west of Pecan Bayou.

Dick's mouth went hard again, and he flipped the reins at the ill-matched team to pick them up a little. He had hoped the long, hot ride might wear down the contempt that stood like an adobe wall between the women and himself. It had not.

He turned the corner by the blacksmith shop, and the trailing dust from the buckboard wheels caught up with him for a moment. Nora Matson sneezed. It was the first sound the girl had made the whole way in, except that she had sobbed quietly when they first pulled away from the stark pile of gray ashes and charred wood that had been the Matson ranch home.

Dick pulled up in front of the hotel on Center Street and climbed down, wrapping the reins around the right front wheel. He held up his callused hands to help Nora's mother down from the buckboard. Her eyes lashed him in scorn. She was a tall, graying woman with a stiff puritan pride.

"I can get down by myself."

Her daughter followed her. Nora was eighteen, slender and pretty, with wide brown eyes that used to dance in laughter. Nora's eyes never touched Dick's face now, not while he was looking.

"I'll bring in your things," he said, nodding toward the small bundle of clothing under the buckboard seat.

Mrs. Matson cut him short. "We can manage that too. There's not much of it, since the fire."

Wincing, Dick stood silently by the buckboard wheel while the two women climbed the steps to the high plank gallery of the frame hotel. The balding proprietor hurried out and took the bundle from Nora Matson's hands. He turned solemnly around to the girl's mother.

"We heard about your son, Mrs. Matson. I'm terribly sorry."

She acknowledged his sympathy with a quick nod of her chin, which suddenly was set harder than ever. Stiffly she went on into the hotel, Nora behind her. The hotel man paused for a quick glance at Dick. His frown showed that he knew. The whole town must know.

Head down, Dick stepped up into the buckboard and flipped the reins. He pulled the team back around and rolled down to the livery barn at the end of the dusty street. He was conscious of idle eyes following him. He drew up within and tried to convince himself that he didn't care.

Mike Lavender walked out through the big open door of the frame livery barn and waited for him. Mike was a stiffened old cowhand who had had to seek an easier way to round out his days. His leather-dry face was expressionless, but Dick felt a quiet friendliness in the faded blue eyes. He leaned eagerly toward that friendliness, needing it for strength.

"Walter Matson's buckboard and team, Mike," Dick spoke. "Walter said let you take care of them."

Dick took his war bag and bedroll from the buckboard and started out. He walked with a faint limp.

Mike Lavender's eyes followed him. "What about you, Dick? What you goin' to do?"

Dick stopped in the open doorway, his saddle slung over his shoulder. "Leave, I reckon. Go someplace where people haven't heard of me. Then maybe I can start over."

Mike Lavender shook his head. "You can't run away from a thing like this, Dick. It'll follow you. Take my advice and stay right here."

Dick dropped the saddle heavily, desperation raising the color in his face. "Look, Mike, I'm a coward. Anybody'll tell you. I lost my head in a fight, turned tail and deserted my friends. And a man died."

He lifted his hands. "Mike, do you think I could stay here and have people lookin' at me the way they will, like I was a coyote or somethin'? Snickerin' at me, maybe callin' me a coward to my face?"

Mike's pale eyes were patient. "Talk's cheap. You don't have to listen to it." The old cowpuncher's voice softened. "Son, these things have got a way of workin' themselves out if you just give them a chance. Now, you pitch your bedroll on that spare cot back yonder. You're stayin' with me for a spell."

59

Dick stood uncertainly, weighing Mike's words. It was going to be tough, staying here with the name the town would give him. But it would be tougher leaving, for the memory would be with him always, haunting him with the image of what might have been, the futile knowledge of things left undone.

If he left now, there would never be any coming back. He thought of Nora Matson, the tinkling music of her voice, the warmth of her cheek against his as they stood in the moonlight, the cool evening breeze searching leisurely across the bayou.

Leave, and anything there might have been between them would be finished. Maybe if . . .

He picked up the bedroll and carried it to the empty cot.

Mike slouched in a cane-bottomed chair, idly whittling a stick of kindling wood down to a sliver. His pale eyes lifted as Dick came back. He said, "I've heard the story the way it's been told around town. I'd like to hear it your way."

Squatting on the ground, Dick stared hollowly at the pile of pine shavings growing around Mike's big, worn-out boots.

"You've probably heard it just the way it happened," he said. "It's the barbed-wire fences that caused it. Ansel Hornby and his free-grassers have been cuttin' Walter Matson's fence, and we've been patchin' it right up again. Three nights ago they cut it and left a placard hangin' on a fence-post. Said if the fence went back up they would end the fight once and for all. Walter tore up the placard, and we fixed the fence.

"They waited till the sheriff had to be out of the country. Then last night they came. They were masked, but I know Ansel Hornby was leadin' them. And I recognized the voice of Branch Collin, that foreman of his. They didn't stop at the fence. They came right on to the house. We were puttin' up a good fight, Walter and his son Lindy and three of us hands. Then they somehow set fire to the house."

Dick's hands began to tremble. "I tried, Mike. I tried to stay there and fight. But those flames got to reachin' at me. My clothes went to smokin'. I couldn't stand it. I jumped out the door and broke to runnin'. All I could think of was to get away from that fire. I didn't quit runnin' till I fell. I laid there till I finally got a grip on myself. I could tell the shootin' had stopped. The fence cutters were gone. The house was gone. And Lindy Matson was dead."

Dick's head was in his hands. "Wasn't a

one of them would speak to me. They all looked at me like I had killed Lindy myself. Came daylight, the cowboys rode after some neighbor help. Everybody went up on the hill to bury Lindy. They wouldn't let me help carry him. They wouldn't even let me help dig his grave.

"And when it was all over, Walter told me to go. I brought the women to town, where they'll be safe. Walter stayed. Swore he was goin' to put the fence back up and fight Hornby's free-grass men till he's dead." His face was grim. "He meant it, Mike. He's got the guts of a Mexican bull. But Hornby'll kill him. He knows the county's watchin' Walter. He knows if Walter's fence stays up, there'll be others, and the free-grass men will be fenced out. He won't quit till Walter's dead."

Sitting on the edge of his cot, trying to figure out what to do, Dick heard the clatter of horses' hoofs coming up from behind the barn. He caught the unintelligible conversation and the lift of careless laughter. Dick glanced at Mike and saw that the old cowboy was bent over in an uneasy nap.

Dick arose and walked toward the front of the barn. The limp was momentarily heavy from his having sat awhile. He heard riders hauling up on their reins and swinging to the ground in a jingling of spurs.

"Hey, Lavender," a rough voice called, "how about us throwin' our horses in a corral here for a while?"

Dick's heartbeat quickened. That voice belonged to Branch Collin. Dick hesitated, looking back at the sleeping Mike Lavender. Then he walked on to the door. Facing Collin, he jerked a thumb toward Lavender's pens.

"Mike's asleep, but I reckon it's all right."

Branch Collin was a medium-tall, slender man with a quick, easy movement and a sharp, sensitive face. There was a hint of green in his eyes that seemed always to contain a devilish laughter. Ansel Hornby was boss of the ranch, but Branch Collin was undisputed boss when it came to trouble. There were people two counties away who broke into a cold sweat at the mention of his name.

Collin seemed momentarily surprised at sight of Dick. Then the laughter came to his eyes. "Richard the Lion-Hearted. I reckon you found where you really belong, swampin' a stable."

Dick gritted his teeth and held his anger inside.

Ansel Hornby kneed a big roan horse up

closer. He had a narrow, intense face. Dick had never seen him smile. Hornby's voice was flat and grim. "Boy, you should never have quit runnin'. You should have kept goin' till you were clear out of the country. I would advise you to move on now."

Anger beat against Dick, but his throat was tight. He could not speak.

Branch Collin said, "He'll leave, Ansel." Collin's smile lingered. His eyes dwelt heavily on Dick's. "But not before he puts up our horses for us."

Dick opened the gate for the men to ride in. There were five besides Hornby and Collin. They unsaddled and turned their horses loose in the corral.

Collin shook his finger under Dick's nose. "You feed them horses good, you hear? Otherwise you'll find yourself runnin' faster than you did last night."

A couple of the men chuckled. Enjoying the approval of the little audience, Collin suddenly pulled Dick's hat down over his eyes, hard. "There, that's just to be sure your hat don't blow off while you're runnin'."

Trembling with anger and humiliation, Dick pulled his hat up. Collin and the men were walking away, laughing. But Ansel Hornby stood there, his humorless eyes on

Dick's blazing face.

"Man down the road said you brought the Matson women in. They put up at the hotel?"

Dick's answer came brittle and sharp. "You leave the women alone!"

Hornby's eyes widened in speculation at this unexpected hardness in the cowboy who had run away. "I'm not here to hurt the women. But sometimes you can reason with a woman when you can't talk to her men." His eyes narrowed again. "You had better consider what I told you, Fladness. You can ride a good way between now and dark."

Hornby turned and broke into a brisk stride to catch up with his men. Their spurred boots raised puffs of dry dust in the street. Dick watched Hornby point toward the hotel. But Collin shook his head and jerked his thumb at the saloon. Pleasure before business.

Dick's mind turned to Nora Matson and her mother. If only Sheriff Adams were in town. . . .

Dick stepped hurriedly back into the barn. In his haste he almost knocked down Mike Lavender. The old man had awakened to the lift of voices and had seen at least part of this.

Dick took his belt and gun from his war bag.

Lavender watched him worriedly. "You sure you know what you're doin'?"

Dick's glance touched him, then dropped away. "I don't know, Mike. I only know I've got to do *somethin'*."

Summer heat clung heavily over the empty street as Dick hurriedly walked up Center. He sensed men watching him. A remark was made just above a whisper, and he knew he was meant to overhear it. The blood rose warmly to his face, but he held his eyes straight ahead.

An idler leaning against the smoky blacksmith shop pointed a crooked finger at him. "You're runnin' the wrong way. They're in front of you, not behind you."

Choking down anger, Dick stepped up onto the long gallery of the hotel. A backward glance showed him Hornby and Collin pushing out of the saloon. Dick moved on in. The proprietor eyed him suspiciously.

"I've got to see Mrs. Matson and Nora," Dick told him.

The hotel man frowned. "Don't you think you'd better move on? I don't believe they'll care to see you."

Dick's nervous hands gripped the desk edge. "I know what you think of me. I know

66

what the town thinks. But that doesn't matter right now. Ansel Hornby and Branch Collin are on their way here to see Mrs. Matson. She ought to know."

The man's eyes widened. "They're upstairs in seven. I'll go with you."

Dick rapped insistently on the door. Mrs. Matson pulled it inward. Her grieved eyes hardened at sight of him. "I thought you'd be gone by now. What do you want?"

He told her. Mrs. Matson's jaw was set like carved stone.

Dick finished, "I'll be here if you need me." He tried vainly to see past Mrs. Matson, perhaps for a glimpse of Nora.

Winter ice was in the tall woman's voice. "We needed you last night. We can do without you now."

Through the open door he watched her move back to a wooden dresser and reach into the drawer. Then Dick turned away. Slowly he walked down the stairs, the hotel man behind him. At the foot of the steps Dick stopped and waited. Ansel Hornby strode through the open front door and stood a moment, adjusting his eyes to the dark interior. Branch Collin came in behind him and stood at his side, mouth fixed in his usual hard grin. His eyes raked Dick in contempt.

A soft, feminine tread on the stairs behind him made Dick step aside. Mrs. Matson came down, and Nora. Dick glanced quickly at Nora. Her brown eyes sharply met his, then fell away. Her lips trembled.

In an empty gesture of politeness, Ansel Hornby removed his broad-brimmed hat and bowed slightly. Branch Collin never moved or changed expression. "Good afternoon, Mrs. Matson, Miss Matson," Hornby said. "I heard about your son. I want to tell you how deeply I regret it, ma'am."

Hatred darkened Mrs. Matson's face.

Hornby went on, "It wasn't necessary, Mrs. Matson. It isn't necessary that there be any more deaths. You could stop it."

Dick saw that her hands were trembling. One was covered by a dark brown shawl.

Hornby's voice intensified. "It's only the barbed wire, ma'am. I think I could talk to the fence cutters, if I had your assurance that the wire would not go up again. Your husband would listen. That's all it would take, just a word from you."

Mrs. Matson's voice was quiet and flat. "It's our land. It's our right to fence it. We'll be there when you're dead!"

Hornby's face began to cloud. "There'll be more killin's, Mrs. Matson. A word from you could save your men. Keep silent, and they may die."

Mrs. Matson's lips curved downward. "No, Ansel. It's *you* who will die!"

The shawl fell away. Gun metal winked a reflection from the window. For just an instant Dick froze. He saw Branch Collin's hand streak upward from his holster.

Dick leaped at Mrs. Matson, putting himself between her and Collin. He grabbed her hand and forced it down. The barrel blazed in his grip as the gun thundered and a bullet bored through the plank floor. In fury Mrs. Matson threw her body against him, struggling for the pistol. But Dick held his grip on the hot barrel and wrenched it away. It clattered to the floor at Hornby's feet. Mrs. Matson fell back against her daughter. Her face was splotched red.

"You *are* a coward. Get out of my sight. If I ever see you again, Dick Fladness, I'll kill you!"

She whirled and hurried back up the stairs. Dick flinched under the lash of contempt in Nora's dark eyes.

Collin's eyes followed the women. "Another second and I'd of shot her. Good thing for her that you did what you did, Fladness."

Dick's face twisted. "I wish I could've let her kill you, Hornby. One way or another,

69

though, you're goin' to lose."

Hornby tried to stare him down. Branch Collin's cold grin came back, and he resembled a cat stalking a mouse. "Maybe you better apologize to Mr. Hornby."

Dick clenched his fists. "I apologize for nothin'."

Collin's hand worked down toward the pistol on his hip. "That's a good-lookin' six-shooter you're wearin', Fladness. Maybe you'd like to try to use it."

Dick went cold. "I couldn't match you, Collin."

Collin's eyes remained on him, hard as steel. "See there? You've crawfished again."

Impatiently, Hornby spoke. "What did you expect, Branch? You knew he was a coward. We'll give the boys another hour at the bar. Then we'll take a ride around the bayou and see about that wire. We're goin' to finish this thing once and for all."

He turned on his heel and strode out, his spurs ringing dully to the strike of his heavy boots. Collin faced Dick a moment more. "Another hour," he said grimly, "then we'll leave. But you better be gone before that. If you're still here, I'll leave you hangin' on the fence like any dead coyote."

A chill on his shoulders, Dick stood and listened to the fading tread of Collin's boots as the man stepped down from the gallery. Cold sweat broke on Dick's forehead and on his suddenly weak hands.

The hotel man's shaky voice broke the stillness. "That was better than I expected of you, Fladness. But you'd best move on. You can get a far piece in an hour."

Woodenly Dick picked up Mrs. Matson's pistol from the freshly swept floor. He handed it to the hotel man. "Take it to her. She's liable to need it."

Dick stood on the hotel porch, steadying himself against a post. The heat of late afternoon rushed against him, stifling him, crushing his lungs. The street seemed stretched out of shape. It swayed back and forth, and it looked a mile long. He knew it was his nerves. They tingled like telegraph wires.

Two men stood in front of the nearby saloon. The words of one came to Dick like the slap of a swinging rope. "Bet you the drinks he lights off of that porch in a high lope."

Dick swallowed hard. Deliberately he stepped down into the street. He started back toward Lavender's barn, his steps measured and slow. He was so scared he was sick at his stomach. But they weren't going to see him run.

71

It seemed an hour before he gained the door of the barn. Mike Lavender's chair was empty. Dick sagged into it. Lavender hobbled up, braced his long arm against the door and leaned on it, looking out across the town and saying nothing.

"You've heard about it?" Dick asked him finally.

Mike nodded gravely. "Collin means it, Dick. I told you a while ago that you ought to stay. I've changed my mind. You better go, son. I got you a horse in the pen back yonder."

Dick stared at the ground. A thousand things hummed through his mind, memories of people he had known and ridden with and liked. He had especially liked Lindy Matson. Maybe Lindy's death was Dick's fault, and maybe it wasn't.

"You goin', or ain't you?" Mike queried anxiously.

Dick shook his head. "Give me time to study."

For a long time he sat there staring vacantly across the town. He watched a lazy cur dog make its leisurely way down the street, checking under high porches, sniffing at every corner. He watched a brown hen out back of a washerwoman's house, scratching around in the thin shade of a mesquite, seeking a cool place to settle herself.

Most of all he watched the saloon where Collin and the Hornby crew were. Occasionally he would see one or two of them come out, look around and go back in. He could feel speculative eyes appraising him from a distance, and he wondered how poor the betting odds were that he might not run.

Mike Lavender tromped back and forth in the barn like a stallion in a small corral. Now and then he would stop in the door and look up the street with Dick. Once he drew an old stem-winding watch from his pocket. "Been half an hour, Dick."

Dick nodded dully.

Mike said, "Son, I know that on a thing like this a man has got to make up his own mind. But anybody would know you ain't got much chance against a man like Branch Collin. Supposin' you leave now, there ain't much people can say that they ain't said already."

Dick never answered. He sat in the doorway, watching.

He saw the flare of a long skirt on the gallery of the hotel. The girl stood looking down the street toward the barn. Her shoulders squared as she saw Dick sitting in the doorway. Quickly she lifted the hem and

73

rushed down the steps onto the street. In a few moments Nora Matson stood in front of him, her young face pale.

"Dick," she said huskily, "are you a fool? I thought you'd be gone by now."

Bitterness coiled in him. "Like last night?"

She flushed. "Dick, it won't help anything for you to stay here and get killed. It's too late to bring Lindy back."

He searched her eyes for some sign of the love he had seen there before. "Does it still matter to you, Nora?"

"It matters. Last night changed a lot of things, but I can't forget what there was between us. I beg you. Go!"

Dick watched her walk hurriedly back toward the hotel, drawing upon her stout pride to keep her shoulders straight and her head high. Dick looked down, staring fixedly at the ground in front of his brush-scarred boots. He heard Mike Lavender stomping around behind him.

"Mike," he said, "is that horse still out there?"

A sigh of relief passed the old cowhand's lips. "He is, and it's high time you used him."

Stiffly Dick stood up. He glanced at the saloon long enough to know he was being watched. Then he moved back into the barn and picked up his saddle and bridle. He flipped a loop over the horse's head, pulled him in, bridled and saddled him. The pen had an outside gate opening west. Going out through it, a man could leave town without using the street. But it wouldn't keep him from being seen.

Mike strode out of the barn with Dick's war bag. "Here's your gear. Good luck to you."

"Thanks, Mike," Dick replied. "But it's not me that's goin'. It's you!"

Lavender's jaw sagged. "Me? What in the —"

Dick said, "Look, Mike, you know I couldn't beat Collin if he came lookin' for me. But I'm a fair enough shot. If I had surprise on my side, I might beat him.

"You're about my size, Mike. You're goin' to spur out of this gate and head west in a lope. They'll think it's me. When Collin comes, he won't expect me. Maybe that'll be enough to give me an edge."

The old man's face was sharp with anxiety. "And maybe it won't."

Dick shrugged. "If it doesn't, I sure appreciate the way you've stuck by me."

Lavender placed his knotty hand on Dick's shoulder. "Son, I know why you ran last night. I knew all along you wasn't no coward. Good luck to you."

Dick opened the gate for him. The old man spurred out and swung westward, the dust rising beneath the horse's hoofs.

Dick watched him a minute. Then he latched the gate and hurried once again through the back door of the barn. In the shadowed interior he picked his spot, about twenty feet inside the barn door, where he would not readily be seen from outside. He pulled up a chair and sat down to wait. Holding the gun, he sat back, his hands cold with sweat, nervousness playing through him like lightning in a stormy sky. His eyes set on the open door, he waited. . . .

He heard the voices before he saw the men. They were laughing voices, lifted high by the warmth of liquor. Dick heard the easy jingling of spurs. Branch Collin and Ansel Hornby swung into view, their men trailing. Collin was laughing, and even Hornby's normally somber face showed a little humor. The sight of the horseman spurring out the back way had been a joke even Hornby could enjoy.

Still in the sunlight, Collin threw back his head and roared, "Hey, Lavender, I see we flushed your quail."

Collin and Hornby walked in through the door and passed into the shadow. Collin blinked away the momentary blindness and sought out Dick Fladness's form in the dark of the barn. Dick stood up and took one step forward from the chair.

Collin's jaw dropped as recognition hit him like the lash of a whip. His hand dipped.

But the surprise had delayed him a moment. In that moment Dick brought his pistol up into line. It exploded twice. Collin's weapon cracked once, raising a puff of dust at the man's toes just before he pitched forward onto his face.

Paralyzed, Ansel Hornby stared foolishly at Collin's sprawled form. He grabbed at his own pistol, then realized belatedly how foolish *that* was. He stopped with it half out of the holster. He stared into the smoking muzzle of Dick's six-shooter, and horror slowly crawled into his eyes as he felt death brush him.

He stammered, his voice failing as panic gripped him. "For God's sake," he managed, finally. "My God, man, don't kill me!"

Dick held his pistol steady. He had every intention of squeezing the trigger, and Hornby must have seen it in his eyes. Hornby let his pistol drop to the dust. "Fladness, for the love of God . . ." His knees gave way, and he sank to the dust, crying.

Dick looked past Hornby at Hornby's men. Muddled with drink, they had sobered quickly at the roar of guns. They stared in disbelief upon the man who had led them, now groveling in the dust, begging for his life.

Other men gathered, and they too, stared, and they knew who was the coward.

Dusk gathered heavily. Dick sat on the broad gallery of the hotel, the cool evening breeze bringing him relief from the heat and ordeal of the day. From inside the lobby Mike Lavender's voice drifted out to him.

"You see, Mrs. Matson," Mike was saying, "it was the fire that chased Dick away last night. It was several years back that me and Dick was workin' for the same outfit. One night one of the hands got careless with a cigarette. We woke up with the bunkhouse burnin' down around us. Smoke had already knocked out a couple of boys in their sleep.

"Wasn't time for us to do anything except run. Dick tried to drag one of the boys out, but part of the roof fell in on him. Dick was pinned under a burnin' timber that broke his leg. He laid there and seen that other boy burn to death. We finally got Dick loose just before the whole place caved in. That's where his limp come from, and his fear of fire. Most anything else he could've stood. But when the fire got to burnin' him last night, he couldn't hold out."

Presently Mrs. Matson came out onto the gallery. Nora was with her. "Dick," Mrs. Matson said, "I wish there was some way to tell you . . ."

Hat crushed in his hands, Dick nodded. "I know."

Mrs. Matson gripped his arm. "I wish you would go hitch the team to the buckboard. I want you to take us home."

Dick shook his head. "There's not much home left out there."

Her shoulders braced. "No house, perhaps, but a house can be rebuilt. It takes more than fire to destroy a home."

Dick stepped down from the porch and started toward the livery barn.

"Wait for me," Nora said, and hurried after him. "I'd like to go with you."

THE BLACK SHEEP

Will Clayton crawled stiffly out from under the blankets into the chill of the dark room, as tired now as when he had gone to bed. Pulling on his khaki clothes and his high-heeled boots, he caught the familiar aroma of Maude's coffee and bacon. But he felt no appetite.

He cupped his hands and splashed icy cold water on his wind-toughened face. Glancing up into the mirror, he felt the sudden surprise that hit him so often lately, as if he were looking not at himself but at the face of some troubled stranger. His gray eyes were weary, and the carved lines were deepening day by day.

He hobbled toward the kitchen, through the hall whose walls were covered by pictures of 4-H Club boys with prize-winning steers and lambs. His legs were slow and sore. He had put in a heap of miles yesterday, checking an ailing milk cow for Jeff Alley, helping Buster Cook mark up his early lamb crop, running terrace lines in old Max Pfeiffer's fallow cotton field. It seemed like the older a county agent got, the more there was to do.

Maude turned away from the stove and glanced at him, her blue eyes soft with concern. She turned his frying egg to harden the yolk the way he used to like it. Lately, nothing seemed to have much taste for him.

"You didn't sleep much last night," she said. He shook his head. "You've got to start sleeping, Will. You'll kill yourself this way."

He didn't much care. "All I need is work." *Work to keep me busy,* he thought, *too busy to remember.*

His tired gaze touched upon two layers of fresh-baked cake cooling on the cabinet, and he knew Maude had been up a while. Lately, she hadn't slept much either.

"For the Stevens family," she said. "Mrs. Stevens is sick." The fact that the Stevens family lived clear across town wouldn't mean a thing to Maude. It was a small town, and she knew everyone in it.

Will poured himself a cup of coffee and sipped, immune to the scalding heat. He stared up at the West Texas Feed and Supply calendar, with its bright print of a Charlie Russell cowboy painting. "Real estate man'll be over this morning," he said. "Maybe you ought to stay around."

Lips tight, she set his egg in front of him. "We don't *have* to go, Will."

"But we *do* have to. And you know why." He picked up the knife and fork, then laid them down again, seeing the glistening in her eyes before she blinked it away.

"Look, Maude, you know the Prairie Land and Cattle Company has been after me a long time to take that manager job. It's a good job, the chance of a lifetime."

"*This* is your kind of job, Will. That isn't. You won't be happy there. And neither will I." She looked straight at him then, her blue eyes firm. "Why don't we be honest about it? You're trying to run away, Will."

He flinched and looked down. "You know why I haven't slept, Maude?" he asked huskily. "I lie there and fight it for hours. I know that when I sleep I'll dream. And there it'll be, all over again, just the way it was. I've dreamed it twenty times."

"It was an accident, Will. Nobody blames you for it, nobody except yourself."

"And John McKenna?"

"You don't know how he feels. You won't go to see him. Look, Will, he's been your best friend for twenty years. Why don't you go talk to him?"

Will stood up and shoved back his chair, leaving his breakfast uneaten. "What do you say to a man when you've killed the only son he had?" he asked miserably.

At the 4-H feeding barn, he slowly stepped out of his pickup truck and turned up the collar of his faded plaid Mackinaw against the chill of the January wind. He stopped in the open barn door and heard the bleating of hungry lambs. He listened to the rattle of buckets and the noisy clamor of happy young voices.

The brisk cold weather was a stimulant to the boys. They ran and jumped and cut up as they swept out troughs and poured fresh feed for eager lambs to push their noses into.

"Morning, Mister Clayton."

"Hi, Will."

He answered quietly as each boy spoke to him, stepping past him with buckets of grain or chips of hay. He knew each kid by his first name, knew the parents of every one. This was the community barn he had worked to get for so many years, so the kids in town could feed livestock and get to know how to handle them, like the boys on the farms and ranches. He and Maude had never had sons of their own.

That new L off the south end of the barn

had been built just last year because of overcrowding. The boys themselves had raised the money for it, selling soft drinks and barbecue at the rodeo and the stock show. And there had been that big 4-H amateur show, with Johnny McKenna as master of ceremonies.

Johnny McKenna. Will Clayton closed his eyes, his fist tightening in the pocket of the Mackinaw. A blowout on a sharp curve . . . the helpless skid and the crash through the guardrail that had thrown Will out of the pickup truck before it pitched off the embankment and smashed onto the rocks below. Johnny McKenna never had a chance.

Will watched six lambs in a little pen run over each other to get to the feed which a red-haired boy was pouring out. They were Johnny's lambs.

Will swung his body around and savagely punched his fist against the yielding bulk of a grain sack. *Why wasn't it me? Why wasn't it me?*

Slowly, then, he became conscious of a commotion around the corner, down at the end of the L. He hobbled down the alley between the sheep pens. He found three club boys angrily confronting a fourth

84

youngster in one of the pens.

"I wasn't gonna hurt nothin'," the dirty-faced kid protested. "I just come to look at the lambs."

"You come here to steal somethin'," one of the boys declared hotly. "That's all you know how to do, is steal stuff."

Will studied the boy. He was 12, maybe 13, dressed in patched, faded blue jeans and a thin woolen coat that had been worn out before it was passed on to him. His grimy fists were doubled, tough as mesquite knots. Defiance shone in his brown eyes.

"I can't place you, son," Will said. "Who are you?"

"I ain't done nothin'. I just wanted to see the sheep."

Patiently Will shook his head. "I didn't say you'd done anything. Just asked who you are. Where do you live?"

"I'm Bo Magee. I live down yonder by the stockpens."

An older club boy named Chester Willis said, "His old man runs Blackie's pool hall. A boozer. His old lady takes in washing to feed them. This Bo's strictly a foul ball."

"That's enough of that kind of talk," Will said firmly. "Turn him loose."

"We better search him first," Chester said.

"Turn him loose!"

85

Free, Bo Magee stepped back with eyes flashing.

Chester said, "Plays hooky half the time, hangs around them tough guys down on the *arroyo.* I'd search him, if it was me."

Will frowned. "You kids better get on to school."

The other boys gone, Bo Magee stood facing Will, nervously shifting his weight from one foot to the other. "You fixin' to call the law?"

Will shook his head. "Why? You haven't done anything wrong. You wanted to look at the sheep. You can look at them with me."

Will slowly started up the alley that divided the L. He stooped down. "Boys left some of their buckets lying around," he said, picking up one. "Mind helping me gather them?"

Bo Magee didn't answer, but he pitched in and helped. His eyes were on the lambs, some just beginning to take on that final bloom that meant they were nearly ready for the stock shows.

"You like sheep, Bo?"

The boy was silent a moment. "Yeah, I reckon." His brown eyes came alive as he watched the lambs eat, and his dirty face seemed to warm.

"Why haven't you ever joined the 4-H Club, fed some lambs or a calf?"

"I got no money. You can't buy nothin' without you got money."

"The bank lends money to 4-H Club boys, Bo. You could get a loan."

The boy pondered that a while, then shrugged hopelessly. "Paw wouldn't let me. I brought home a puppy once. Paw said it costs too much to feed a family, much less an animal. He took it out and killed it."

Will looked away quickly, a flush of anger rushing to his face. In a moment he said quietly, "Well, you come over and watch the lambs any time you take a notion, Bo."

A tall man appeared in the alley and stopped there. Going out, Bo Magee gave him a quick, fearful glance and hurried his step. A tiny metal badge on the man's coat winked a spot of light. Eyes narrowed in suspicion, Deputy Chuck Standefer watched the boy hurry out.

"What's that Magee button doing around here?"

"He was just looking at the lambs," Will answered.

Standefer nodded confidently. "I'll bet. He was casing the outfit to find out what he could pick up. That's what I came to see you about. You keep this room locked up when there's nobody around, Will?"

"No," Will said. "Who'd steal from a bunch of kids?"

Standefer was the kind who watched every stranger as if he suspected him of stealing the county courthouse. But maybe he felt that was necessary to offset the openhanded, easy-going policy of the sheriff, John McKenna.

The deputy said, "You better put you a lock on it. Been some feed stolen around lately. Nothing big, just a little two-bit pilfering. Big store of feed like this, though, they might haul off a truckload."

When Standefer left, Will finished straightening up around the barn. What he had to do, he did woodenly. He took a final look at Johnny McKenna's lambs and wished he were already moved out.

Will drove to the tall old sandstone courthouse that had been built in the days of domed clock towers and multiple cupolas. Climbing the stairs, he paused for a quick, nervous glance into the office of Sheriff John McKenna.

He hadn't seen John since the funeral. He'd tried to talk to him then but he hadn't been able to speak, and he guessed John wouldn't have been able to listen. For a long time, then, he had consciously avoided John.

Will found Jeff Alley waiting in the office for him, patiently flipping through one of the college bulletins on the feeding of ensilage. Jeff was a middle-aged stock farmer with gray-shot hair and a smile warm as the stove in an old-fashioned country store. He rolled the bulletin and shoved it in the pocket of his faded shirt. "Taking this," he said. "Take anything I can get for free, even advice." He paused. "I still got trouble."

For 20 years, when the farmers or ranchers around here had troubles, they sent for Will Clayton. He usually knew the answer. And if he didn't, he knew where to find it.

"That milk cow you looked at," Jeff said, "she didn't give any milk again this morning. Not hardly enough for the old woman's coffee. Derndest thing I ever saw. She gave a barrelful last night."

Will rubbed his jaw. "Beats me, Jeff," he said. "You sure her calf's not getting to her of a night?"

Jeff said, "I doubt it. He's already wrapped up in my freezer box."

Walking back downstairs with Jeff, Will anxiously watched the hallways, half hoping, half dreading that he would run into John McKenna.

They got into Jeff's pickup and drove out

away from the courthouse and down through the main street of the little town. Will leaned against the door, looking out the frosty window at the stores, the houses, the people he had known so long.

Jeff Alley's smile was gone. "It's not the cow I'm really worried about. It's you. I can always get me another cow. But there ain't another Will Clayton."

Will kept looking out the window, watching the street that was giving way to a graded road, the houses giving way to mesquite pasture and small-grain patches.

Jeff said, "I hear you're leaving. I reckon I know how you feel. But folks don't want you to go, Will."

Will's voice came tight. "You ought to walk down the street with me, Jeff. See the people looking at me, thinking about that boy. And me knowing they're thinking it. We'll all be better off when I'm gone from here."

Jeff Alley said, "I saw you looking in John McKenna's office as we came out. You haven't talked to him, have you?"

Will's fists clenched in his lap. "No, I haven't."

"Then maybe it's John you're really worried about. Go talk to him, Will."

Will sharply shook his head, making it

plain that he didn't want to discuss the subject any further.

Jeff Alley's farm lay just beyond the city limits. The sight of something green always lifted Will up. He felt better now, seeing the fine stand of small grain, waving its rich deep green in the morning wind, the field seeming to flow in the rhythmic pattern of gently curving terraces.

Jeff slowed down suddenly and grunted. "Another of Vince Yancey's heifers in my oak patch," he said. "But I'll let her get her belly full before I put her out. She looks as poor as a whippoorwill, poor thing. She's starving."

Will could see the Yancey ranch from here, where one of the pastures bordered on Jeff Alley's. Bare as a hardwood floor. Eternally overstocked and grazed off to a nub. Yancey was always having trouble with his sheep and cattle.

Will checked Jeff's milk cow, and again he couldn't find anything wrong with her. "Whatever it is, maybe it'll pass."

They started back toward the courthouse.

"We'll stop at the Wagonwheel and have us some coffee," Jeff said.

They hadn't driven far before Will spotted a boy walking down the road toward a big brush thicket. It was Bo Magee. Will stepped out of the truck, his left foot still on the running board. "Bo," he spoke, "I thought you went on to school."

The boy stopped short at the sight of him. He stood uncertainly a moment, his mouth open. Then he turned and sprinted toward the thicket.

"Bo!" Will called after him. "Come back!"

But the boy disappeared into the brush.

Worriedly shaking his head, Will climbed stiffly into the pickup again. "Some boys," he said, "you just can't figure out."

"You've done a good job of figuring them out the last 20 years," Jeff said. "And you're needed as much now as you ever were. Don't quit us, Will."

The rest of the morning, and all afternoon, he spent running terrace lines for old Max Pfeiffer. But his mind wasn't on the job. Twice he had to go back and reset some of the stakes.

"Today you don't look so good, Will," Max said worriedly. "Look, we got plenty of time. Maybe you go home and rest, we do it another day, yeah?"

"No, Max," he said, knowing there might not be another day. "We'll finish it."

And when he finished, he had made up

his mind. He drove by the courthouse to leave the equipment at the office. That done, he walked back down the stairs and stopped in front of Sheriff John McKenna's door. He stood there bracing himself, the excited rush of blood in his ears as loud as the crackling of the state police radio he could hear inside the office.

A hundred times during the afternoon, he had planned how he would say it. Now suddenly, before he had a chance to go inside, John McKenna stepped out the door.

The two men stared at each other in surprise, almost like strangers. Will felt his mouth go dry. His heart thumped so fast it hurt, like a band tightening around him. "John, I came to tell you —" The words stopped. Will tried, but they wouldn't come. Then, numbly, he turned away. Head bowed, fists drawn up in knots inside his Mackinaw pockets, he walked down the corridor and into the chilly winter air.

At home, he closed the back door behind him and turned his burning eyes toward Maude, standing over the kitchen stove. "We're going to finish packing tonight, Maude," he said hopelessly. "I can't stay here another day."

Next morning he'd started stacking things in the borrowed truck as soon as it was light enough. Now, with the morning sun an hour high, he had the suitcase and the cardboard packing boxes ready to put on the truck. He picked up the biggest box and balanced it on his hip. Then he heard the knock on the door.

Will eased the box down again and straightened, rubbing his hip in an effort to work the stiffness out. He pulled the door open and stepped back in surprise. "Morning, Will," said John McKenna.

Will tried to answer him but he found no words. Maude walked in, and she too stopped in surprise. Self-conscious about the handkerchief tied around her head, she pulled it off and dusted it against her apron. "Come in, John," she said. "Get out of the cold."

The sheriff stopped in the middle of the bare room, his hat in his hand, and looked at the packed belongings scattered about. "It's true, then, what I've heard. You're leaving."

Will's voice came back. "It seems like the best thing to do."

His hands suddenly were shaking. "I tried to tell you yesterday, John. I wanted to explain everything to you. But what could I say? That I'm sorry? That I wish it hadn't

94

happened?" He shook his head wearily. "I found out there just weren't any words for what I wanted to say, John. So I couldn't say anything."

John McKenna nodded gravely. "I know, Will. For days I've wanted to see you. But I haven't known what to say. Then I saw you last night. I saw your eyes. You've been killing yourself for what happened to Johnny. Don't do it, Will. *I* don't blame you. Those things just happen sometimes, and there's nothing any man on earth can do to stop them. There's nobody to blame. Least of all you."

Will felt his knees giving way. He sat down heavily on a packing box.

John McKenna said, "He was my son, Will, but he was one of your boys. You taught him things, gave him things in life that even a father couldn't. Sure, he died young. But he died rich because of you. I'll always remember that."

Will stood up again, walking slowly to the window and looking out into the morning. He took a handkerchief from his pocket and blew his nose.

The sheriff said, "I came here for something else, Will. I've got a boy out there in my car. Manny Nixon caught him just before daylight this morning, taking a short sack of feed out of his barn. Boy's name is Bo Magee."

Will nodded regretfully. "I know him."

"Not the first time the kid's been in trouble," McKenna said. "Manny was roaring mad and wanted to send him off to the reformatory. But then the boy showed us what he took the feed for — and Manny wouldn't even press charges. Will, that boy has got him a little pen fixed up out there in a brush thicket. Used old chicken wire and stuff. Built him a shed out of scrap iron and old lumber. He's got four baby lambs in there. They're some of Vince Yancey's dogies that he found starving to death along the fence by the town section."

The sheriff was shaking his head in admiration. "Sure, he was stealing. But he's got too much of the makings in him to ship him off. With somebody to guide him a little, he could grow up into a real man, Will. And you're the one can help him."

Will was silent a moment. "I'm leaving, John," he said.

The sheriff ignored that. "The boy loves livestock, and that's what we'll work on. If that shiftless old man of his tries to interfere, I'll lower the boom on him. How about turning Johnny's lambs over to him, Will? Let him finish them out and show them."

Will felt a warmth growing inside him. "You mean you'd let him have your son's lambs, John?"

The sheriff nodded. "Johnny's gone. But that kid's here." He lifted his hand and placed it on Will's shoulder. "Look, Will, we've lost a boy, you and me. Now we've got a chance to save one. You coming with me?"

Will looked into McKenna's deep, friendly eyes, and the weight was gone from his shoulders for the first time in weeks. He turned back to Maude, and he managed a smile. "I'll be back, Maude, and help you unpack."

He opened the door and went out with the sheriff toward the car where the boy sat waiting.

97

A BAD COW MARKET

The loudspeaker above the livestock auction ring carried the auctioneer's chant over the clanging of steel gates and the shuffle of cattle's hooves in the soft sand. Most of the words had no meaning, but George Dixon could hear the price being asked, and he understood *that* meaning all too well; these calves were not going to pay the cost of their raising.

Sitting on a wooden bench high up toward the sale ring's acoustical-tile ceiling, he stared glumly at the last calves of his trailer-load, a couple of cutbacks the yard crew had sorted off to keep them from lowering the value of the others. If the rest had been cheap, these were being stolen. He reached to his shirt pocket for cigarettes before he remembered he had given them up, not so much for his health as to save the money.

He jotted the price of the final calves in a shirt-pocket tallybook and reviewed what the other lots had brought. He would have to wait awhile for the bookkeeping staff to make out his check. He dreaded taking it to the production credit office for application against his loans. The PCA manager would not say much, but George could anticipate the look in his eyes; he had seen it many times the last few years as the prices for what he sold kept going down and the prices for what he had to buy kept going up.

Damned sure takes the romance out of the ranching business, he thought sourly.

Two thin crossbred cows came charging into the ring, eyes wide and heads high in anxiety over this unaccustomed place and the noise and the fast handling in the alleyways behind the auction barn. George stood up, glad they weren't his. The market was no kinder to cows than it was to calves. He made his way to a set of steps, begging pardon of other ranchers who pulled their booted feet back to let him pass. They looked no happier than he felt. He walked out into the auction's lobby and glanced at the glass behind which the office staff worked. There was no way he could rush his check. He pushed through a glass door into the restaurant, the smell of fried onions slapping him in the face like a damp, sour towel.

Someone spoke his name. He turned toward a row of booths and saw a man of about his own age, in his early forties, his waist expansive where George's was lean. George wore old faded jeans and a blue work shirt, and his hat looked as if it had been run over by his pickup truck. Bubba Stewart resembled an ad in a Western-wear catalog. A big platter of chicken-fried steak and French fries gave off steam in front of him.

"Sit down, George," Bubba invited jovially. When a man had Bubba's wide grin and open manner, it was hard to resent him for being so damned wealthy. "I was havin' a little bite of dinner. I'd like to buy yours and not eat by myself."

George had figured a cup of coffee and a piece of pie would hold him until Elizabeth fixed supper. He didn't spend much these days on cafe chuck. "You go ahead and eat," he said. "I'll just settle for coffee." He decided against the pie because he didn't want Bubba spending that much on him. He would feel obligated to return the favor the next time. Bubba stabbed the steak with his fork. "You sellin' today, or buyin'?"

"I'm givin' them away," George responded flatly.

Bubba nodded sympathetically. "I thought

last year it couldn't get no worse. So much for my fortune-tellin'." His smile showed his pleasure in the steak. Bubba Stewart had always drawn pleasure from life and seemed never to be struck by the arrows of outrageous fortune. "You sure ought to order one of these. It ain't like Mama makes. It's better."

George looked up as the waitress brought his coffee. "Thanks. This'll do." He blew across the cup.

Bubba said, "Gettin' tougher and tougher to stay a cowman. You thought any more about that proposition I made you?"

George hoped his eyes did not betray how much he had been thinking about it. Maybe if Bubba thought he was not interested he would raise the ante. "That ranch has been in the family a long time. My old granddaddy bought it back in aught-nine."

Bubba nodded. "Mine was already here. A man could make a good livin' then, raisin' cows on a little spread like that. Now it's like a life sentence to hard labor with no parole."

George could offer no argument.

Bubba talked around a mouthful of steak. "I've given up worryin' about cows. I keep a few for ornamentation, like my wife keeps a pair of peafowl, just to look at their feathers. But recreation — that's where it's at nowadays, George. Cater to hunters out of Dallas and Houston. Not just oilfield rough-necks, either. Go for the rich dudes that just ask where it is, and not what it costs."

Bubba had done well at that. In recent years he had gradually trimmed his livestock numbers and in their place had introduced exotic game animals such as black-buck antelope and sika deer that could legally be hunted the year around. He had built a large rustic hunting lodge where paying guests could rough it with comforts they didn't even have at home. Much of the year he had people waiting in line to get in.

George remembered that local cowboys used to snicker at Bubba because he wasn't much of a hand with cattle and horses. He had been a disappointment to his father and grandfather. But he had been a good student in arithmetic class. Bubba said, "I've got an architect workin' on a second lodge. I could use the extra huntin' acreage your place would give me." George had lain awake nights, thinking about it. When his restless stirring had roused Elizabeth, he had told her he was having a touch of rheumatism. In reality, it was the cattle that were giving him pain.

He had considered trying to do in a small

way what Bubba was doing in a large one, but he knew he could not. He took in a few hunters from East Texas during the fall whitetail deer season, but he could never find financing for facilities like Bubba had built. His ranch was too small. Bubba said, "I'll raise my offer a little. You could pay off your debts and put the rest out on interest. It wouldn't be a full livin', but you're sure not makin' a livin' now." George moved his hands from the tabletop and down into his lap so Bubba could not see them tremble. "I don't know. It'd have to be all right with Elizabeth. And I'd have to get approval from my brother Chester in San Antonio. Dad left the place to both of us, you know."

Bubba nodded. "I imagine Chester would be tickled to get shed of the old place and have the cash to put into his business. Plumbin', isn't it?"

"He contracts air-conditionin' and heatin'." George frowned. "If I'd had any judgment, I'd've gone partners with him years ago and left the cow business to somebody else. He offered to take me in."

"Kind of hard to picture you as a city slicker. It fits Chester, a little, but you was always the cowboy of the family."

"And look where it got me." George's voice had a rough edge. Bubba pushed his

103

empty plate aside and signaled the waitress that he needed his ticket. "Well, you holler if you decide. See you around, George."

George stared absently at the cold gravy on Bubba's plate and did some mental calculations for the hundredth time. He could settle his accounts and buy the family a house in town, maybe San Antonio, where Chester was. Then he could find himself a paying job for a change. There were lots of things he could do besides wet-nurse a bunch of feed-loving cows or the runny-nosed sheep that helped subsidize the cows' feed bill.

He sipped the last of his coffee and watched Bubba paying the cashier. Bubba's father and grandfather would turn over in their graves if they knew the direction Bubba had taken their ranch. But financially it was a sensible direction. Bubba was still building and buying while the old-line ranchers who stayed by tradition were losing their butts and all the fixtures. He had the judgment to change with the times. George begrudged him nothing.

He picked up his check and found it was even a bit less than he had expected after commission, feed and yardage. He walked out onto the auction yard to his pickup and long gooseneck trailer. One of the trailer tires had gone halfway down. It was so slick the original tread barely showed. The ranch business had come to a hell of a pass when a load of calves wouldn't even buy a new tire. He passed Bubba Stewart's ranch entrance before he came to his own. Bubba had built a large stone archway with the Lazy-S brand displayed at top center. Many people used to make a joke of the brand, claiming it fitted Bubba all too well, but some of the scoffers were gone now, while Bubba was growing stronger.

George's entrance had no architect-designed archway. It had only a pair of chest-high stone pillars he and his brother Chester had helped their father to build thirty-odd years ago. They were plain and simple, but each time he drove between them across the cattleguard he remembered his father's pride in a job that had required two days of back-bending work. A mailbox just off the road shoulder was the only thing bearing the Dixon name. George had never thought he needed anything more. About the only people who ever hunted him up were feed and mineral salesmen.

He drove to his barn first and unhitched the trailer, then waded through the mud to a water trough that was overflowing onto the ground. A lifetime of water shortages had given George a contempt for waste. The old float had sprung a leak and filled, leaving the water to run unchecked. He unwired it from the valve and fetched an empty plastic sheep-drench bottle from the barn. It was less efficient than a commercial float, but it did not cost anything.

George had long operated on a principle of thrift: never buy a new nail if a bent one could be straightened. Disgustedly he hurled the old float as far as he could throw it, thinking, I'm getting damned sick and tired of this.

He saw a yellow school bus stop on the farm-to-market road. Shortly his fourteen year-old son Todd came pedaling to the barn on a bicycle he had left hidden in a clump of brush near the cattleguard. The bicycle frightened a couple of calves too young to haul to town, and they stampeded away with tails hoisted.

George's frustration boiled over. He gave his startled son a dressing down for needlessly scaring the stock. "Now you get your clothes changed and start your chores!"

Face red, Todd said, "I've got to be back in town tonight for a 4-H Club meetin'."

"We'll talk about that later. Right now you do what I told you!" Regret arose as he watched the boy walk the bicycle to the house, shoulders hunched under the weight of the reprimand. The boy hadn't deserved that. It had just been one of those days. Better for all of us, he thought, if we get away from this place.

He tinkered around the barn as long as he could, knowing that when he went to the house Elizabeth would want to know what had made him ride the boy so hard. Todd came back with his old clothes on, milk bucket in his hand. He gave the barn a wide berth as he went to the pen where he had started a new calf on feed for the county stock show next January. Feeding show calves was one thing Todd would have to give up when they moved to town. It was too expensive anyhow; once a boy got past the county show and moved up to the big ones where the real money was, he went against the professional steer jockeys who dominated the circuit. That was simply one more thing gone wrong with the cattle business.

Todd finished milking the Jersey cow and trudged back to the house, followed by a red dog that was like a shadow to him. Presently Elizabeth came out onto the front porch, searching with her eyes. Hands clasped over her apron, she watched George make the long walk from the barn. The sight of her usually lifted his spirit, but not today. He studied the way she looked, framed between the porch posts that George's grandfather had put up. She deserved better than that old house, he thought.

He supposed she saw the answer to her question in his face, but she asked it anyway. "Did the calves sell all right?" He handed her the sale sheet. "They sold." She did not look at the paper. "It'll be better next year." That was always her response to bad news: things'll be better tomorrow, or next week, or next year. He wondered how she found strength for that faith. His had about played out.

"Supper's on the table," she said, and moved toward the door. He caught her arm. She turned to face him, but it took a minute for him to bring out the words. "Bubba Stewart made me an offer again today."

He caught a flicker of reaction in her eyes, but she covered it so quickly he could not read it. She asked, "What did you tell him?"

"Told him I'd have to talk to you, and to Chester. I'll call Chester after supper."

"You're really serious this time?"

"The times are serious."

Elizabeth looked past him, toward the barns, the corrals, toward the road that led out to the highway. "Supper's getting cold."

She turned abruptly and led him into the house.

Todd was already seated at the table. He avoided his father's eyes. George tried to think of something that would ease the sting of rebuke. "What time's that 4-H meetin'?"

"Seven-thirty."

"We can make it without rushin' our supper."

That was the extent of conversation. Elizabeth offered no comment at all. Finished, George glanced at the clock on his grandfather's old mantel and decided Chester should be home from work by now. He dialed the number. The telephone rang a couple of times. A man answered in a voice George recognized as his brother's, though its tone was oddly somber, as if Chester had just heard bad news, or expected to. "Hello. Chester? This is George. How's things in the big city?" Chester said he had seen them worse, but he did not remember when. George said, "They aren't good here, either. That's what I'm callin' you about. I was wonderin' if you could come out this weekend. I need to talk to you."

Chester hesitated a long time before sayin' it would be hard to get away and asking if they couldn't talk about it on the phone. "No," George told him. "It's not going to be simple. We may need time to talk it out."

Chester hedged, saying he did not know how he could leave the business. But finally he relented, though his voice carried no pleasure. "I'll come."

"Bring the family. The kids haven't seen each other in a while."

Chester was silent another long moment. "I'll just have to see about that, George. I can't promise."

Todd brightened as his father hung up the telephone. "You mean Allan'll be out to see us?"

Allan was fifteen, just enough older that Todd had always looked to him for leadership, like the brother he had never had. Allan through the years had always come out from the city each summer to spend a few weeks. Todd would follow him like the red dog followed Todd. This year Allan had not come. Too many things to do, his father had explained to a disappointed Todd. George had reasoned it was natural for boys, even those who had been close, to drift apart as they became older. Each was developing his own interests and pointing himself toward the lifestyle he would follow as an adult. George remembered a cousin who had been his best friend until they were both about Todd's age. They had not seen each other in ten or fifteen years now, and the cousin rarely even crossed his mind.

He said, "Son, I wouldn't count on Allan. Even if his folks come out, and his sister too, he might not be with them. City boys his age have got football and girlfriends and such as that."

"He'll be here," Todd said enthusiastically.

George frowned. "You ever wish you could live in the city where you could do the things Allan does?"

Todd nodded. "Sure, I've thought about it. I've wished I could go to all the football games and to the picture show when I wanted to. I've wished I could go hang out at the mall like Allan does, and check out the girls." He gave his mother a quick glance. "Just look, though. That's all I'd ever do." He pondered a moment. "But there'd be things I couldn't do. I couldn't ride a horse. I couldn't feed our show calves. Those are things Allan wishes he could do."

"You might not miss them all that much. You'd have a lot of things you can't get in the country. You'd probably have a bigger and better school."

Todd's eyes widened. "You're not thinkin' about havin' me go live with Uncle Chester and Aunt Kathleen, are you?"

George blinked. He had not expected his

son to misread him so badly. "No. That never crossed my mind."

Todd seemed relieved. "I'd probably get tired of the picture show. I might even get tired of hangin' out at the mall. I'd rather have my horse and my show calves."

"We can get used to anything if we want to bad enough."

"I suppose. I just don't think I'd want to." Todd shrugged off the subject as easily as he would slip out of his coat. "You still got any of that pie left, Mama?"

George glanced at Elizabeth. She had that look in her eyes again, that frustrating mask she could draw down at will to cover what she was thinking.

From experience he knew Chester and his family should reach the ranch about noon Saturday. That morning he took advantage of Todd's day off from school to repair a section of the fence he shared with Bubba Stewart's ranch. Some kind of animal had run into it and had broken off an old cedar post, leaving the fence to sag. He could only guess what it might have been; Bubba had a regular menagerie over there. While George put his shoulders into driving a set of posthole diggers against the resisting hard ground, Todd leaned on a crowbar and said, "If we'd waited till afternoon, we could've

112

had Allan to help us."

George answered, "You know how goofy you and Allan get when you start playin' around. One boy can be good help. Two boys are like one good man had got up and left you."

He heard something crashing through a cedar brake. A long-legged animal with twisting black horns burst into the open, saw the two people and whipped back, disappearing as quickly as it had come. George said, "One of Bubba's exotics. I swear, there are as many on our side of the fence as on his."

"If they come over here, does that make them ours?" George shrugged. "In a way, I guess. They go where they want to go and eat our feed. But Bubba paid for the breedin' stock. I'd hate to be a judge and jury."

"I still think they're ours."

"It won't matter long anyway." Todd gave him a quizzical look, but George had said too much already. There would be time enough to tell him when the deal was made. "Here, let's see you hit the bottom of this hole with the point of that bar."

They finished the fence repair a while before noon, and they were still unloading the tools into a frame shed beside the barn when the red dog started barking. George saw Chester's blue automobile raising dust along the graded road. The car was three years younger than the one in George's garage. Todd jumped up into the pickup bed for a better look. "It's Allan!" he exclaimed, and ran toward the house, shouting to his mother. George finished putting away the tools and half-smiled, remembering that he used to make much the same fuss over his own cousin thirty-odd years ago. He paused at the windmill to rinse the dirt and grime from his hands, then walked to the house amid the dust settling from the passage of Chester's car.

Chester had a tired look in his face, as if he had not slept. His voice had the same dark and pained quality George had heard on the phone. "Howdy, George. Good to see you." George reached out, and Chester's handshake startled him. It was strong, almost crushing, but it was not the strength of pleasure; it was like the desperate grasp of a drowning man. George pulled away, looking back to his brother even as he gave sister-in-law Kathleen an obligatory hug. Through the years she had been the bubbly sort, but she also seemed subdued, troubled. The couple's daughter Pamela, at nine too young to play with boys, stuck close beside her mother.

George turned to his brother's son, who had shoulders like a football player. "Allan, we needed your muscles with us this mornin'. We had a couple of mean postholes to dig."

He expected some joking rejoinder, for that had always been the boy's way. Like his mother, he had an answer for everything, and usually a funny one at that. But he offered no reply. He turned away from Todd as if trying to avoid him and stared silently back down the road.

Probably got chewed out about something, and he's pouting, George thought. He had no intention of saying anything to make it appear he was butting in. "You-all come on into the house. I expect Elizabeth's about got dinner ready."

Kathleen and the girl hurried ahead. Chester held back, glancing uneasily at his son. "You made it sound pretty urgent on the phone, George."

George did not know exactly how to start. "It'll keep. Let's go have dinner."

They visited over the table, talking weather and rain and dry spells, exchanging gossip about old friends and acquaintances, studiously avoiding the subject that had brought Chester and his family all the way out here.

Nobody smiled much, and nobody laughed. After they had eaten, George and Chester walked out onto the porch and seated themselves on the steps. They were silent for a time. At length George ventured, "I guess business must be pretty bad in the city." That would account for the somber mood in his brother and sister-in-law.

Chester nodded. "But there's a lot of people worse off." He rubbed his hands nervously against his knees. "I think I can guess what you wanted to talk about, George. I keep up with the cattle market. If you want to cut the lease you're payin' me for my half of the ranch, I'd have no objection."

George's jaw dropped. He had not considered that Chester would misconstrue his intentions so badly. He fumbled for words but found none.

Chester went on, "We're brothers, George. Sure, I can use the money, but I don't want it comin' out of your hide." He stared out across the pasture. "Hell, let's just eliminate the lease payment altogether till the cattle market goes up. I wouldn't want you hurtin' this old place by over-stockin' it so you could pay me. I remember how much our daddy and granddaddy loved it."

George stared at the ground. He felt as if

116

Chester had punched him in the belly. He had lain awake for hours last night trying to plot out just how he was going to put this proposition to his brother. Suddenly his whole plan had gone up in smoke.

Chester said, "Would you mind drivin' me around, George? Sometimes when the traffic is heavy and all the phones are ringin' at the same time, I get to thinkin' about this ranch. It's like a tranquilizer to me, with no bad side effects."

"The side effects come when you try to raise cattle on it," George said dryly. He stood up. "You boys want to go?"

Todd was eager, but Chester's son seemed distant and cold. Todd grabbed his arm. "Come on, Allan. We'll ride in the back of the pickup, like we used to."

Allan hung back, like a dog reluctant to follow the leash. His father said brusquely, "Come on, son. You've got nothin' better to do." The boy burst out, "I did have, if you'd just left me alone."

"I've left you alone too many times. Get in the pickup!" Chester's face was flushed, his hands clenched. He glanced uncomfortably at George. Allan climbed into the pickup bed, his eyes angry and downcast. Todd hesitantly followed. His questioning gaze touched George, asking for an answer

George did not have.

It struck George that Allan looked different, somehow adult, yet somehow lost, even bewildered. Todd'll be at that stage in another year or two, he thought. Damned if I know how we're going to handle it.

They drove through what had always been known as the horse pasture, now used mostly for young heifers being grown out to join the breeding herd. At one end was a surface tank built to catch runoff after a rain. For the first time since they had left the house, Chester spoke. "Remember how we loved to fish in that tank, George? Never caught much of anything, but we sure did drown a lot of worms."

George nodded soberly. His problem was getting no easier.

Chester said, "Doesn't seem like it took much to keep us happy. A horse to ride, a tank to fish in, a .22 to hunt rabbits with. We never gave Dad a lot of trouble, did we, George?"

George shook his head. "Not much, I guess. We ran some weight off of his calves, learnin' how to rope when he wasn't lookin'. I remember once we ran his pickup into a rockpile and ripped the oil pan out from under it."

"But that wasn't real trouble. Not like

118

today. Livin' out here, George, you've got no idea . . ."

Chester turned away from him and covered his eyes with his hand. "God, George, why couldn't things stay simple like they used to be? Sure, me and you pulled some stunts, but we never really hurt anybody. These days . . ."

George glanced through the back window. Allan was staring moodily to the rear. Todd was watching him in silent disappointment. So far as George was able to tell, there had been little communication between these two boys who used to roll and tumble and tear together. "Is he in trouble, Chester?"

"He will be, if he's not already. He's fallen in with a wild bunch. He's usin' somethin'; I can't tell what, but somethin'. You can't talk to him half the time. He flies into a wild rage at nothin'. He's even got his mother and sister scared of him. I'm about at the end of my rope."

Chester went quiet, but George could almost hear him crying inside. "I'm sorry, Chester. I had no idea."

"Wherever these kids turn, there's temptation and trouble. They can buy stuff me and you never even heard of, and do it in the school hallways. Nights, no matter what we tell him, he slips out of the house and is gone. The telephone rings, and I'd rather die than answer it. I'm afraid they've picked him up and hauled him to jail. Or worse, that they've hauled him to a hospital.

"I know even the little towns aren't immune anymore, but at least people can keep track of things better. Where we're at, you don't know who's livin' three houses down the street, or what they're up to. Be thankful you've got Todd out here so you can always know where he is and who he's with."

George could see his brother's hands tremble. He said, "I wish there was somethin' I could say or do. I've never been up against that kind of situation."

"You were always the cowboy, George. I always had two left hands when it came to ranch work. I used to think the happiest day of my life would be when I could go to the city for a nice clean line of work where I'd never have to look another cow in the face. I thought my kids were better off than yours because the city had so much more to give them." He made a bitter laugh. "Look what it gave my boy. I'd've been better off livin' out here somewhere in a line shack, workin' for cowboy wages, and they'd've been better off."

George said, "We make our choices the best way we know how. We can never tell what's ahead of us."

"Well, I sure made the wrong one. I know I'll never come back here to live; I've got too much of my life invested where I am. But it's a comfort to know I could. Maybe somehow we'll pull through this thing with Allan, and he'll outgrow it. Maybe we'll be able to keep his sister from fallin' into the same trap; we'll try our best. But just knowin' this place is out here helps keep me and Kathleen from climbin' the wall sometimes. It's like an anchor in a rough sea.

"So keep your lease payments, George. Even get a part-time job in town if that's what it takes to pull through, so long as you've got this place to come to of a night, and for your boy to come home to. Hang on to our anchor."

George turned to look through the rear window again. Todd was talking, pointing, hopefully enthusiastic. If Allan was even listening to him, he gave no sign.

George said, "I reckon there's worse things than a bad cow market."

No more was said about Allan, or about the low value of cattle. Chester and Kathleen and their two youngsters left Sunday afternoon. Allan had not said fifty words to Todd, so far as George ever heard. Todd ventured, "I think he's probably got girlfriend trouble."

George said, "I expect that's it."

"It'll never happen to me."

George smiled. "No, it probably never will."

He expected to hear from Bubba Stewart by Sunday night, but Bubba did not call. Monday morning Bubba was sitting in front of George's house when George and Todd came out after breakfast. Bubba grinned at Todd as the boy mounted his bicycle and started up to the road to catch the school bus.

"Don't let that old bronc throw you," he warned.

Todd laughed. "I've got him broke gentle."

Bubba watched Todd pedal away. "Good boy you got there."

"I know."

"I seen Chester on the road yesterday, headin' back to the city. What did he say about sellin' the place?"

George's face twisted. "I never got up the nerve to ask him."

Bubba pondered a moment, then nodded. "Figured it was somethin' like that."

"He's got troubles. I couldn't burden him with any more."

Bubba gave the old place a long study, from the barn to the corrals and back to the house. "Goin' to try to hang on a while longer, are you?"

"Seems like the thing to do. The market'll turn around one of these days. It always has."

Bubba shrugged. "Well, I'd've liked to add this place to mine. It would've been good for my hunters. But I reckon I know how you feel."

George could see Todd way down by the road, putting his bicycle into a shielding clump of brush. The yellow bus was waiting for him, and Todd trotted across the cattle-guard afoot to catch it. "It's not for me, Bubba. It's for him."

Bubba had both hands shoved into his pockets. George had learned years ago that this was his horse-trading stance. Bubba said, "I saw one of my black bucks out yonder by your fence."

"They're all over the place," George replied. "You'll have to put them on a leash if you figure on keepin' them at home."

"It gave me a notion, George. I was thinkin' maybe there's a way for me to add this place to mine without you losin' it. How about you leasin' the huntin' rights to me so I can bring my hunters over? It wouldn't make any difference to them whether I own the place or not, so long as they're in my lodge come dark. I could even pay you to guide them, if you was of a mind to agree to it."

George was enough of a horse trader himself not to let the smile he felt inside come out and betray itself on his face. "I owe you a cup of coffee, Bubba. Come on in the house."

DUSTER

Hamp Bowdre listened to the auctioneer's machine-gun voice as a dozen drouth-stricken sheep clattered out onto the scales. A chilly west wind whistled through the cracks in the plank siding of the auction barn. His corded right hand squeezed his left shoulder. Damned rheumatism — sign of another norther coming. It'd be a dry one — like the rest of them had been.

One of the ring men grabbed a ewe and peeled her lips back.

"Now, boys," the man said enthusiastically, "most of these ewes has got good mouths. They been on hard West Texas country, but they're bred for March lambs and worth ten dollars if they're worth a dime."

"Five dollars!" the bid starter shouted. The auctioneer picked it up from there. He wheedled and bluffed and let a sour-faced

125

San Angelo trader have them for five-and-a-half.

Hamp took a tally book from his pocket and jotted a note. He was conscious of a knotty old cowpuncher beside him.

"Howdy, Hamp. They've sure lowered the boom on the livestock market."

Hamp frowned at the intrusion.

Eby Gallemore prodded, "What you keepin' books for?" Hamp drew up within himself. Eby could ask more questions than a prying old woman.

"You ain't figgerin' on buyin' some sheep for yourself, are you, Hamp?" Eby laughed as if he had just told a big joke. "You'll never own a sheep or a cow-brute as long as you live. You're just a wore-out old ranch hand who'll work for wages till they nail you up in a box. Like me."

Sudden impatience lashed at Hamp. "If I was like you, Eby, I'd poke a rag in my mouth and keep it there!" He stood up stiffly and hobbled out.

Eyes narrowed against the bite of dust, he watched wind whip sand off the road and whisk it away. He clenched his fist. Dammit, if it would only rain!

Eby Gallemore's words were still running through his mind. *Wore out. Never own a sheep or a cow-brute as long as you live.*

Hamp's jaw ridged under his wrinkled brown skin. They'd soon see if Hamp Bowdre was wore out.

The boss came for him by and by. Crawling into the rattly old pickup truck, Hamp could see bad news carved deep into Charlie Moore's young face.

"It's all over with, Hamp," the boss finally spoke. "They're closin' me out."

Hamp couldn't say he was surprised. After four years of bare ranges, ruinous feed bills, and plummeting livestock prices, the wonder was that the bank had stayed with Charlie this long.

"I told old Prewett my lease contract is up at the end of this month — that I'd be needin' feed money besides. But he couldn't go, Hamp. Bank examiner's been crawlin' all over him about these big livestock loans he's stuck with. Well, I flipped my lid — told him if that's the way it stood, they're his sheep, and his cattle."

Moore's chin was low, his gray eyes sick. "Prewett's been good to me, and I oughtn't to've done it, Hamp. But I did. So it's the bank's outfit now — soon as they get out and take count."

Hamp didn't say anything. He didn't know anything that would help.

Moore said, "I'd rather pull my own teeth

127

than tell Vera. She really loves that ranch — her and the kids."

Hamp nodded sympathetically. The ranchman was in his mid-thirties, fully twenty years younger than Hamp. The year Moore had come home from the war he'd borrowed money to buy livestock and lease this ranch from old Whisky Sam O'Barr. The next year, he'd hired Hamp.

"Gonna hate to part with you, Hamp," Charlie said disconsolately. "We've been a great team."

Yes, Hamp thought, they sure had. Well, it wasn't the first time drouth had done him out of a job.

As they drove over the cattle guard onto Moore's mesquite-dotted pasture, Hamp thumbed at a windmill whose tower barely showed through the haze of dust. "We better take a look at that Lodd mill. It's been weakenin'."

Out of habit, Hamp first boogered two sheep away from a feed bunk and peeped under the lid to see how much cottonseed meal and salt mixture was in it. Enough for three or four days, he noted. Sheep couldn't last long on bare range without supplemental feed. The salt was to keep them from taking too much at one time. But it took lots of water, or a sheep would dehydrate on meal and salt.

They found the mill pumping a weak stream about the size of a pencil. "Drouth's droppin' the water table," Hamp observed. "The well needs to be deepened fifteen, twenty feet."

Moore shrugged. "That's Sam O'Barr's worry now — and the bank's."

Hamp cast a worried glance at Charlie. He'd never heard that grudging tone from the boss before. He walked over and looked in the concrete storage tank. Half empty. Sheep were drinking up the water faster than it was coming out of the ground.

A cloud of dust boiled toward them on the two-rut road. An oil-field pump truck with a big water tank on back pulled up beside the windmill. A college-age kid in oil-stained work clothes stepped out from behind the wheel and eyed the two ranchmen warily. "Truck's heatin'. Needs some water in the radiator."

Suspicion began working in Hamp. That concrete tank ought not to've been so low on water. Casually he edged over to the truck and put his hand on the front of it. Warm, but not hot. Anyway, a big twenty-gallon can of drinking water was strapped on the side.

"You're from that drillin' outfit over across

the fence, ain't you?" he queried. The youngster nodded.

"You-all have got a contract to take what water you need from Old Man Longley's wells. But it's a far piece over to Longley's, and it's just a mile over here. Ain't that right?"

The youngster looked as if he'd been caught sport roping another man's calves.

Hamp shook a stubby finger at him. "Now you hop in that truck and git! You ain't gonna steal another load of water here just because you're too triflin' lazy to go git it where you're supposed to."

Hamp watched until the truck was gone. "Two more truckloads would drain that tank. And we'd have a bunch of salt-poisoned sheep."

"The bank's sheep," Moore said.

Hamp eyed him sharply. Charlie acted as if he wouldn't care.

At the ranch Charlie drove the pickup into the shed. "Would you feed the stock for me, Hamp? I've got to talk to Vera."

Hamp forked some hegari bundles across the fence to a half-dozen saddle horses and a couple of potbellied dogie calves. Charlie's cowboy sons, Mackey and Jim, had finished milking the Jersey cow and were feeding their lambs. Hamp leaned against the fence

130

and watched them with a glow of satisfaction. It was almost as if they were his own boys.

"Hey, Hamp, looky here at old Hungry," called ten-year-old Jim, proudly petting a thick-bodied Rambouillet lamb. "County agent was out today. He said you did a good job of doctorin'. Old Hungry's gonna win that San Angelo show."

Hamp nodded, but he didn't grin with Jim. Chances were they wouldn't be making the San Angelo show now. He hobbled off to the frame bunkshack that served him as a home. It was bare except for an old dresser and a cot, and a table in the corner. But it was all Hamp needed — all he wanted. He pulled the light cord and sat down at the table.

He tore a sheet off of a writing tablet and began scrawling figures. One thousand sheep at five-and-a-half — five thousand five hundred dollars. Fifteen sections of land at forty-five cents per acre lease — four thousand three hundred twenty.

He had done it so many times lately that he had all the figures in his head. But it brought him satisfaction to mark them down on paper.

Old. Wore out. Never own a sheep or a cow-brute as long as you live.

131

He grinned without knowing it. They wouldn't say that again.

He wondered how Eby Gallemore's eyes would pop if Hamp showed him a savings account book adding up to more than twenty-three thousand dollars.

Hamp Bowdre still had sixty cents out of every dollar he'd ever made. While Gallemore and his kind had drunk up their wages, or spent them on women, or pooped them off around the rodeos, Hamp Bowdre had been living like a monk, saving against a time when he could be his own boss.

He'd had many chances these last few years, but Hamp was a cautious man. He'd seen this boom-and-bust business before. Wait till the bust. Wait till everybody else wants to sell.

Well, they wanted to sell now. Four years of drouth and demoralized markets had done that.

It was going to rain this spring. Hamp had been through drouths before, and somehow he knew. It would rain, and the livestock business would start a slow but steady upward climb.

Maybe he could get *this* place, he was thinking. Now that Charlie Moore was dropping out, it was possible. Talk around town was that hard-drinking Sam O'Barr had spent all his money and was getting desperate. Since that wildcat oil bunch had drilled two dry holes on his ranch, the oil-lease money had petered out. Only the land lease was left. Charlie had been paying sixty cents an acre — too high the way things had turned out.

I'll offer Sam forty-five cents, Hamp thought. *He'll snuff and stomp, but bare and dry as the place is, he won't find anybody else to take it. Maybe someday I'll even find me a rich partner. . . .*

The two boys came to the shack to call Hamp for supper. A tear rolled down Jim's freckled cheek. Mackey, a year older, was gravely quiet.

"Hamp," Jim burst out, "what am I gonna do with old Hungry? Daddy says we're fixin' to move to town."

Hamp patted the boy on the head. Sure tough on the kids.

Tough on Vera too. With dancing blue eyes, and a little on the plump side, she was usually quick to laugh, but there was no fun in her tonight.

Hamp ate the cobbler pie she had baked especially for him, but he couldn't enjoy it. Vera had always been as concerned about him as if he belonged to her family. She had often made him regret he'd never married.

133

Hamp thought he'd probably hire him a Mexican couple if he got this place. But he was going to miss the Moores.

The next morning Charlie Moore was sick. Moody and sleepless, he had taken a long walk in the night air. Now he was fighting off the flu.

Banker Prewett was out shortly after noon the second day and found him sitting up in the living room. "Mind if I look the sheep over?" he asked.

"Have at it," Charlie answered, a little curtly. "They're your sheep."

Hamp frowned. He'd never seen Charlie act this way before, and he didn't like it. He'd thought better of Charlie.

The wind buffeted the pickup around as Hamp slowly drove the banker over the bare, dusty pastures. Prewett was studiously silent during most of the ride. "I hate to do this," he said finally. "Charlie Moore's a good man, Hamp. I'd like to've helped him."

Hamp nodded. He'd thought about lending Charlie enough money to pull him through. But it would take Charlie years to pay it back, and Hamp was getting too old to wait. If he was to get a place for himself, it had to be soon.

Hamp said suddenly, "Mr. Prewett, would the bank take five-and-a-half a head for these sheep — the whole outfit?"

Surprised, Prewett straightened. "It might. Who's interested?"

"I am." Briefly Hamp explained his idea. Prewett nodded in silent admiration. Hamp had it figured out to a T.

Their last stop was the Lodd mill. Hamp knew something was wrong — the sheep were all gathered around it.

"She's gone dry," he exclaimed.

The mill had stopped pumping. Sheep nuzzled vainly at the dried mud in the trough. The concrete tank was drained.

Hamp's face flushed red as he saw where the truck had backed up to the tank. Water had sloshed out over the side, and the heavy tires had left deep prints in the dried mud.

Anger clenched Hamp's knotty fists as he walked out through the bleating sheep, the blowing sand gritty in his eyes, nose, and ears. He knew it would take days to get anything out of the drilling company.

But these ewes were already drawing up. They had been without water a day or two — and with all that salt in them. They had to be taken somewhere today or they'd begin losing some unborn lambs.

Hamp made good time in getting back to the house. The banker stood by while Hamp told Charlie what had happened.

Pale, sitting weakly in his chair, Charlie frowned, looking out the north window. "It'd be hard to drive them in this norther, mighty hard. It'd be blowin' up a storm by the time anybody could get to that well a-horseback."

The banker spoke up, "Like you said, Charlie, they're the bank's sheep. I wouldn't ask you to ride out in the face of that storm. We'll just write off those lambs."

Charlie kept frowning. Suddenly he stood up and headed for the coat rack. "Catch up the horses, Hamp," he said. "The quicker we start, the quicker we get those sheep to water."

Vera grabbed Charlie's arm. "Charlie, you're sick. You can't. . . ."

But Charlie was pulling on his coat. Watching him, Hamp felt a glow begin inside him. He forgot he'd ever been disappointed in Charlie Moore.

The huge brown dust cloud was rapidly swelling out of the north. For the three horsemen, riding into it was like heading into the mouth of a gigantic howling cave. Prewett rode with Charlie and Hamp — he had been a ranch hand before he had been a banker. It took an hour or more to reach the mill. By that time Hamp's sand-burned eyes were afire with pain.

136

Throwing the sheep into a bunch was a hard job. It's the nature of sheep to drift into the wind, unless it's too strong. Heading the ewes away from it at an angle took the hardest chousing Hamp had ever done in his life. The only way to turn them was to ride along beside them, whipping at their faces with an empty gunnysack.

The wind lifted to a new fury, the dust so thick that sometimes Hamp couldn't see Charlie fifteen feet away. It became too much for the sheep. They wanted to stop and huddle in helpless confusion.

Desperation swelled and grew in Hamp. He dismounted, and leading his horse, went to shoving against them, slapping at them with his bare hands. Hope flagging, he pulled over beside Charlie and shouted, "It's no use. Let's let them go."

Charlie was walking too, bent painfully, stumbling over his own feet. But doggedly he shook his head. "No! We'll fight them a little longer."

Hamp pulled back and went to shoving again, shouting until the voice finally left him. But somehow they were getting the job done. They had the sheep angled toward the house. And they were keeping them moving.

They finally struck a net-wire fence, and

it was easier after that. Through one gate, then another, dragging one ewe so the others would follow.

It was dark when they shoved the last ewe through the gate at the headquarters, and the sheep bunched up around the two long water troughs in the holding corral. Hamp saw that Charlie was smiling. Then Charlie's legs buckled.

In the house, Vera had a pot of coffee on the stove, hot and waiting. Wearily Hamp and Prewett sat with steaming cups in their hands, watching Vera go back and forth to and from the room where they had put Charlie. The kids sat quietly with their lessons, but they weren't studying much. Hamp coughed from deep in his throat. Vera hovered over him worriedly, telling him she'd better put some medicine down him or he would be sick like Charlie.

"I'll be okay," Hamp told her hoarsely, his throat raw. "I'm just give out, and got a chestful of dust. It's the same with Charlie. He'll cough it out."

She forced a smile. "Maybe, Hamp, maybe. The point is, he just doesn't care now. Losing this ranch and all . . ."

The idea had come to Hamp somewhere in that long drive, and it had grown with every step he had taken back toward the house. He'd need a good partner — and right here he could get a partner who had something better than money. Charlie had been sick. He hadn't had to go out there in the face of a duster, to save sheep that didn't belong to him anymore. But he had gone.

"Looky here, Vera," Hamp said, "you-all don't have to lose this place. You could take on a partner."

Her blue eyes widened. "A partner?"

"Me." He explained to her about the money he had saved, about the plan he'd had to take over the ranch when they left. "With the money I've got, we can pay Mr. Prewett here enough to satisfy the examiner. We can feed these sheep till it rains in the spring. And leave it to me to whittle Sam O'Barr down on the lease; I can be mean when I have to.

"It'll take the range a long time to recover, but the sheep that're still on the place now can be a foundation for us to start with. We can let the flock grow back as the range does."

Excitement bubbled within him. "What do you think, Vera? Reckon Charlie would take me on as a partner, fifty-fifty?"

The two kids were grinning. Vera's round face was all mixed up, her eyes laughing and crying at the same time. "He will, Hamp," she said. "I know he will."

Hamp walked out onto the front porch where the wall sheltered him from the wind. Prewett followed him. Hamp rolled a brown-paper cigarette while the banker stuffed his pipe. The wind howled as if there was nothing between there and the North Pole but a barbed-wire fence.

Well, let it blow. Pretty soon it would be spring, and things would change.

In the darkness he could sense the banker smiling at him.

Defensively Hamp said, "I always *have* wanted a place of my own. And I used to wish I had me a family. Well, sir, I've got that too. What better could a wore-out old ranch hand ask, for just twenty-three thousand dollars?"

No Music for Fiddle Feet

This would be remembered in west Texas as the year of the drought. Even more, it would be remembered as the year of the fence-cutting war. The war had been brewing a long time, but the drought brought it to a boil. It left its black mark in dozens of forlorn gray tombstones. They all ended the same way: died 1883.

It wasn't worrying young Johnny Clayton as he jogged along the dusty old wagon road on his bay gelding. Nothing was worrying Johnny. A few more months and he would be twenty-one. The only things he owned were the bay horse, a saddle, a bedroll and an old fiddle. He drew his wages every month, and the world was peaches and cream.

A new fiddle tune was leisurely working itself out in Johnny's mind. The fingers of his left hand played upon his bridle reins as if they were fiddle strings. He grinned. He knew Dottie Thurmond would like it when he played it for her at the square dance next Saturday night.

Clyde Thurmond, Johnny's boss, reined up his horse a little way ahead and looked back. He lowered the leather blab that protected his chapped lips from the sun and hot wind.

"What do you think we are, Johnny," he grinned, "a couple of Indians riding along single file? Come on and catch up."

Johnny grinned back. Clyde was middle-aged now, at least thirty-five, and his mind was always on cattle. But Johnny was young and his mind was on music, or on Clyde's younger sister.

His thoughts went back to the fiddle tune after he caught up with his boss. An oath from Clyde snapped him to reality right in the middle of a bar.

"The fence, Johnny! The fence cutters have been here!"

Clyde hit a lope toward a new wire gate just ahead. Johnny spurred after him. The older man reined up at the gate and began to swear.

The wire was cut between every post for fifty feet on each side of the gate. The soft dirt showed tracks of a dozen horses. A crudely-printed placard was nailed to one of the cedar gate posts.

Clyde Thurmond was quick to grin or quick to anger. Fury showed scarlet in his face now. Johnny could see Clyde's knuckles turn white as he clenched his work-roughened fists.

"So they finally got here. They've hit nearly every fence in the county. I wondered when they'd get to me."

Clyde stretched out of his saddle and snatched the placard from the post. His gray eyes smouldered as he read it, then handed it to Johnny. The penciled sign read:

You have three days to tear the fence down. If you don't, then we'll be back!

"Free range men," Clyde gritted bitterly. "They wouldn't buy the land when they had a chance. Thought there would always be free grass. And now they cut down our fences so they can crowd cattle and sheep onto our range."

Johnny knew. It hadn't meant much to him one way or the other, but he had seen it come on. Even he could remember when there hadn't been a wire fence in west Texas. Range had been free to any man strong enough to hold it.

But in the last few years, Texas state, school and railroad lands had started going on the market, and men had bought them.

Fences had sprung up.

Now drought had come to west Texas. Free range men suddenly found that the best range and the best waterholes were under private ownership and fenced off. Men with no range of their own were being crowded together on poor, sun-baked land where watering places were nothing but bogholes. In desperation they had turned to wire pinchers and sixguns.

Clyde Thurmond was still swearing. "I have to pay for my grass. It's me that's got to pay the interest and meet the bank note on this land. It's my family that's got to eat rabbit stew if I don't make a go of it.

"My dad brought us kids out here when his old buffalo gun was the only thing between us and a Comanche scalp pole. He hasn't bowed under the fence cutters and I'm not going to either."

His hard gaze bore into Johnny's eyes. "It's liable to mean some fighting, Johnny. I don't want you running out on me when I really need you. If you don't want any part of it, you better quit now."

Johnny felt a faint irritation and wished Clyde wouldn't look at him that way. He didn't want to fight anybody.

But he couldn't quit now. Dottie Thurmond had called him a fiddlefoot. When he had gone to work on her brother's ranch, which neighbored that of her father, she had laughed at him. He hadn't stayed two months on any other outfit — liked to fiddle and play too much. She had said he couldn't stay here.

But he had stayed six months already. Dottie was beginning to look at him as if she thought he might amount to something.

So he just couldn't quit now. Maybe this would all blow over, like stormclouds do sometimes in March.

Remembering the placard, Johnny started counting on his fingers. "Thursday, Friday — why, the third day's Saturday, Clyde. This might even make us miss the dance."

Clyde was looking at him queerly. "We're liable to miss a lot of dances before this is through, Johnny. But my fence is staying up! Come on. We got some patching to do!"

On the way home, Clyde told him he wanted to keep this from his wife as long as he could.

When they rode into the corral and dismounted at the barn, Helen Thurmond stepped out of the raw lumber ranch house and came walking out to meet them. Their three-year-old son came toddling along behind her, stopping to throw a rock at an old white hen.

Clyde avoided her eyes, and it didn't take her long to sense trouble. "There's something wrong, Clyde. I can tell. What is it?"

Clyde looked back at Johnny an instant, as if for help. Then he told her what happened. She didn't speak for a while, just dabbed at her eyes with a handkerchief.

Finally she said, "Maude Tatlock's husband tried to stop them on his place. They killed him."

Johnny felt sorry for his boss. One child was already depending on Clyde, and another was on the way. It must have been tough to tell Helen about this. Johnny wondered. If life got so hard for people with responsibilities, why did they look down on a man who didn't have any?

The next couple of days Johnny could feel the tension mounting. Helen had usually been as cheerful as her little son Bobby. After supper she usually sat beside Clyde on the front porch, while they watched the night come on.

But now Helen Thurmond had little to say. Hollow fear showed in her blue eyes as she sat down at the table and said grace at meals. At night Clyde sat on the porch alone. Johnny could see Helen in the parlor, reading her family Bible by lamplight.

Saturday morning Helen broke. At breakfast she set the steaming coffeepot on the table, then stood there gripping the cloth she had used to protect her hand from the hot handle. Her face was the palest Johnny had ever seen it. Her hands trembled.

"The dance tonight, Clyde," she said tightly. "I want you to take me."

Clyde stared at her, his mouth open. "But you're not in any condition — Helen, this is the third day. They may come tonight."

She began to sob. "That's why I want you with me. There'll be too many. They'll kill you like they did Jed Tatlock. Oh Clyde, please take me to town!"

Clyde tenderly put his arms around her shoulders, and Johnny watched a brave man give in.

It looked as if half the county had come out to the dance. Orange lamplight shone through the schoolhouse windows and fell on tied horses and buckboards. Johnny happily untied from his saddlehorn the sack in which he always carried his fiddle. In front of the schoolhouse door, Clyde was carefully helping Helen down from the buckboard.

Dottie was already there. Her father, old Floyd Thurmond, had come in from his ranch earlier in the day. Dottie broke away from an admiring group of young cowboys as Johnny came in the door.

Johnny thought his heart would melt when she came up, smiling at him. He tried to hold back that foolish grin he always seemed to get when he was around her.

"I composed you a tune, Dottie," he said, and he felt that grin come on. "I'm going to name it after you."

She stood there smiling at him. His knees got weak. "I can't believe it, Johnny," she said. "You've been out at Clyde's place six months now. Dad used to keep telling me you'd never amount to anything but a fiddlefooted saddle tramp. But he's wrong. You've proved that."

Johnny nervously shifted his weight from one foot to another and studied his polished boots.

Finally he looked back up at her and said, "I'd like to keep proving it to you, Dottie. From now on."

The thought of what he had just said scared him. A tinge of red crept into Dottie's cheeks. But he knew she had liked it.

Then the guitar player called him. "Come on, Johnny, we need us a fiddler. Quit making eyes. Come on up here and make music."

It was a while before midnight when the word started spreading through the crowd.

Ten or fifteen of the free range men suspected of wire cutting had been hanging around the Golden Eagle saloon most of the evening. Now they were all gone. And it was too early for them to leave on Saturday night.

A worried look was on Clyde's face as he trotted up to the fiddlers' stand. "They've ridden out to cut somebody's fence, Johnny," he said grimly, "and it's liable to be mine. We better get out there in a hurry."

Johnny lowered his fiddle and looked at Helen. She was trembling. There was a prayer in her eyes.

"Look here, Clyde," Johnny reasoned for Helen's sake. "You can't take Helen home now, and you sure don't want to leave her here in town by herself. If they cut the fence, we can fix it."

Clyde stared at Johnny unbelievingly. Then that red anger crept into his face, and his eyes were hard. "You're getting scared. That's what's wrong. You're trying to get out of it."

Anger flared in Johnny, too. "Now hold on, Clyde. I'm just trying to make you think about Helen. What if you got yourself killed? Look at her, and answer me that!"

But Clyde didn't look around at Helen. His gray eyes smouldered. "I thought you'd changed, Johnny. I ought've known you'd quit when things got tough. Well, I don't want a coward in my way. You came here to fiddle. Now fiddle your head off!"

Clyde turned on his heel and strode toward the door. Helen called him, but he didn't look back. He was probably afraid to. Helen almost fainted. Dottie caught her and helped her sit down.

For a second Johnny's eyes met Dottie's. He saw nothing there but scorn. He started to go after Clyde. But drumming hoofs fading into the distance told him Clyde had borrowed a horse and was already gone.

Other ranchmen who had fences were gathering up their cowboys and getting ready to go home. Johnny half wanted to go too. But a stubborn pride gripped him. Clyde had jumped off the deep end, like he often did, and hadn't given Johnny a chance.

Well, Johnny wouldn't go now and give in in a quarrel where he had been falsely accused. There was slim chance the fence cutters would be going to the Thurmond ranch, he told himself disconsolately. There were a dozen other fenced ranches in the county, and they had all had threats.

Maybe in the morning Clyde would be over his sudden anger. Then Johnny could go back and talk sense to him.

The dance crowd was quickly depleted to about half. Johnny had seen old Floyd Thurmond take his one cowboy out. Then Dottie started escorting Helen out into the night. Johnny put down his fiddle and ran to help.

Dottie turned on him with contempt. "Get away from us. Leave us alone, fiddle-foot!"

Numb, Johnny stood in the door and watched Dottie take Helen down the street to the little hotel.

Johnny stayed on and fiddled. But he seemed to have lost his taste for it. The exhilaration he usually felt just wasn't there now.

He decided a fiddle string was loose. He tried to turn the peg, but it seemed stuck. With impatience sharpened by the last hour's experience, Johnny braced the fiddle against his shoulder and gave the peg a sudden hard twist.

The string snapped and hit his face. He quickly rubbed his cheek to ease the burning.

His stomach for music was gone now. Gloom settled over him. He said good night to the other musicians and wearily made his way to his horse. He swung into the saddle and trotted dejectedly toward a burning lantern that marked the livery stable down the street. He unsaddled and rolled out his single blanket on top of some straw in the back of the stable.

He lay there a long time, trying to go to sleep. In the distance he could hear the sound of music from the schoolhouse and an occasional whoop from a celebrating cowboy. There were people all around him, Johnny thought moodily. But never in his life had he felt so lonely.

The Sunday morning sun was high when rapid hoofbeats awakened Johnny. He heard someone slide a horse to a stop at the doctor's home near the livery stable, and start pounding on the door.

Johnny swayed sleepily to his feet and rubbed his eyes. He was surprised he had slept so late. But it had taken him hours to get to sleep. He rolled up his blanket and tied it to his saddle. Then he strolled out and took a look down the street.

Old Floyd Thurmond's rider came out of the doctor's door and worriedly stepped down off the front porch. Apprehension quickly rose in Johnny. He trotted over to the doctor's house.

"What's wrong, Harvey?" he asked the rider. "What's happened?"

The cowboy eyed him coldly. "So this is where you spent the night. When he really needed you, you weren't there to help him."

Johnny felt weak. Clyde!

"We guarded the old man's fence last night," the cowboy said. "When sunup come and nothing had happened, the old man decided to go over to Clyde's and see how he made out. We found the fence jerked down and cut in places for a quarter of a mile. And Clyde was shot."

Shame flooded through Johnny. He stared down at the toes of his boots. "Is he — is it bad?"

The cowboy nodded. "Looks bad. We didn't dare bring him to town. The doc's going out to the ranch. I got to go to the hotel now and break the news to his wife and Dottie. If I was you, I'd keep out of their sight."

Harvey turned contemptuously and mounted his horse. He rode on up the street.

Johnny choked. He wanted to cry, something he hadn't done in years. They had all been right, he told himself bitterly. He was just a no-good, fiddlefooted loafer that wasn't worth his weight in river rocks. For the first time in his life, people had begun to have confidence in him. And he had let them down.

He turned and started back toward the

livery stable, kicking up dust as he went.

The anger against himself slowly turned into anger against the fence cutters. Gunning down a man for trying to protect his own land and feed his own family! They probably figured they had licked the Thurmond outfit now — gunned down Clyde and scared off the kid cowboy.

Well, it wasn't going to be that easy, Johnny told himself. Even a fiddlefoot takes root sometimes, and Johnny was going to do it right here. If they wanted to tear down the fence, they'd have to gun him down first. He'd show the fence cutters, and he'd show Clyde and Dottie.

He swung a fist at a horsecollar hanging on a peg and knocked it ten feet across the stable. He saddled up, tied on the sack containing his fiddle and paid the grinning hostler. He struck a brisk trot down the sleepy street. He shot one quick glance at the Thurmond buckboard beside the hotel.

Idly his gaze settled on the Golden Eagle saloon. He reined up a moment, then angled his horse across to the saloon. He tied him loosely, stepped briskly up onto the sidewalk and pushed through the swinging doors into the empty saloon.

A swamper looked up in surprise and stopped mopping the floor. Johnny saw the saloon owner idly wiping the wooden bar.

"Selkirk," he said evenly, not moving, "I'm going to put up Clyde Thurmond's fence where the wire cutters dropped it last night."

Selkirk stared at him, a trace of a smile on his bland face. "So what? Why come to me about it?"

Johnny doubled his fists. "Everybody knows the fence cutters hang out in here — and that you're a friend to them. Well, you can tell them that if they want to come back tonight and tear down what I put up, I'll be there waiting. And they won't do it cheap!"

He turned and walked out. The doors were still swinging as he mounted and rode on toward the wagon road.

The fiddle kept bouncing against his knee as he jogged along. If it hadn't been for the fiddle, people might not have regarded him as shiftless ever since he had started out on his own, he thought bitterly. Clyde and Dottie might not have condemned him. And maybe Clyde wouldn't be lying there in the ranch house now, possibly dying of bullet wounds.

Johnny untied the sack. He hefted the fiddle a minute in indecision, then hurled it away. It landed in a bush at the side of the trail. Johnny glanced at it blackly, then rode on.

At the ranch he wanted to go into the house and see how Clyde was. But he recognized old Floyd Thurmond's horse tied in front and knew he had better not. The old man would turn on him like a bear. Clyde likely wouldn't want to see him either.

Johnny stopped at the little bunkhouse. He found a couple of cans of tomatoes and some sardines he had bought on another trip to town and hadn't eaten. He dropped them into a sack. At the barn he picked up a pair of wire pinchers, a sackful of staples and as much barbed wire as he could carry coiled up across his saddlehorn. Then he struck out for the fence.

He didn't have any trouble finding where the fence cutters had been. In their haste to tear down as much of the fence as they could, they had not done much actual cutting. Instead, it looked as if they had tied ropes to the wire and pulled down big sections of it, jerking staples out of the posts.

All the rest of the day he worked in the blazing sun, stopping only to eat a can of sardines and gulp down the canned tomatoes. He untangled the snarled-up wires and stapled them back to every fourth or fifth post, splicing where necessary. By dark he had much of the damage repaired in a temporary way.

But the coming of darkness made him reconsider his problem. He had been angry when he had made his little speech in the saloon. He hadn't given any real thought to the consequences.

But now the anger was gone. In its place was a cold realization of the danger he had stepped into. The wire cutters were sure to come tonight. If Clyde Thurmond hadn't been able to stand them off, what chance did a footloose kid have?

One thing sure, he couldn't just ride away. He would be branded a coward wherever he went. He had to stay.

Cold sweat popped out on his face and a clammy fear rose in him. He rubbed his hand across his face and remembered the burn of the fiddle string.

The fiddle string! He caught a sharp breath. If a little string did that, what might a big wire do? His heart raced as an idea struck him. A slim chance, but it might work. He had to try something.

Johnny decided to make his stand at a gate. He cut off a fifty-foot piece of wire. He wrapped the wire around the gate post about chest-high to a man on horseback and fastened it down securely with four staples.

The riders would likely come down the fence looking for him, he reasoned. No matter from which direction they came, he would have the wire and pivot post waiting for them.

As the full moon rose, Johnny squatted on the ground to wait. Every night sound quickened his pulse as he listened for hoofbeats. Jack rabbits rustled the scattered dry mesquite beans. Night birds called. A coyote came close, then bounded away. One hour went past, then two.

Finally he heard them. They were coming down the fence from the west. They didn't seem to be trying to keep from making noise. Maybe they hoped to scare him away.

Johnny was scared, but he wasn't leaving. He swung into the saddle, grabbed the end of the wire and wrapped it twice around his saddlehorn. He moved back and out from the fence until the fifty-foot wire was drawn fairly taut. Then he sat quietly and waited.

They showed a moment against the moon-lit skyline as they topped a rise. There weren't many. They probably figured it wouldn't take many to booger a kid like Johnny.

Apparently they didn't see him until they were within fifty feet of him. "There he is, boys," the man out in front said cautiously.

They rode up to within twenty feet. They sat there and eyed Johnny a full minute. He counted six men. He didn't think they could see the wire tied to his saddlehorn.

"Well, button," the leader said, "you had your chance to clear out. Now you'll take what's coming to you."

Johnny tried to keep his voice even. His hands trembled a little. "And just what is that?"

The leader rested his hands on his saddlehorn and leaned forward on them, his arms straight. "Well, in the first place, we brung along an extry set of wire pinchers. We're going to make you help us cut that wire."

Another rider pushed up even with the leader. "Say, Jake, ain't he that fiddling kid?"

The one called Jake nodded.

"Well, then, I got a good notion to stomp them fiddling fingers when we git through with him."

The leader grunted. "All right, button. Let's git started. And don't reach for your six-shooter. We'll do what we done to Thurmond."

Johnny acted as if he was going to dismount. Suddenly he leaned low over the right side and spurred his horse. He let out an ear-splitting yell and started a wide swing around the fence cutters.

"Stop him!" the leader yelled. "He's getting —" The wire caught him across his chest and jerked him off the saddle before he knew what had happened. The second man clawed at his gun, but the wire dragged him down.

Johnny knew he had caught them by surprise. Shouts and curses rose in the night as the cutting, gouging wire hit man after man and dragged each one off. In a few seconds only one man was left in the saddle. He was outside the wire's range.

Johnny knew it was time to get out of there. Desperately he struggled to get the wire loose from his saddlehorn. The jolt of hitting the men had drawn it taut.

Some of the downed men were feeling on the ground for guns that had fallen from their holsters. One was firing wildly at Johnny.

Now the mounted man was coming in. Johnny freed the wire just as the moving rider fired at him. He stood his ground, jerked out his own gun and triggered two fast shots at the man. The rider twisted in the saddle, then fell to the ground.

Not waiting a second, Johnny spurred back around behind the wounded man's horse and hazed it toward the others. The gunfire had scared the horses. Not a man had been able to get back in the saddle.

Johnny bent low over the horn as the men

on the ground fired at him. He wanted their horses now, all of them.

One man had managed to catch a horse and had one foot in a stirrup. Johnny spurred by him. He swung the barrel of his gun down across the man's head. Then he was in the clear — with all six horses in front of him!

Behind him, two or three men were still firing. He snapped back a couple of parting shots as he loped away. Suddenly he felt as if someone had hit his arm with a hot branding iron.

He swayed in the saddle, sickened and dizzy from pain.

Somehow he managed to stay astride. He got the horses headed for town and let them slow down to a fast trot. His head swirled, and he was sick at his stomach. He gripped the saddle horn grimly with one hand and kept himself on.

Much later he reined up in front of the sheriff's house beside the jail. He tried to swing down, but sprawled weakly in the street. He struggled to his feet and staggered to the front steps. After a long minute's pounding on the door, he got the sheriff out.

Johnny sank down onto the edge of the porch and quickly told his story. "You'll find

161

them all out there afoot some place."

The sheriff put his big hand on Johnny's shoulder.

"I'm taking you over to the doc, son. Then I'll get me some men together and we'll round up your fence cutters."

The doctor found that the bullet had gone on through Johnny's arm. As he cleansed the wound and bound it, he told Johnny that Clyde was going to pull through.

"You've lost a lot of blood, youngster. I've got an extra cot in the back room. You'd better lie down and get you some sleep."

Wearily Johnny lay down. Later on he couldn't even remember his head hitting the pillow.

The midday sun was bright when something awakened him. He blinked a minute and saw old Floyd Thurmond standing in the door.

"Didn't mean to wake you up, son," Thurmond said quietly, hat in hand. "How you feel?"

Johnny tried to raise up, but nausea pulled him down again.

"That's all right, son. Stay there. You know, it looks kind of like you've stopped the fence cutting in this country. The sheriff found your six men."

The old man went on. "One of them was

162

shot up pretty bad. He got scared he was going to die and told about how they shot Clyde and killed Jed Tatlock, and who all was with them. The sheriff's out now rounding up the whole bunch."

Suddenly Dottie came into the little room. Johnny felt his pulse quicken. She looked at her father, grinned sheepishly, and leaned over and kissed Johnny. She stayed there a long moment, looking proudly at him.

Finally she said, "I've got something for you, Johnny."

She stepped out of the room, then came back carrying something. She held up his fiddle and bow, and laid them across his cot.

"We found them where you had thrown them into a bush, Johnny."

His eyes burned a little. His throat was choked. He let the fingers of his good hand rove lovingly over the fiddle.

"When your arm gets well," Dottie was smiling, "I want you to play that tune for me. You know, the one you made up for me."

A warm glow spread through Johnny, and he grinned. Sure, he would play it for her, play it as many times as she wanted him to.

With a little luck, he might be playing it for her the rest of his life.

THE DEBT OF
HARDY BUCKELEW

I guess you'd call him crazy. We did, that spring of '78 when old man Hardy Buckelew set out to square his account against the Red River.

That was my third year to help graze the Box H steer herd from South Texas up the Western Trail toward Dodge. The first year I had just been the wrangler, bringing up the remuda to keep the riders in fresh mounts. A button job, was all. The second year they promoted me. Didn't matter that they put me back at the dusty tail end of the herd to push up the drags. It was a cowboy job, and I was drawing a man's wages, pretty near.

Old Hardy Buckelew had only one son — a big, raw-boned, overgrown kid by the name of Jim, wilder than a Spanish pony. They used to say there was nothing Jim Buckelew couldn't whip, and if anything ever did show up, old man Hardy would

164

whip it for him. That's the way the Buckelew were.

I never did see but one thing Jim couldn't whip.

He was only nineteen the first time I saw him. That young, he wasn't supposed to be going into saloons and suchlike. He did anyway; he was so big for his age that nobody paid him much mind. Or if they did notice him, maybe they knew they'd have to throw him out to get rid of him. That wouldn't have been much fun.

One time in San Antonio he fell into a card game with a pair of sharpers, and naturally they fleeced him. He raised a ruckus, so the two of them throwed together and lit into him. They never would have whipped him if the bartender in cahoots with them hadn't busted a bottle over Jim's head.

Now, a man who ever saw old Hardy Buckelew get mad would never forget it as long as he lived. He was one of those old-time Texas cowmen — the likes of which the later generations never saw. He stood six feet tall in his brush-scarred boots. He had a hide as tough as the mesquite land he rode in and a heart as stout as a black Mexican bull. When he hollered at a man, his voice would carry a way yonder, and you could bet the last dollar you owned that whoever he hollered at would come a-running too.

Old Hardy got plenty mad that time, when Jim came limping in broke and bruised and bloody. The old man took him way off to one side for a private lecture, but we could hear Hardy Buckelew's bull voice as far as we could see him.

Next day he gathered up every man he could spare, me included, and we all rode a-horseback to San Antonio. We marched into the saloon where the fight had taken place and marched everybody else out — everybody but the bartender and the two gamblers. They were talking big, but their faces were white as clabber. Old Hardy busted a bottle over the bartender's head and laid him out colder than a wedge. Then he switched those fiery eyes of his to Jim Buckelew and jabbed his stubby thumb in the direction of the gamblers.

"Now this time," he said, "do the job right!"

Jim did. When we left there, three men lay sprawled in the wet sawdust. Jim Buckelew was grinning at us, showing a chipped front tooth like it was a medal from Jeff Davis himself. His knuckles were torn and red-smeared as he counted out the money he had taken back from the gamblers' pockets.

Old man Hardy's voice was rough, but you couldn't miss the edging of pride in it. "From now on, Jimbo, whether it's a man or a job, don't you ever take a whippin' and quit. No matter how many times it takes, a Buckelew keeps on comin' back till he's won."

Now then, to the debt of Hardy Buckelew. Late in the summer of '77 we finished a cow hunt and threw together a herd of Box H steers to take to Kansas and the railroad before winter set in. Hardy Buckelew never made the trip himself anymore — too many years had stacked up on him. For a long time now, Will Peril had been his trail boss. Will was a man a cowboy liked to follow — a graying, medium-sized man with the years just commencing to put a slump in his shoulders. His voice was as soft as the hide of a baby calf, and he had a gentle way with horses and cattle. Where most of us might tear up enough ground to plant a potato patch, Will Peril could make livestock do what he wanted them to without ever raising the dust.

He handled men the same way.

This time, though, Hardy Buckelew slipped a joker in the deck.

"Will," Hardy said, "it's time Jimbo took

on a man's responsibilities. He's twenty-one now, so I'm puttin' him in charge of this trail herd. I just want you to go along and kind of keep an eye on him. You know, give him his head but have one hand on the reins, just in case."

Will Peril frowned, twisting his mule-hide gloves and looking off to where the cook was loading the chuckwagon. "Some men take longer growin' up than others do, Hardy. You really think he's ready?"

"You want to teach a boy to swim, you throw him in where the water's deep. Sure he'll make some mistakes, but the education he gets'll be worth the price."

So we pointed them north with a new trail boss in charge. Now, Jim was a good cowboy, make no mistake about that; he was just a shade wild, is all. He pushed too fast and didn't give the cattle time enough to graze along and put on weight as they walked. He was reckless too, in the way he rode, in the way he tried to curb the stampedes we had before we got the cattle trail-broke. He swung in front of the bunch one night, spurring for all he was worth. His horse stepped in a hole and snapped its leg with a sound like a pistol shot. For a minute there, we thought Jim was a goner. But more often than not a running herd will split around a man on foot. They did this time. Jim just walked away laughing. He'd have spit in the devil's eye.

All in all, Jim did a better job than most of us hands thought he would. That is, till we got to the Red River.

It had been raining off and on for three days when we bunched the cattle on the south bank of the Red. The river was rolling strong, all foamy and so muddy you could almost walk on it. You could hear the roar a long time before you got there.

The trail had been used a lot that year, and the grass was grazed down short. Will Peril set out downriver to find feed enough that we could hold the cattle while we waited for the water to run down. He was barely out of sight when Jim Buckelew raised his hat and signaled for the point man to take cattle out into the river.

"You're crazy, Jim!" exclaimed the cook, a limping old Confederate veteran by the name of Few Lively. "A duck couldn't stay afloat in that water!"

But Jim might have had cotton in his ears for all the attention he paid. When the point man held back, Jim spurred his horse out into that roaring river with the same wild grin he had when he waded into those San Antonio gamblers. Him shaming us that way, there was nothing the rest of us could do but follow in behind him, pushing the cattle.

The steers didn't like that river. It was all we could do to force them into it. They bobbed up and down, their heads out of the water and their horns swaying back and forth like a thousand old-fashioned rocking chairs. The force of the current started pulling them downriver. Up at the point, Jim Buckelew was fighting along, keeping the leaders swimming, pushing them for the far bank.

For a while there it looked like we might make it. Then, better than halfway across, the lead steers began to tire out. They still had heart in them, but tired legs couldn't keep fighting that torrent. Jim Buckelew had a coiled rope in his hand, slapping at the steers' heads, his angry voice lost in the roar of the flood. It was no use; the river had them.

And somehow Jim Buckelew lost his seat. We saw him splash into the muddy water, so far out yonder that no one could reach him. We saw his arms waving, saw him go under. Then we lost sight of him out there in all that foam, among those drowning cattle.

The heart went out of all of us. The main

part of the herd milled and swam back. It was all we could do to get ourselves and the cattle to the south bank. Not an animal made it to the far side.

It was all over by the time Will Peril returned. We spent the next day gathering cattle that had managed to climb out way yonder down the river. Along toward evening, as the Red dropped, we found Jim Buckelew's body where it had washed in with an uprooted tree. We wrapped him in his blankets and slicker and dug a grave for him. A gentle rain started again like a quiet benediction as Will Peril finished reading over him out of the chuckbox Bible.

The burial done, we stood there numb with shock and grief and chill. Will Peril stuck the Bible inside his shirt, beneath the slicker.

"We haven't got a man to spare," he said tightly, "but somebody's got to go back and tell Hardy."

His eyes fell on me.

It had been bad enough, watching Jim Buckelew die helpless in that boiling river. In a way it was even worse, I think, standing there on the gallery of the big house with my hat all wadded up in my hand, watching old Hardy Buckelew die inside.

He never swayed, never showed a sign of a tear in his gray eyes. But he seemed somehow to shrink up from his six feet. That square, leather face of his just seemed to come to pieces. His huge hands balled into fists, then loosened and began to tremble. He turned away from me, letting his gaze drift out across the sun-cured grass and the far-stretching tangle of thorny mesquite range that he had planned to pass down to Jim. When he turned back to me, he was an old man. An old, old man.

"The cattle," he whispered, "did Jim get them across?"

I shook my head. "No, sir, we lost a couple hundred head. The rest got back to the south bank."

"He never did quit, though, did he? Kept on tryin' all the way?"

"He never quit till he went under, Mister Buckelew."

That meant a lot to him, I could tell. He asked, "Think you could find Jimbo's grave for me?"

"Yes, sir, we marked it."

The old man's voice seemed a hundred miles away, and his mind too. "Get some rest, then. We'll leave at daylight."

Using the buckboard, we followed the wide, tromped-out cattle trail all the way up to the Red River. We covered more ground in one day than the herd had moved in three or four. And one afternoon we stood beside Jim Bucklelew's grave. The cowboys had put up a little brush fence around it to keep trail cattle from walking over it and knocking down the marker.

The old man stood there a long time with his hat in his hand as he looked at his son's resting place. Occasionally his eyes would lift to the river, three hundred yards away. The water had gone down now. The Red moved along sluggish and sleepy, innocent as could be. The dirty high-water marks of silt and debris far up on the banks were all that showed for the violence we had seen there.

Then it was that I heard Hardy Buckelew speak in a voice that sent fingers of ice crawling up my spine. He wasn't talking to me.

"I'll be back, Jimbo. Nothin' has ever beat a Buckelew. We got a debt here, and it's goin' to be paid. You watch, Jimbo, I'll be back!"

I had never really been afraid of Hardy Buckelew before. But now I saw something in his face that made me afraid, a little bit.

He turned toward the buckboard. "Let's go home," he said.

All those days of traveling for that single hour beside the river. And now we were going home again.

The old man wasn't the same after that. He stayed to himself, getting grayer and thinner. When he rode out, he went alone and not with the boys. He spent a lot of his time just puttering around the big house or out at the barn, feeding and currying and petting a roan colt that had been Jim's favorite. He never came to the cookshack anymore. The ranch cook sent his meals up to the big house, and most of the food would come back uneaten.

When the trail crew finally returned from Dodge City, old Hardy didn't even come out. Will Peril had to take his report and the bank draft up to the big house.

Will was shaking his head when he came to the cookshack for supper. Worry was in his eyes. "The thing's eatin' on him," he said, "turnin' him in on himself. I tell you, boys, if he don't get off of it, it'll drive him out of his mind."

Knowing how much Will loved that old cowman, I didn't feel like telling him what Hardy had said at the grave by the Red River. The way I saw it, Hardy Buckelew was pretty far gone already.

When winter came on, he just seemed to hole up in the big house. He didn't come out much, and when he did we wished we hadn't seen him. For a time there, we didn't expect him to live through the winter. But spring came and he was still with us. He began coming down to the cookshack some-times, a living ghost who sat at the end of the long table, deaf and blind to what went on around him.

Time came for the spring cow hunt. Hardy delegated all of his responsibility to Will Peril, and the chuckwagon moved out.

"He won't live to see this roundup fin-ished," Will said. You could see the tears start in his eyes. "One of these days we'll have to quit work to come in and bury him."

But Will was wrong. As the new grass rose, so did Hardy Buckelew. The life that stirred the prairies and brought green leaves to the mesquite brush seemed to touch the old man too. You could see the change in him from one day to the next, almost. He strengthened up, the flesh coming back to his broad shoulders and his square face. He commenced visiting the wagon more and more often, until one day he brought out his bedroll and pitched it on the ground along with ours.

We thought then that we had him back —

the same old Hardy Buckelew. But he wasn't the same. No, sir, he was another man.

The deep lines of grief that had etched into his face were still there, and we knew they would never fade. Some new fire smouldered in his eyes like camp coals banked for the night. There was hatred in that fire, yet we saw nothing for him to hate. What had happened was nobody's fault.

As the strength came back to him, he worked harder than any man in the outfit. Seemed like he never slept. More often than not, he was the one who woke up the cook of a morning and got the coffeepot on to boil. He was always on the go, wearing out horses almost as fast as we could bring them up for him.

"Tryin' to forget by drivin' himself into the grave," Will Peril said darkly. "I almost wish he was still mopin' around that ranch house."

So did some of the others. Hardy got so hard to follow that three of his cowboys quit. Two reps for other outfits left the Box H wagon and swore they wouldn't come back for anything less than his funeral. Hardy didn't even seem like he noticed.

We finished the regular spring works, and we had a sizable bunch of big steers thrown together for the trip up the trail to Dodge. For those of us who usually made the drive, it was a welcome time. We were tickled to death at the idea of getting away from Hardy Buckelew awhile. I think even Will Peril, much as he thought of the boss, was looking forward to a little breathing spell himself.

We spent several days getting the outfit ready. We put a fresh trail brand on the steers so that if they ever got mixed up with another bunch we could know them easy. We wouldn't have to stretch a bunch of them out with ropes and clip away the hair to find the brands.

You could tell the difference in the men as we got ready. There wasn't much cheer among those fixing to stay home, but the trail crew was walking around light as feathers. Trail driving being the hard, hot, dusty, sleepless, and once-in-a-while dangerous work that it is, I don't know why anybody would look forward to it. But we did.

The night before we started, Hardy Buckelew dropped us the bad news. He was going too.

Will Peril argued with him till he was blue in the face. "You know what it's like to go up that trail, Hardy — you've done it often enough. You're not in any condition to be makin' the trip."

Will Peril was the only man Hardy Buckelew ever let argue with him, and even Will didn't do it much.

"Who owns this outfit?" Hardy asked.

"You do," Will said.

"What part of this outfit is yours?"

"None of it," Will admitted.

"Then shut up about it. I'm goin', and if you don't like it you can stay home!"

Right about then I imagine Will was tempted to. But you could see the trouble in his eyes as he studied Hardy Buckelew. He couldn't let the old man get off on that trail without being around someplace to watch out for him.

Hardy didn't bother anybody much the first few days. It was customary to drive the cattle hard the first week or so. Partly that was to get them off the range they were used to and reduce the temptation for them to stray back. Partly it was to keep them too tired to run at night till they were used to trail routine.

Hardy rode up at swing position, leaving everybody pretty much alone. Once in a while you would see him turn in the saddle and look back, but he didn't have anything to say. Seemed like everything suited him — at first.

But one morning after we had been on the trail a week he changed complexion. As we strung the cattle off the bedgrounds, Will Peril told the point man to slow them down. "We got them pretty well trail-broke," he said. "We'll let them start puttin' on a little weight now."

But Hardy Buckelew came riding up like a Mexican bull looking for a fight. "You don't do no such of a thing! We'll keep on pushin' them!"

Will couldn't have been more surprised if Hardy had set fire to the chuckwagon. "Hardy, if we keep on like we started, they won't be nothin' but hide racks, time we get to Dodge."

Hardy Buckelew didn't bother to argue with him. He just straightened up and gave Will that "I'm the boss around here" look that not even Will would argue with. Hardy rode back to the drags and commenced pushing the slow ones.

From then on, Hardy took over the herd. The first couple of days Will Peril tried every way he could to slow things down. But Hardy would just run over him. Will finally gave up and took a place at swing, his shoulders slumped like he had been demoted to horse wrangler. In a way, I guess you might say he had.

Hardy Buckelew was as hard to get along with on the trail as he had been on the cow hunt — harder, maybe. He was up of a morning before first light, rousing everybody out of bed. "Catch up on your sleep next winter," he would growl. And he wouldn't let the drive stop till it was too dark to see. I remember an afternoon early in the drive when Few Lively set up camp on a nice little creek. It was about six o'clock when the point came even with the place. If Will had been bossing the outfit, right there's where we would have bedded the herd. But Hardy Buckelew rode up to the wagon in a lope, looking like he was fixing to fight somebody.

"What're you doin' here?" he demanded.

Few Lively swallowed about twice, wondering what he had done wrong. "I always camp here. Good water, plenty of grass. Ain't nothin' ahead of us half as good."

Hardy's face was dark with anger. "There's two more hours of good daylight. Now you git that team hitched up and that camp moved a couple more miles up the trail."

As cook, and as one of the old men of the outfit, Few wasn't used to being talked to that way. "There ain't no good water up there, Mister Buckelew."

180

"We'll drink what there is or do without. Now you git movin'!"

Hardy was like that, day in and day out. He would wear out four or five horses a day just riding back and forth from drag up to the point and back again, stopping every little bit to cuss somebody out and tell him to push them harder. We rode from can-see to can't, Hardy's rough voice never very far away. Not able to fight Hardy Buckelew, and having to work it off someway, some of the boys took to fighting with one another. A couple of them just sneaked off one night while they were on night guard. Didn't ask for their time or anything. Didn't want to face Hardy Buckelew.

Time we got to the Red River, the whole outfit was about ready to bust up. I think if one man had led off, the rest of us would have ridden out behind him, leaving Hardy Buckelew alone with all those steers. Oh, Will Peril probably would have stayed, but nobody else. That's the way it usually is though. Everybody waits for somebody else to start, and nobody does.

Like the year before, it was raining when we got to the Red. The river was running a little bigger than usual as Will Peril rode ahead to take a look at it. He came back and told the point man to keep on going till he reached the other side.

Hardy Buckelew had loped up right after Will Peril and took a long look at the river. He came back holding his hand up in the air, motioning the men to stop.

"We're campin' right here."

Middle of the day, and Hardy Buckelew wanted to camp! We looked at each other like we couldn't believe it, and I think we all agreed on one thing. He'd finally gone crazy.

Will Peril said, "Hardy, that river's just right to cross. Got enough water runnin' to swim them and keep them out of the quicksand. Not enough current to give them much trouble."

Hardy shrugged his shoulders as if he had already said all he wanted to say about it. "We're goin' to camp — rest up these cattle."

Will was getting angry now, his face red and his fists clenched up. "Hardy, it's rainin'. If we don't get them across now, we're liable to have to wait for days."

Hardy just turned and gave him a look that would melt a bar of lead. "This is *my* herd. I say we're goin' to rest these cattle."

And rest them we did, there on the south bank of the Red, with the rain falling and the river beginning to swell. Will Peril would go down by the river and pace awhile, then come back and try arguing again. He had just as well have sat down with the rest of us and kept dry under the big wagonsheet stretched out from the wagon. He couldn't have moved Hardy Buckelew with a team of horses.

We were camped close to Jim Buckelew's grave. Old Hardy rode off down there and spent a while. He came back with his eyes aglow like they had been the fall before, when I had brought him here in the buckboard. He spent little time under the wagonsheet, in the dry. He would stand alone in the rain and stare at that mud-red river.

"He'll catch his death out there," Will Peril muttered, watching the old man like a mother hen watches a chick. But he didn't go out to get him.

The old man had never said a word to anybody about Jim. Still, we knew that was all he was thinking of. We could almost feel Jim right there in camp with us. It was an eerie thing, I'll tell you. I would be glad when we got out of that place.

The second day, after standing by the river a long time, Hardy walked in and spoke to Will Peril. "Is the river the way it was the day Jim drowned?"

Will's eyes were almost closed. "No, I'd

say it was a little worse that day."

The old man went out in the rain and watched the river some more. It kept rising. He came back with the same question, and Will gave him the same answer. Now alarm was starting in Will's face.

Finally the old man came back the third time. "Is it as big now as it was that day?"

Will Peril's cheekbones seemed to stand out as the skin drew tight in his whiskered face. "I reckon it is."

The look that came into the old man's gray eyes then was something I never saw before and have never seen again. He turned toward his horse. "All right, boys," he said evenly, "let's go now. We're puttin' them across."

Talk about surprise, most of us stood there with our mouths open like we'd been hit in the head with the flat side of an ax. But not Will Peril. He must have sensed it coming on. He knew the old man better than anybody.

"You've waited too long, Hardy," he said. "Now it can't be done."

"We couldn't go across earlier," spoke Hardy. "We'd have been cheatin' Jimbo. No Buckelew ever started anything but what it got finished. We're goin' to finish this job for *him.*" Hardy shoved his left foot in the stirrup and started to swing into the saddle.

Will Peril took three long strides toward him. "Listen to me, Hardy, I'm fixin' to tell it to you straight. Jim rode off into somethin' too big for him and knew it. He was playin' the fool. You've got no call to take it up for him."

Hardy's eyes blazed. If he had had a gun, I think he might have shot Will.

"He was my boy. He was a Buckelew." Hardy's eyes left Will and settled on the rest of us. "How about it, you-all comin'?"

We all just stood there.

Hardy looked us over, one by one. We couldn't meet his eyes. "Then stay here," he said bitterly, pulling himself into the saddle. "I'll do it alone!"

Will Peril was close to him now. Will reached out and grabbed the reins. "Hardy, if you won't stop, I'll stop you!"

"Let go, Will!"

"Get down, Hardy!"

They stared hard at each other, neither man giving ground. All of a sudden the old man swung down and waded into Will.

Will wasn't young, but he was younger than Hardy Buckelew. Most of us thought it would be over with in a hurry. It was, but not the way we expected. Hardy was like a wild man, something driving him as we had

185

never seen him driven before. He took Will by storm. His fists pounded Will like mallets, the sound of them solid and hard, like the strike of an ax against a tree. Will tried, but he couldn't stand up under that. Hardy beat him back, and back, and finally down.

The old man stood over him, swaying as he tried for breath. His hands and face were bloody, his eyes afire. "How about it now?" he asked us again. "You comin'?" When we didn't, he just turned and went back to his horse.

You had to figure him crazy, the way he worked those cattle, getting them started, forcing the first of them off into the water. We stood around like snake-charmed rabbits, watching. We'd picked Will Peril up and dragged him under the wagonsheet, out of the rain. He sat on the muddy ground, shaking his head, his gaze following Hardy Buckelew.

"You tried," I told Will. "You can't blame yourself for what he does now."

Will could see that Hardy was going to take at least a few of those cattle out into the water, with or without us. The trail boss stood up shakily.

"You boys can do what you want to. I'll not let him fight it alone!"

We looked at Will, catching up his horse,

then we looked at each other. In a minute we were all on horseback, following.

It was the same as it had been the last time, the water running bankwide and strong. It was a hard fight, just to get those cattle out into the river. They were smarter than us, maybe — they didn't want to go. I don't really know how we did it, but we got it done. Old Hardy Buckelew took the point, and we strung them out.

Time or two there, I saw the leaders begin to drift, and I thought it was over for Hardy the way it had been for Jim. But Hardy Buckelew was fighting, and Will Peril moved up there to help him.

I can't rightly say what the difference was that we made it this time, when we hadn't the time before. Maybe it was the rest the cattle and horses had before they started across. Maybe they were tougher too, the way they had been driven. But mostly I think it was that determined old man up there ahead of us, hollering and swinging his rope and raising hell. He was crazy for going, and we were crazy for following him.

But we made it.

It was a cold and hungry bunch of water-soaked cowboys who threw the herd together on the north bank of the Red. We couldn't get the chuckwagon across —

187

didn't even try — so we went without supper that night and slept without blankets.

But I don't think anybody really minded it much, once it was over. There was the knowledge that we had taken the Red's challenge and made it across. Then too, there was the satisfaction we got out of seeing peace come into Hardy Buckelew's face. We could tell by looking at him that he was one of us again, for the first time in a nearly a year.

Next morning we floated the wagon over and had a chance to fill our bellies with beef and beans and hot coffee.

At Few Lively's fire, Hardy Buckelew looked at Will Peril and said: "From here on, Will, I'm turnin' it back over to you. Run it the way you want to. I'm goin' home."

Surprised, Will said, "Home? Why?"

Hardy Buckelew smiled calmly. "You were right, Will, I'm too old for this foolishness. But I owed a debt for Jimbo. And I'd say that you and me — all the boys in the outfit — have paid it in full."

THE BURIAL OF
LETTY STRAYHORN

Greenleaf Strayhorn frowned as he rode beyond the dense liveoak motte and got his first clear look at Prosperity. The dry west wind, which had been blowing almost unbroken for a week, picked up dust from the silent streets and lifted it over the frame buildings to lose it against a cloudless blue sky. He turned toward the brown pack horse that trailed the young sorrel he was riding. His feeling of distaste deepened the wrinkles which had resulted from long years of labor in the sun.

"Wasn't much of a town when we left here, Letty, and I can't see that it's got any better. But you wanted to come back."

Prosperity had a courthouse square but no courthouse. Even after voting some of its horses and dogs, it had lost the county-seat election to rival Paradise Forks, a larger town which could rustle up more horses and dogs. Greenleaf hoped the dramshop was still operating. He had paused in Paradise Forks only long enough to buy a meal cooked by someone other than himself, and that had been yesterday. He was pleased to see the front door open. If the sign out front had been repainted during his twelve-year absence, he could not tell it.

" *'Finest in liquors, wines and bitters,'* " he read aloud. " *'Cold beer and billiards.'* Our kind of a place. Mine, anyway. You never was one for self-indulgence."

The sorrel's ears poked forward distrustfully as a yellow dog sauntered out to inspect the procession. Greenleaf tightened his knee grip, for the young horse was still prone to regard with great suspicion such things as dogs, chickens and flying scraps of paper. It had pitched him off once already on this trip. Greenleaf was getting to an age when rodeoing was meant to be a spectator sport, not for personal participation. The dog quickly lost interest in rider and horses and angled off toward the liveoak motte to try and worry a rabbit or two.

Greenleaf tied up the horses in front of the saloon, loosening the girth so his saddlehorse could breathe easier. He checked the pack on the brown horse and found it still snug. Seeing no others tied nearby, he knew the saloon was enjoying another in a long succession of slow days.

He stepped up onto the board sidewalk, taking an extra-long stride to skip over a spot where two planks had been removed. Somebody had evidently fallen through in the relatively distant past. The rest of the boards were badly weathered, splintered and worn. It was only a matter of time until they, too, caused someone embarrassment, and probably skinned shins.

The whole place looked like the tag end of a hot, dry summer. Whoever had named this town Prosperity was a terrible prophet or had a wicked sense of humor, he thought.

A black cat lay curled in the shade near the front door. It opened one eye in response to Greenleaf's approach, then closed the eye with minimum compromise to its rest.

The bartender sat on a stool, his head upon his arms atop the bar. He stirred to the jingling of spurs and looked up sleepy-eyed.

"Beer," Greenleaf said. "A cold one if you've got it."

The man delivered it to him in a mug and gave him a squinting appraisal. "Ain't your name Greenleaf Shoehorn?"

"Strayhorn."

"A name like Greenleaf ain't easily forgot.

The rest of it . . ." He shrugged. "Didn't you used to work on Old Man Hopkins' place?"

"And married his daughter Letty."

Memory made the bartender smile. "Anybody who ever met Letty would remember her. A mighty strong-willed woman. Where's she at?"

"Outside, on a horse."

The bartender frowned. "You'd leave her in the hot sun while you come in here for a cool drink?"

He walked to the door. "All I see is two horses."

"She's under the tarp on the packhorse, in a lard can. Her ashes, I mean."

The bartender's face fell. "She's dead?"

"Took by a fever two weeks ago. Last thing she asked me was to bring her back here and bury her on the homeplace alongside her mama and papa. It was so far, the only way I could do it was to bring her ashes."

Soberly the bartender refilled the mug Greenleaf had drained.

"Sorry about Letty. Everybody liked her. Everybody except Luther Quinton. He hated all the Hopkinses, and everybody that neighbored them."

"It always makes it easier when you hate the people you set out to rob. Less troublin'

192

on the conscience."

"He still owns the old Hopkins place. He may not take it kindly, you buryin' Letty there. Asked him yet?"

"Wasn't figurin' on askin' him. Just figured on doin' it."

The bartender's attention was drawn to the front window. "If you was thinkin' about askin' him, this'd be the time. That's him comin' yonder."

Greenleaf carried his beer to the door, where he watched as the black cat raised up from its nap, stretched itself luxuriously, and meandered out into the windy street, crossing Quinton's path. Quinton stopped abruptly, turning back and taking a path that led him far around the cat. It stopped in the middle of the deserted street to lick itself.

The bartender remarked, "Superstitious, Luther is. Won't buy anything by the dozen because he's afraid they may throw in an extra one on him. They say he won't even keep a mirror in his house because he's afraid he might break it."

"He probably just doesn't like to look at himself. I never liked lookin' at him either." Quinton had long legs and a short neck. He had always reminded Greenleaf of a frog.

Quinton came to the door, looking back

to be sure the cat had not moved. He demanded of the bartender, "How many more lives has that tomcat got? I've been hopin' a wagon might run over him in the street."

"She ain't a tomcat, and there ain't enough traffic. She's liable to live for twenty years."

"I'd haul her off and dump her, but I know she'd come back."

Quinton's attention shifted to Greenleaf, and his eyes narrowed with recognition. "Speakin' of comin' back . . ." He pointed a thick, hairy finger. "Ain't you the hired hand that married the Hopkins girl?"

"Letty. Yep, I'm the one."

"There's no accountin' for some people's judgment. Wonder she ain't killed and scalped you before now. Has Indian blood in her, don't she?"

"Her mama was half Choctaw."

"Probably some kind of a medicine woman. That Letty laid a curse on me the day I took over the Hopkins place. Cow market went to hell. Calf crop dropped to half. Rain quit and the springs dried up. I had nothin' but bad luck for over a year."

"Only a year? She must not've put her whole heart into it."

Dread was in Quinton's eyes. "She back

194

to cause me more misery?"

"She died."

Relief washed over Quinton's round, furrowed face like sunshine breaking through a dark cloud. He was not one to smile easily, but he ventured dangerously near. "I'm mighty sorry to hear it." He gulped down a glass of whiskey in one long swallow. "Mighty sorry."

Greenleaf grunted. "I can see that." He turned to the bartender. "Old Brother Ratliff still doin' the preachin'?"

The bartender nodded. "You'll find him at the parsonage over by the church. My sympathies about Letty."

Greenleaf thanked him and walked out. He had not expected this to be a pleasant homecoming, and running into Luther Quinton had helped it live down to his expectations. Untying the two horses, he looked a moment at the pack on the second animal, and a catch came in his throat. He had worked his way through the darkest of his grief, but a lingering sadness still shadowed him. He wanted to fulfill his promise to Letty, then put this place behind him for once and all. His and Letty's leave-taking from here had created a residue of memories bitter to the taste.

Not all the fault had been Quinton's.

Letty's father should have known he was dealing himself a busted flush when he tried farming on land where the average rainfall was only about fifteen inches a year, and half of that tended to come in one night if it came at all.

Letty's stubborn nature was a natural heritage from both sides of her family. She had tried to keep on farming even though her father had accomplished four crop failures in a row. He had died of a seizure in the middle of a diatribe against the bank for letting him borrow himself so deeply into the hole and refusing to let him dig the hole any deeper.

All Quinton had done, really, was to buy the notes from the frustrated banker and foreclose on Letty. Quinton had acquired several other properties the same way. He was not a hawk that kills its prey but rather a buzzard which feeds on whatever has died a natural death.

Greenleaf had not considered Brother Ratliff an old man when he had lived here, but like the town, the minister had aged a lot in a dozen years. Greenleaf had to knock on the door a third time before it swung inward and a tall, slightly stooped gentleman peered down at him, cocking his head a little to one side to present his best ear.

From Ratliff's gaunt appearance, Greenleaf judged that the Sunday offering plate had been coming back but little heavier than it went out.

"May I be of service to you, friend?"

"I'm Greenleaf Strayhorn. You may not remember, but you tied the knot for me and Letty Hopkins a long time ago."

The minister smiled broadly and made a gesture that invited him into the spare little house. "I do remember. Quite a beautiful bride, she was. Have you brought her with you?"

"In a manner of speakin', yes sir. I was wonderin' if you'd be kind enough to say some fittin' words over her so I can put her ashes in the ground?"

The minister's smile died. "The Lord calls all of us home eventually, but it would seem He has called her much too early. I hope she had a good life to compensate for its shortness."

"We did tolerable well. Got us a nice little ranch up north, though we wasn't blessed with kids. She just never could shake loose from her old family homeplace. The memory of it was always there, itchin' like a wool shirt. She wanted me to bring her back."

"It's a sad thing to preach a funeral, but part of my calling is to comfort the bereaved

197

and commend the soul to a better land. When would you want me to perform the service?"

"Right now, if that's not too soon."

The minister put on his black coat and walked with Greenleaf to the church next door. "Would you mind pulling the bell rope for me, son? The devil has afflicted my shoulder with rheumatism."

Afterward, Greenleaf unwrapped the pack and fetched the lard can containing all that was left in the world of Letty Strayhorn. He placed it in front of the altar. A dozen or so citizens came, curious about the reason for the bell to ring in the middle of the week. Among them was the bartender, who knew. He had removed his apron and put on a coat, though the church was oppressively warm. Its doors and windows had been kept shut because the wind would have brought in too much dust.

The sermon was brief, for Brother Ratliff did not know all that much to say about Letty's past, just that she had been a hard-working, God-fearing woman who held strong opinions about right and wrong and did not easily abide compromise.

At the end of the closing prayer he said, "Now, if any of you would like to accompany the deceased to her final resting

198

place, you are welcome to go with us to the old Hopkins farm."

A loud voice boomed from the rear of the church. "No you ain't! The place is mine, and that woman ain't fixin' to be buried in any ground that belongs to me!"

The minister was first surprised, then dismayed. "Brother Quinton, surely you would not deny that good soul the right to be buried amongst her own."

"Good soul? A witch, I'd call her. A medicine woman, somethin' from the Indian blood in her."

"She has passed on to another life. She can do you no harm now."

"I'm takin' no chances. You want her buried, bury her here in town. You ain't bringin' her out to my place."

Apologetically the minister looked back to Greenleaf. "I am sorry, Brother Strayhorn. I may argue with Brother Quinton's logic, but I cannot argue with his legal rights."

Greenleaf stood up and studied Quinton's physical stature. He decided he could probably whip the man, if it came to a contest. But he would no doubt end up in jail, and he still would not be able to carry out Letty's final wish.

"She's goin' to be disappointed," he said.

The town cemetery was a depressing

place, the site picked for convenience rather than for beauty. His sleeves rolled up, Greenleaf worked with a pair of posthole diggers that belonged to the minister. Brother Ratliff, looking too frail to help in this kind of labor, sat on a marble gravestone and watched as the hole approached three feet in depth. The length of the handles would limit Greenleaf's digging. The bartender had come to the cemetery but had left after a few minutes to reopen the saloon lest he miss out on any thirsty customers. Or perhaps he had feared he might be called upon to lend a hand with the diggers.

Ratliff said, "It matters not where the body lies."

"So the old song says," Greenleaf responded, turning into the wind. Though its breath was warm, it felt cool against his sweaty face and passing through his partially soaked shirt. "But I feel like I'm breakin' a promise. I never got to do everything I wanted to for Letty while she was livin', but at least I never broke a promise to her."

"You made your promise in good faith. Now for reasons beyond your control you cannot fulfill it. She would understand that. Anyway, you brought her back to her hometown. That's close."

"I remember a couple of times my stomach was growlin' awful at me, and I bore down on a whitetail deer for meat but missed. Close wasn't good enough. I was still hungry."

"You've done the best you could."

"No, I ain't." Greenleaf brought the diggers up out of the hole and leaned on their handles while he pondered. "Mind lendin' me these diggers a little longer, Preacher?"

Ratliff studied him quizzically. "You'd be welcome to keep them. Should I ask you what for?"

"A man in your profession ain't supposed to lie. If I don't tell you, you won't have to lie to anybody that might ask you."

Greenleaf used the diggers to rake dirt back into the hole and tamp it down. The lard can still sat where he had placed it beside a nearby gravestone. "We had a full moon last night. It ought to be just as bright tonight."

The minister looked up at the cloudless sky. "Unless it rains. I would say our chance for rain is about as remote as the chance of Luther Quinton donating money for a new church. Would you like for me to go with you?"

"You've got to live here afterward, Preacher. I don't." Greenleaf finished filling the hole. "If I was to leave you the money, would you see to it that a proper headstone is put up for her?"

"I would consider it a privilege."

"Thanks." Greenleaf extended his hand. "You don't just know the words, Preacher. You know the Lord."

Even if the moon had not been bright, Greenleaf could have found the old Hopkins place without difficulty. He had ridden the road a hundred times in daylight and in darkness. Nothing had changed in the dozen years since he had last traveled this way. He rode by the deserted house where the Hopkins family had lived while they struggled futilely to extract a good living from a soil that seemed always thirsty. He stopped a moment to study the frame structure. The porch roof was sagging, one of its posts buckled out of place. He suspected the rest of the house looked as desolate. The wind, which had abated but little with moonrise, moaned through broken windows.

"Probably just as well we've come at night, Letty. I doubt you'd like the looks of the place in the daytime."

Memories flooded his mind, memories of coming to work here as hired help, of first meeting Letty, of gradually falling in love with her. A tune ran through his brain, a tune she had taught him when they had first known one another and that they had often sung together. He dwelled at length upon the night he had brought her back here after their wedding in town. Life had seemed golden then . . . for a while. But reality had soon intruded. It always did, after so long. It intruded now.

"I'd best be gettin' about the business, Letty, just in case Luther Quinton is smarter than I think he is."

The small family cemetery lay halfway up a gentle hillside some three hundred yards above the house. Rocks which the plow had turned up in the field had been hauled to the site to build a small protective fence. Greenleaf dismounted beside the gate and tied the saddlehorse to the latchpost. He let the packhorse's rein drop. The brown would not stray away from the sorrel. He untied the rope that bound the diggers to the pack, then unwrapped the pack.

Carefully he lifted down the lard can. He had been amazed at how little it weighed. Letty had never been a large woman, but it had seemed to him that her ashes should represent more weight than this. Carrying the can under one arm and the diggers under the other, he started through the gate.

He had never been of a superstitious nature, but his heart almost stopped when he saw three dark figures rise up from behind the gravestones that marked the resting places of Letty's mother and father. He gasped for breath.

The voice was not that of a ghost. It belonged to Luther Quinton. "Ain't it strange how you can tell some people no and they don't put up an argument? Tell others and it seems like they can't even hear you."

The shock lingered, and Greenleaf had trouble getting his voice back. "I guess it's because no doesn't always make much sense."

"It don't have to. All that counts is that this place belongs to me, and I don't want you on it, you or that woman of yours either. Lucky for me I set a man to watchin' you in town. He seen you fill that hole back up without puttin' anything in it but dirt."

"Look, Luther, you hurt her enough when she was livin'. At least you could let her rest in peace now. Like the preacher said, she's in no shape to do you any harm. She just wanted to be buried next to her folks. That don't seem like much to ask."

"But it is. You heard her when she laid that curse on me after I took this place. She

204

named a dozen awful things that was fixin' to happen to me, and most of them did. Anybody that strong ain't goin' to quit just because they're dead." Quinton shook his head violently. "I'm tellin' you, she's some kind of an Indian medicine woman. If I was to let you bury her here, I'd never be shed of her. She'd be risin' up out of that grave and hauntin' my every move."

"That's a crazy notion. She never was a medicine woman or anything like that. She wasn't but a quarter Indian in the first place. The rest was white."

"All I know is what she done to me before. I don't aim to let her put a hex on me again."

"You can't watch this place all the time. I can wait. Once she's in the ground, you wouldn't have the guts to dig her up."

"I could find twenty men who'd do it for whiskey money. I'd have them carry her over into the next county and throw her in the river, can and all."

Frustration began to gnaw at Greenleaf. Quinton had him blocked.

Quinton's voice brightened with a sense of victory. "So take her back to town, where you ought to've buried her in the first place. Since you seem to enjoy funerals, you can have another one for her."

"I hope they let me know when your funeral takes place, Luther. I'd ride bare-back two hundred miles to be here."

Quinton spoke to the two men beside him. "I want you to ride to town with him and be sure he doesn't do anything with that can of ashes. I want him to carry it where you can watch it all the way."

One of the men tied up Greenleaf's pack and lashed the diggers down tightly against it. The other held the can while Greenleaf mounted the sorrel horse, then handed it up to him.

Quinton said, "If I ever see you on my place again, I'm liable to mistake you for a coyote and shoot you. Now git!"

To underscore his order, he drew his pistol and fired a shot under the young sorrel's feet. That was a bad mistake. The horse bawled in fright and jumped straight up, then alternated between a wild runaway and fits of frenzied pitching in a semicircle around the little cemetery. Greenleaf lost the reins at the second jump and grabbed at the saddlehorn with his left hand. He was handicapped by the lard can, which he tried to hold tightly under his right arm. He did not want to lose Letty.

It was a forlorn hope. The lid popped from the can, and the ashes began streaming out as the horse ran a few strides, then whipped about, pitched a few jumps and ran again. The west wind caught them and carried them away. At last Greenleaf felt himself losing his seat and his hold on the horn. He bumped the rim of the cantle and kicked his feet clear of the stirrups to keep from hanging up. He had the sensation of being suspended in midair for a second or two, then came down. His feet landed hard on the bare ground but did not stay beneath him. His rump hit next, and he went rolling, the can bending under his weight.

It took him a minute to regain his breath. In the moonlight he saw one of Quinton's men chasing after the sorrel horse. The pack horse stood where it had been all along, watching the show with only mild interest.

Quinton's second man came, finally, and helped Greenleaf to his feet. "You hurt?"

"Nothin' seems to be broke except my feelin's." Greenleaf bent down and picked up the can. Most of the ashes had spilled from it. He waited until Quinton approached, then poured out what remained. The wind carried part of them into Quinton's face.

The man sputtered and raged and tried desperately to brush away the ashes.

"Well, Luther," Greenleaf said, "you really

done it now. If I'd buried her here, you'd've always known where she was. The way it is, you'll never know where she's at. The wind has scattered her all over the place."

Quinton seemed about to cry, still brushing wildly at his clothing. Greenleaf thrust the bent can into his hands. Quinton made some vague shrieking sound and hurled it away as if it were full of snakes.

The first Quinton man brought Greenleaf his horse. Greenleaf's hip hurt where he had fallen, and he knew it would be giving him unshirted hell tomorrow. But tonight it was almost a good pain. He felt strangely elated as he swung up into the saddle. He reached down for the packhorse's rein.

"This isn't what Letty asked for, but I have a feelin' she wouldn't mind. She'd've liked knowin' that no matter where you go on this place, she'll be there ahead of you. And she won't let you forget it, not for a minute."

Riding away, he remembered the old tune Letty had taught him a long time ago. Oddly, he felt like whistling it, so he did.

HORSE WELL

The Jigger Y chuckwagon was camped at Horse Well the night the showdown finally came between Jeff Bowman and Cleve Sharkey. I was just a button then, not yet ten years old. The first excitement of the Crane County oil boom had simmered down in the wake of the Depression, as every Texas oil boom did sooner or later. The place had almost settled into the calm that permanency brings, as much permanency as there can ever be for a community that depends on anything as hard to put a handle on as cattle and oil.

The times were still tight, and there were some around who would turn a fast dollar whenever the opportunity arose. A Jigger Y steer butchered in the dark and peddled out by the chunk in town and in the oil camps was one way to do it.

My dad was foreman of the Y. It was his job to make the cattle operation turn a profit whether beef prices were good or not. He usually went to Midland when it came time to hire cowboys; the men in Crane were mostly working in the oil fields. Dad knew a lot of people in Midland, and there were usually some job-hunting hands waiting around the Scharbauer Hotel for a ranch owner or a foreman to show up. That was where he hired Cleve Sharkey.

The next day Cleve Sharkey came sliding his shiny green Model A coupe to a stop on the gravel in front of the L-shaped kitchen and bunkhouse. As he stepped out, I decided he was the ideal cowboy to fit all those stories the old-timers used to tell about the good old days, back when they were young. He appeared to be seven feet tall, but of course I was looking up at him from pretty low down to the ground at that time. He wore his Levi's jeans tucked into the tall tops of a fancy-stitched pair of high-heeled boots made for dancing, not for cow work. He was good-looking too, I thought, like the people in the stories I had heard old Wes Reynolds and Daddy George Lee and those others tell.

That was an early age for a boy to learn that you shouldn't judge people by what they looked like. My old pet cat Blue Boy came ambling across the bunkhouse porch, full of curiosity about the new hand, and put himself right between Cleve's feet. Cleve came near falling, and he gave Blue Boy a kick that boosted him off into the little patch of Bermuda grass at the edge of the porch.

Right there I got off to a bad start with Cleve. I told him what I thought about anybody who was mean to cats. He in turn told me what he thought about kids who mouthed off to grown-ups. My dad stepped out of our house about that time and came walking across the yard, still too far away to see that anything was wrong. Cleve carried his bedroll and war bag on into his room, and I left before Dad had a chance to challenge me about being at the bunkhouse without any business. I picked up Blue Boy and carried him out to the barn to satisfy myself that he was all right. Actually, he was too fat to hurt.

I made it a point after that to stay out of Cleve's way, though I watched him from a safe distance. He was a good cowpuncher, even if his behavior didn't fit the model I had been led to expect in a top hand. Dad had bought some rank young broncs over on the Pecos River, and Cleve rode the worst of them. He could rope a runaway cow and stand her on her rump about as

211

well as anybody I had seen.

But he was hard on his horses. Some of the broncs lost a lot of hair where his spurs raked them.

After Cleve had been on the ranch awhile, he took to going to town pretty often. I never was much of a hand with a rope, but at the time I thought it was because I never had a chance to practice with a really good one. One Saturday evening after he had gone, I borrowed the rope from his saddle in the barn and practiced roping fenceposts. I forgot to take it in, and that night it rained.

Next afternoon Cleve found his ruined rope where I had left it hanging on a fence. It was as limber as a dishrag. But it still had plenty of sting left in it when he doubled one end and applied two or three smart licks where I would feel them the most.

One day Buddy Green quit us, and Dad had to go to Midland to hunt another cowhand. Buddy didn't say why he was leaving, but I thought I knew. For three months, when Dad wasn't around, I had seen Cleve bullying him. Buddy was a little feller who looked like he had been weaned short of his time. Cleve could have hurt him bad if he had ever taken the notion, and Buddy probably decided sooner or later he would take the notion.

I never did tell Dad about any of that. One of the first lessons he had ever taught me was to keep out of other people's business.

I was a little disappointed when Dad came back from Midland, bringing Jeff Bowman. I followed Dad's rattling old ranch pickup to the barn and watched dismally as Jeff unloaded his saddle and other tack. I had hoped Dad might bring out somebody who would whip Cleve Sharkey. At a glance I knew Jeff Bowman wasn't likely ever to do it.

He was almost as short as Buddy had been, though he was some wider in the shoulders. His clothes were nothing like Cleve's. He wore a wrinkled blue work shirt, patched khaki pants, not even Levi's, and an old hat that looked as if he had let twenty-seven horses run over it. His boot heels leaned in two directions.

He wouldn't have fit the stories I had heard from Wes and Daddy George.

Cleve rode in from the beef pasture about milking time. I happened to be making mighty quiet in the barn at the moment because Dad had been threatening to teach me to milk our Jersey cow, about as un-cowboylike an activity as I could imagine. That is how I happened to be perched out of sight on top of the feed sacks when Cleve walked in carrying his saddle, his big spurs jingling. Jeff Bowman was standing by a rack, patching a broken bridle rein. Both men stiffened as they saw each other. Cleve dropped his saddle unceremoniously to the floor.

"Jeff!" he said, after a minute. "I thought they had you in the —"

Jeff Bowman had both of his fists clenched. "I got a parole."

Cleve stammered a little. "Dammit, what did you have to come here for? You tryin' to ruin me?"

Bowman's voice cut like barbed wire. "I didn't know you were here. But anyway, you like to've ruined *me*. You didn't even have the decency to come forward and tell them the truth."

Cleve's face clouded up, as I had seen it do more than once. His fists doubled, he stepped closer to Bowman. "You ain't stayin'. You're goin' to tell the foreman you don't like the looks of this place and you want to go back to Midland."

I had always thought when people laughed, they saw something funny. Bowman laughed, and there wasn't anything funny about it. "There was a time you'd of scared me, Cleve, but not anymore. Ain't nothin' you could ever do to me worse than you've already done. I need this job. If anybody leaves, it'll be you."

Cleve bristled like a porcupine, but Bowman stared him down. Finally Cleve picked up his saddle, flung it onto a rack, and stomped out. I didn't have much idea what they were talking about. I wasn't even sure exactly what a parole was. I just knew I was going to try my best to get along with Jeff Bowman.

It turned out he was a better hand than Cleve, and he wasn't hard on his horses. More important than that, he took a lot of time trying to teach me how to use a rope. It didn't do much good, but the fault was mine, not his. I never did get the knack for it, then or later.

One day Morgan Lambert of the Cross L dropped by for a visit. He brought his daughter Ellie along. She was probably just one side or the other of twenty then. I considered her pretty old. But I considered her *pretty,* about on a par with a little girl who had sat at a desk next to mine in the third grade, one who made my face turn warm every time she spoke to me.

Jeff and Cleve felt the same way about Ellie, seemed like. Before Jeff had come, I had seen Cleve trying to butter up to her. He had no better luck with her than I had with the girl in school. But somehow it was different with Jeff. He was a long way from handsome, but she appeared to overlook that from the start. The two hit it off well as soon as my dad introduced them.

Before long Jeff was borrowing the company pickup and making trips over to the Cross L every few nights. Once in a while I would catch Cleve watching the pickup as it bounced out across the needle-grass flat to the east and disappeared around the jog in the horse-pasture fence. He looked as if he was festering up a sore.

One night a little before the Y started its fall roundup, a big dance was thrown over at the Mayfield place. Mother and Dad took us kids along. Jeff borrowed the pickup, as usual, and went after Ellie. Cleve headed for town in his Model A coupe, and after a while he brought out a town girl who wore enough rouge and lipstick to paint a barn door. She created some comment among the grown-ups, but I couldn't understand why. She reminded me of a birthday package.

It didn't take me long to get on the outs with the big Thompson boy, who was two years older and a hand-and-a-half taller than me. He was always looking for somebody to be on the outs with, and he usually won whatever contest resulted. I stayed close to the grown-ups to keep my nose clean, and listened to the fiddle music.

Cleve's girl seemed to make a lot of trips to the kitchen, and pretty soon she was wobbly on her feet. She was dancing with just about every unattached man there, though I noticed the married men didn't seem to ask her. Cleve quit asking her too.

Jeff and Ellie took most of their dances with each other. Cleve was watching them, and the devil was looking out of his eyes. Presently Jeff went to the kitchen to get Ellie some punch. Cleve pulled Ellie out onto the dance floor. She put up a little quiet resistance, but not enough to attract much notice. There was anger in her face.

The sight made me ashamed. I pushed through the crowd and went out into the cool night air. In front of the house the big Thompson boy was daring anybody to come and wrestle with him. I had been through that with him once and didn't want any more, so I walked on out into the darkness, away from the yellow lamplight. The door opened, and Cleve came out, holding Ellie by the wrist and pulling her along.

"Now, looky here," he said, with his voice full of indignation, "I was always nice to you, but you always treated me like I was a

217

dog with the mange. That Jeff Bowman comes along, and you take right up with him. Now I want to know, what's the matter with me?"

Cleve acted like he had been in the kitchen too many times himself.

Ellie was not one to raise her voice, but she left no doubt where she stood. "If you could see yourself right now, you'd know what's the matter. You're an egotistical —"

That was all she got to say, because Cleve pulled her to him and kissed her. She was making an angry noise and beating her little fists against him.

The door opened, and Jeff Bowman stood there against the bright lamplight. He took three or four long strides and spun Cleve around like he was a bottle-fed calf. "You take your hands off of her!" He had his fist drawn back, but Ellie grabbed his arm.

"No, Jeff, please. Let's don't have a fight and get everybody out here. It isn't worth that."

Cleve stood there looking like a whipped dog. He was sobering up in a hurry, realizing what he had done. "I'm sorry, Ellie," he said. "I've had too much to drink, or I wouldn't of touched you. I'd cut off my arm before I'd hurt you. I don't want *him* hurtin' you either, so I'm goin' to tell you. He ain't long out of jail."

Ellie looked as if he had hit her. She turned toward Jeff. "Jail?"

Cleve said, "Not just no little old county jail either. He's been in the pen at Huntsville."

Ellie stood waiting for some kind of word from Jeff, and no word came. She sounded as if she was about to cry. "Why didn't you tell me?"

"I've tried. I just couldn't. I didn't know how you'd take it."

She turned and ran back into the house, sobbing.

Cleve said, "Well, now you know how she took it."

I was awfully disappointed in Jeff, not because he had been in jail, but because he didn't hit Cleve. Jeff stayed out there a long time, rolling a cigarette, smoking it, then rolling another. Ellie's father and mother went home early, and she went with them. Pretty soon I recognized the sound of the company pickup, hitting the road back to the ranch.

Jeff and Cleve kept their distance the next day. Dad must have smelled a storm brewing up. He sent them out on separate jobs and kept them that way until time for the roundup.

It was his custom to go to Midland for extra day-help to add to the regular ranch hands and the helpful neighbors during the "works" each year. He brought back five or six, plus Tom Grammer, who had been wagon cook for the Y roundups about as long as I could remember. Dad and Tom went to work bolting the chuckbox to the wagon, and Dad sent me to fetch a monkey wrench.

I couldn't find one in any of the usual places where such tools were apt to stray. I went to the big garage and looked in the back of our car, but we didn't have one either. Cleve's green coupe was sitting there, and it occurred to me a man with a car that nice was bound to have a monkey wrench in it in case he ever had to fix a flat tire. All I found in the front was a shiny-barreled rifle he always kept there. I ran my fingers back and forth over the wonderful cold steel of it and wished I had gotten off to a better start with Cleve, so he might've let me fire it sometime.

I thought I heard Dad holler all the way from the barn. He probably hadn't, but I was always listening for him to. That reminded me about the wrench. I got up on the back bumper and opened the trunk. It surprised me. Unlike most cars that had to travel over our dusty roads, this one was as spotless as a washerwoman's scrub board. It looked like it had been cleaned out often.

There wasn't any wrench. There was a short-handled shovel, though, and a carpenter's saw. I wondered what Cleve wanted with a saw. He never did any carpenter work.

Rolled up and shoved way back was an old section of tarpaulin. Curiosity around our place had not been restricted to the cat. I pulled the tarp out and found it had been washed lately, but it still had some dark stains. Blood-stains, they looked like, the kind on the tarp Dad always used to wrap fresh-killed beef. I was so interested in what I had found that I didn't hear Cleve come into the garage.

He grabbed me and jerked me off of the bumper, then let me fall to my knees. He bent down, and his face looked black with a flash of anger there in the half darkness. He grabbed the front of my shirt and demanded, "What do you think you're doin', prowlin' in my car?"

I tried to stammer that I was just looking for a wrench, but something was in my throat as big as an apple. My heart was pumping like the old gasoline engine that was used sometimes to pump water when the wind wasn't blowing enough to turn a windmill.

I thought Cleve was going to draw back and hit me, so I saw a little daylight off to the left side of him and ran for it as hard as my legs would carry me. I fell once and hit the ground with my face, but I was back on my feet and running while the dust still swirled. I was so scared I didn't realize I was bleeding until Jeff Bowman caught me at the corner of the bunkhouse and looked at me with a deep concern.

"Good Lord, button," he exclaimed, "what happened to you?"

I guess I looked scared, and I glanced back toward the garage in time to see Cleve come out of it. Jeff saw him too. I didn't tell him anything, but he put two and two together. He stood there and flexed his hands while his face went dark with anger.

"He hit you?" he asked.

I had to admit Cleve hadn't, but he had made me think he was going to. Jeff nodded grimly. "I wouldn't go tellin' your dad about it, if I was you. Just tell him you stumbled and fell. Cleve'll pay, when we get him where we want him."

My heart sank in disappointment. I didn't know where Jeff wanted Cleve, but *I* wanted him gone. A sharp suspicion began to gnaw at me. Jeff hadn't done anything about Cleve at the dance, and he wasn't doing anything about him now. Maybe Cleve had finally run his bluff on Jeff, like he had done on Buddy, not to mention *me.* I tried to shake the doubt from my mind, but it clung there like a grass burr.

As the roundup got started, camp moved from the ranch headquarters to the Mayfield place, to the Crier windmills, then over to the Magnolia trap. It was there that I heard Cleve make some remark about Ellie at the campfire. A couple of the cowboys hung their heads, embarrassed. Jeff jumped up with his fists clenched and his back stiff, but he just stood and looked at Cleve for a minute, then walked out away from the campfire, kicking soft sand with his worn-out boots.

My face burned with shame. I went off and crawled into my bedroll and pulled the tarp up over me like I expected rain. It was a long time before I went to sleep.

Finally the chuckwagon moved across the sand country and onto the chalky alkali flat toward Horse Well. That place had always fascinated me. It wasn't any different in appearance from the other camps except that it probably had the dustiest pens to brand calves in. But there *was* a difference.

About as far back as I could remember, I had heard the legend about Horse Well. One of the hands had shown me an unmarked grave over in the big south pasture. In it was buried a cowboy from way back in the 1880s, he said, killed by a band of horse thieves. The cowboy's friends had trailed the murderers, shot them all, then dumped their bodies into the deep hand-dug hole over which the windmill tower now stood at Horse Well.

Cowboys claimed that if you listened on a dark night, you could hear the dead men's spirits moan from down deep in that black hole. I had been to school and didn't really believe that kind of thing anymore. Still, that old windmill used to groan enough to make your hair stand on end, especially at night. Greasing and releathering it didn't seem to help much. Any time we camped at Horse Well I always stayed close to the wagon and kept my bedroll on the off side of it.

It was a comfort to know that Tom Grammer kept a .45 pistol in the chuckbox, though what good that would do against spirits I never had taken time to worry out.

The day the wagon moved to Horse Well, Dad sent me with Jeff on drive. Any other time that would have made me proud, because Dad usually kept me close to him so he could give me Hail Columbia when I made a mistake a-horseback, which was usually. But now I couldn't hold my eyes to Jeff without feeling that he and I shared a guilty secret.

We weren't far from camp when my horse Blackjack suddenly shied and jumped sideways. I gulped a mouthful of air and grabbed at the saddle horn too late. I got up spitting sand as Jeff caught my horse.

Smelling something putrid, I looked around to see what had boogered Blackjack. Off to the left was a hole where the wind had blown the sand away. Holding both snorting horses, Jeff swung down and took a look at it. He handed the reins to me, then poked around in the hole with a dead mesquite limb. He dragged out two sandy but fairly fresh cowhides. Beneath them were the heads and guts of two butchered cattle.

"Bet some thievin' oil fielders done it," I said indignantly, as I figured a good cowboy ought to. Anything that went wrong, it was the custom of the times to blame it on the oil fielders. Usually it turned out they had nothing to do with whatever it was.

Jeff's jaws bulged out a little, and his mouth was grim. "Yeah," he said quietly, "probably some oil fielders."

After supper, and before it got dark enough to be spooky, I borrowed Jeff's rope and went off toward the mill to practice roping fenceposts. I wanted to be far enough from the wagon that the real punchers couldn't watch me and hooraw me for missing most of my loops.

My brother Myrle came out directly. He was only about shoulder high to a Shetland pony then, and too young to know he was supposed to be scared of the place. He quickly tired of watching me miss and walked on over to peer at the old well. Pretty soon I dropped the rope and followed him, leaving the loop still attached to a fencepost, which I had caught from a distance of at least five or six feet. I thrilled as I looked at the wooden tower, and let my imagination carry me back to the good old days of high adventure.

Myrle spoiled it. He leaned over the wide hole and said eagerly, "Bet you if we had us a lantern we could look down there and see the skeletons."

The hair on the back of my neck began to bristle, and I suddenly noticed dusk was gathering around us. I said, "Tom probably wants us to help him dry up the utensils."

Not until we were back at the wagon did I

remember that I had left Jeff's rope hanging from a fencepost. I had no intention of going back for it, because dark was closing in.

Car lights began showing through the gloom. A man from Crane came bouncing up in a Model T. I had seen him at some ball games, selling people something to drink out of a fruit jar, and I remembered once seeing him and Cleve talking together on the sidewalk in town. He called Cleve off to one side. I could hear them arguing, though the words were not clear, and Cleve was waving his arms a lot. In a little while Cleve came up to the campfire and said to Dad, "I got some business in town that won't wait. Be all right if I go with Albert here?"

Dad nodded, and Cleve rode off in the bootlegger's old car. A look passed across Jeff's face, one I had seen a few times in camp when some cowboy won a big poker hand and raked in all the matches.

I didn't sleep very well that night. The mill got to groaning louder and louder, and I could almost hear those old horse thieves crying for help. The night closed in on me, thick as pudding and dark as a sack of black cats. I could hear voices, fighting voices. I awoke and sat straight up, throwing back the tarp. It had all been a dream.

Or maybe it hadn't. The voices were still there, muffled and distant, but I could hear them though I had both eyes wide open. I recognized Jeff's voice. For just a second a fanciful notion struck me that the spirits had come up out of that well and somehow gotten ahold of him. The notion passed as I came completely awake.

Somebody was fighting with Jeff, though; I could tell that by the sounds. My pulse racing, I pulled on my boots to keep from stepping barefooted into a patch of goat-heads, then moved cautiously toward the voices, my throat as dry as old leather. I had slept in my shirt, but a cool night breeze brought goose pimples to my bare legs.

It was not so dark as I had thought. A full moon was up. In a minute I could tell the other voices didn't belong to any spirits. They were Cleve's, and the bootlegger Albert's. Jeff held Tom Grammer's big .45 in his hand and had the two men backed up against the Model T.

"I was ready to forget about goin' to jail for what you did, Cleve," he said bitterly, "but you changed my mind for me the night of the dance. I've taken a lot from you since then because I was waitin' for you to make a real mistake. It's plain to me what you've been doin' with the stuff the kid found in your car. These nights folks thought you was in town, you've been out spot-lightin' and shootin' Y cattle for your friend here to peddle."

I was so relieved that I almost forgot and showed myself. It had hurt, thinking Jeff was letting Cleve put a bluff across on him.

Jeff said, "You haven't had time tonight to clean up that Model T. I expect a cattle inspector is goin' to be awful interested in what he finds there. And you can't move it without this key." He held the key up for Cleve to see, then pitched it off into the brush.

Cleve had quit talking, and I thought Albert was going to sink into a dead faint. "Now looky here, cowboy," he begged, his voice quavering, "don't you wake up the foreman. I'll pay you every cent I got in my pocket — close to a hundred dollars."

Jeff shook his head. "The only pay I want is to see Cleve go to jail, like he let me do."

Somehow it didn't seem to me that Cleve looked as worried as he ought to. He looked past Jeff and said, "All right, boys, I reckon you've heard it all."

Jeff was a cowboy, not a lawman, or he probably wouldn't have fallen for that stunt. He looked back, thinking some of the hands had come up behind him. Cleve bowled him over with his fist. The pistol fell to the ground.

Jeff and Cleve waded into each other, fighting like a couple of strapping big bulls. To be as much smaller as he was, Jeff was putting up a mighty good scrap. The brush popped and cracked as they struggled back and forth through it.

The gun still lay on the ground, its barrel gleaming in the moonlight. My heart pounded as I looked at the thing, deadly as a rattlesnake. I reached for it twice, then drew back my shaking hands. Finally I made myself pick it up.

The bootlegger was on his hands and knees, frantically searching for the key Jeff had thrown away.

I didn't know much about pistols, and I never had touched Tom's .45 before. In my nervousness I must have touched the trigger, because it exploded in my hands with a great roar and the biggest flash of fire I had ever seen. The recoil sent it flying off into the dry weeds. Not for a hundred dollars in silver would I have picked it up again.

A commotion started down at the wagon as the shot woke everybody up.

Jeff and Cleve were still fighting. Cleve had picked up a piece of a discarded windmill sucker rod and was swinging the heavy metal end of it. A good lick with that thing could brain a mule. Jeff was backing away, trying to keep beyond reach. He stumbled over something — his rope that I had left hanging from a post. For a second it looked as if Cleve had him, but Jeff jumped to his feet, one end of that rope in his hand, and made a run around Cleve. Cleve got the sucker rod caught in that rope and dropped it.

They were fighting again then, slugging it out, moving closer and closer to the old well. Boards had been nailed around the base of the tower to keep cattle from falling into the hole, but the boards were rotten. Jeff took some hard licks from Cleve but finally ducked, leaned down, and came up with a hard fist from about the level of his boot tops. It slammed Cleve back against those old boards, and he broke through. With a wild yell he tumbled backward into that deep, dark hole.

His body hit the big pipe casing as he slid down, and somehow he managed to get his arms around it. I could hear his shirt ripping as he hugged the casing and tried to stop his fall.

In a moment his voice floated upward, broken with panic. "Throw me a rope! Hurry up, or I'll lose my hold."

Several cowboys got on Jeff's rope and helped haul Cleve up out of the well. He was dirty and torn, trembling and sniffling. It was a poor time to think of such things, but I desperately wanted to ask him if he had seen anything of those old horse thieves while he was down there. I had the good judgment not to bring the matter up.

Cleve was too shaken to talk, but his friend Albert wasn't. He told it about the way Jeff had guessed.

The Y lost two hands then, Cleve to the sheriff, Jeff to the man he had worked for before he had been sent away for the cattle stealing Cleve had done. The rancher came down to the Y and apologized for past misunderstandings. He offered Jeff a foreman's job at top pay — what passed for top pay in those days anyway.

We kept seeing Jeff regularly for a while after that because he had to come through the Y to get over to the Lambert place and visit Ellie. After they were married he didn't have that excuse anymore.

We never did see Cleve after that, so I never had the chance — if I had ever gotten the nerve — to ask him about the horse thieves in that old well.

232

CONTINUITY

Ed Whitley would always remember where he was and what he was doing when the old man had his heart attack: in the dusty corrals behind the barn, preg-checking a set of Bar W black baldy heifers.

It was not a dignified job for a cowboy who would much rather be on horseback, doing something else — anything else. It was not the pastoral western scene depicted on calendars or Christmas cards, and certainly not the stuff of song and story. It was messy work and smelled a little, but it had become an economic necessity of life for a rancher in a time of tight or negative profit margins. A dollar saved was better than a dollar earned, for it was not subject to income tax.

To Ed's knowledge, his father had had no previous indications that a coronary was imminent. If there had been, the old man had remained tight-lipped about them. Tom

Whitley had always regarded aches and pains as a personal affront, to be borne in silence. To complain was to give them importance.

Ed's probing fingers had just confirmed the presence of a developing calf when he saw Tom fall against the steel squeeze chute, one hand grasping for a rail, the other clutching at his chest. The old man's eyes were wide in surprise and pain and confusion, his mouth open for a cry that choked off before it started. Ed jerked his arm free and ripped off the shoulder-length plastic glove that had covered his hand and sleeve. He caught Tom and eased him to a sitting position on the ground.

Ed's grown son Clay vaulted over the crowding-pen fence and came running, along with ranch hand Miguel Cervantes.

The old man wheezed, "I'm all right. It's just that sausage I had for breakfast."

Ed knew better. He had seen that look before, when his neighbor Alex Hawkins had collapsed and died at the bankruptcy auction that sold out his cattle and rolling stock two years ago.

"Help me get him to the pickup," he shouted. He had never understood how doctors could have such a dispassionate attitude in the face of suffering and human mortality. With no more emotion than if he was reading the cafeteria menu, the emergency-room doctor confirmed Ed's opinion that his father had suffered a heart attack.

"We will not know the extent of muscle damage or blockage until we have done an angiogram. We must assume, though, that it has been severe. I do not wish to sound alarmist, but you had better prepare yourself and your family for the worst."

"Dad's got a constitution like a horse. He hasn't had a sick day in his life, hardly."

"With an eighty-year-old heart, it may take only one."

Tom was eighty-two, if one wished to be technical about it, but he acted as if he was twenty or thirty years younger. He rode more miles a-horseback than Ed and far more than Clay, who lived in town and held down an eight-hours-a-day job at the feed mill. Clay helped at the ranch on weekends.

Tom persisted in wrestling fifty-pound feed sacks two at a time when Ed was not looking. Somewhere in his sixties he seemed to have made up his mind not to get any older, but not to die, either. He had gotten away with it, except for a little arthritis in his joints that occasionally forced him into minor retreat but never into surrender. He had also come into increasing reliance on reading glasses. But he still ate beef for dinner and supper every day, using his own teeth.

In the back of his mind Ed had known his father could not live forever, but he had never allowed himself to dwell upon that. He could not visualize the ranch without Tom Whitley. From Ed's earliest memories, Tom and the home place had been one and the same, inseparable. Tom's father, Ed's grandfather, had acquired the nucleus of the ranch around the turn of the century, homesteading four sections under Texas law. Tom had been born there and over the years had more than doubled the size of the place. With Ed's help he had cleared the land debt so that the ranch now was free and clear.

"Ready to pass on, without no encumbrance," Tom had said when they paid the final note. But Tom had shown no inclination to pass it on. Now Ed had to face the shattering probability that the time had come. Nothing would ever again be as it had been. He could see no continuity between the past and the future. Losing Tom would be like cutting a tree off from its roots.

They moved Tom into the intensive care unit. The hospital had rules about visitation, but it was lax on enforcement in regard to family members. Ed never asked permission to stay in the room with his father, and nobody contested him.

For a long time Tom seemed to be asleep. He was hooked to a monitor, its green screen showing heartbeats as a series of bobbles up and down from a straight line. Ed would watch the screen awhile, then stare at Tom, forcing up old memories as if he had to retrieve them now or lose them as he was losing his father. Most were pleasant, or at least benign.

He could not remember a great deal about his grandfather. The face that came to his mind's eye owed more to old photographs than to life. He knew that Morgan Whitley had come of age in the waning years of the great trail drives and the open range. The ranch's outside fence still retained segments of the original wire and posts that Morgan had installed some ninety years ago, though the toll of time had caused most to be rebuilt in recent years. Even when replacing it, Tom and Ed had coiled and saved some of the rusty old wire and hung it on the barn wall as a keepsake, for Morgan's strong hands had once gripped it. A lively imagination could fantasize that his fingerprints were still fixed upon the steel strands.

Many ranches had unbroken family ownership into the third, fourth, and fifth generations. It conveyed, in a peculiar way, a sort of immortality to those who had gone on. This continuity fostered a reverence for the land as if it were a living member of the family. It engendered in the later generations a strong urge to protect and improve rather than to mine the land for immediate gain at the expense of the future.

But Ed feared for that continuity when Tom was gone. Tom's boots made big tracks, as his father's had before him. Ed felt inadequate to fill them. His life had been relatively easy compared to Tom's and to Morgan's. Most of the building had been completed before he had come of age. He had inherited the fruit without having to dig through the rock and plant the tree.

This was Saturday, so Clay was not on duty at the mill. He had remained at the corrals to finish the day's job. It was an unwritten tenet of ranch life that not even an emergency should interrupt work in progress if any alternative was available. Ed arose from the hard chair as Clay and Ed's wife Frances came into the room. Neither asked aloud, for they could not be certain that Tom would not hear. Ed answered just as silently with a shrug of his shoulders, followed by a solemn shaking of his head. Frances slipped her arm around his waist, offering him emotional support. Clay said his young wife Susan was downstairs with their five-year-old son. The hospital did not allow children into ICU.

Clay moved close to his grandfather's bedside and stared down gravely into the lined face that had been a part of his daily life as far back as memory went. Tears welled into his eyes. When Ed had been a boy, Tom had been demanding of him — often unreasonably demanding, in Ed's view. He remembered a time when Tom had taken a dislike to Ed's way of mounting a horse and had made him practice getting on and off until Ed had thought his legs would collapse. Tom had drilled him mercilessly in the art of roping, making him do it over and over, day after day, until he rarely missed a loop. Not until years later did Tom confide that his own father had done the same thing to him. It was not enough to pass on property. It was necessary to pass on knowledge and skills if the property was to have meaning and continuity.

Tom had mellowed by the time his grandson had come along. He had shown infinitely more patience in teaching Clay the cowboy trade. At those rare times when discipline was called for, Tom had walked away and left that painful duty to Ed.

Odd, Ed thought, how sometimes the further apart people were in age, the closer they seemed in their relationships with one another. The boy had learned diligently, polishing the horseback skills passed down from his great-grandfather Morgan through Tom, then through Ed and finally to Clay.

Frontier realities had limited Morgan Whitley's formal schooling to a couple of years, though he had acquired a liberal education in the school of practical experience, with graduate honors in hard knocks. Better times had allowed Tom to finish high school before turning to a full-time career as a working cowpuncher and eventual partnership with his father.

Ed, the third generation, had gone on to earn a degree in animal husbandry at Texas A&M. It was an accomplishment Tom had always regarded with a conflicting mixture of pride and distrust. "Most of what I know about a cow," he had often declared, "you ain't goin' to find in no Aggie textbook."

Tom's eyelids fluttered awhile before he opened his eyes, blinking as his vision adjusted itself to the fluorescent lights of the hospital room. He focused first on Tom and Frances, then let his gaze drift to Clay.

At first he seemed confused about his surroundings. Ed grasped his father's hand to keep him from tearing loose the tube that fed him glucose.

Anyone else might have asked how he had come to be where he was or what kind of shape he was in, but not Tom. He had always been one to take care of business first. "You-all finish with them heifers?"

Clay said, "We did, Granddad — Miguel and me. They were all settled but three."

"Hell of a note, stoppin' work to rush me in here like this when there wasn't nothin' wrong except that sausage. I could tell the minute I ate it . . ."

Ed said, "It's a lot more than the sausage. Doctor says it's your heart." He stopped there. He thought it best not to tell his father how serious his condition really was unless it became necessary to prevent him from climbing out of bed. It would be like Tom to get in the pickup and head for the ranch in his hospital gown if they wouldn't give him his shirt and Levi's.

Tom grumbled, "Probably just overdone myself workin' that squeeze chute. Never did see that we need to preg-test those heifers. You can tell soon enough which ones come up heavy with calf and which ones don't."

Ed could have told him, as he had before, that checking the heifers early for pregnancy allowed for culling of the slow breeders before they had time to run up an unnecessary feed bill. Moreover, high fertility was a heritable characteristic. The early breeders were the kind a rancher wanted to keep in his herd, for they passed that trait on to their offspring. The slow ones were a drag on the bottom line.

But to Tom, that had always been an Aggie textbook notion. He distrusted selection judgments based on records or mechanical measurements. He preferred to rely upon his eyes. He had not thought much of artificial insemination either, when Ed had first brought it to the ranch.

Tom had not always been so reluctant to try new ideas. Neither, for that matter, had Ed's grandfather Morgan, up to a point. Though Morgan had been a product of the open range, he had built a barbed-wire fence around the perimeter of his holdings as soon as he had been financially able to buy cedar posts and wire. That had allowed him to keep his own cattle in and his neighbors' out. He had gradually upgraded the quality of his herd through use of better sires without his cows being subject to the amorous attentions of inferior stray bulls.

But as the years went by, Morgan had become increasingly conservative, content with things as they were and quick to reject the innovations of a younger generation. He had looked askance upon the advent of the automobile and truck as tools of the ranching trade. He argued that anything he needed could be carried by a good wagon and team. As for cattle and horses, they could walk anywhere it was needful for them to go; they didn't have to be hauled.

He and his son had almost come to a fist-fight over Tom's purchase of a light truck. In time he became accepting enough to ride in a truck or car, but to the end he stubbornly refused to place his hands on the wheel of one.

Tom often told about building his first horse trailer. He had long wished for a way to eliminate the waste of time involved in riding horseback to a far corner of the ranch to do a job, then returning home the same slow way. It took longer to get there and back than to do the work. He acquired the chassis of a wrecked Model T and stripped it down to the wheels and frame. Atop this he built a three-sided wooden box with a gate in the rear. Crude though it was, it could haul two horses, pulled by the truck.

Morgan had ridiculed the idea. "First

thing you know, you'll never see a cowboy ridin' anymore, or a horse walkin'."

Gradually, however, the horse trailer became a regular and accepted fact of survival in the ranching business. It allowed more work to be done in less time and with less labor.

Through thrift and careful borrowing, Tom had managed to add on to the ranch, each addition and each mortgage coming over Morgan's strong objections and predictions of imminent ruin. He had brought a telephone to the ranch, and a gasoline-driven generator to furnish limited 32-volt power so the two houses and the barn could have electric lights. He had even bought Morgan a radio in hopes it would keep his widowed father from feeling so lonely when he sat alone at night in the original old ranch house. At least, he argued, Morgan could keep up with the world news.

"You're wastin' your money," Morgan had declared. "I won't ever listen to the thing. I won't even turn it on."

Tom had often delighted in telling about the time a few weeks later when conversation somehow turned to country music, and old Morgan exclaimed, "Say, that Uncle Dave Macon can sure play the banjo, can't he?" The aging open-range cowboy had died just before the outbreak of World War II, leaving Tom to run the ranch after his own lights. Tom had sometimes wondered aloud how his father would have reacted to the technological innovations that war and its aftermath had wrought upon the ranching industry.

Tom had cross-fenced the ranch for better control of grazing. He had replaced the generator with REA electricity. But in time he had settled into the same brand of conservatism as his father when it came to modern innovations. He treated with skepticism many of the ideas Ed brought home from A&M.

"Aggie textbook notions," he would snort. Some he accepted after a time. Others he never did.

Despite heavy medication, Tom awoke in the early morning hours, as he was accustomed to doing at home.

Ed's back ached from sitting up all night in the straight hard-backed chair. He suspected that hospitals purposely installed uncomfortable furniture to discourage visitors from staying too long. Tom stared at his son with concern in his eyes.

"You ever get anything to eat last night?"

"I slipped away for a bite with Frances while Clay was here."

"You better go and get you some breakfast, else you'll be the one sick in here instead of me."

"Later. I don't want to miss seein' the doctor."

"Ain't no doctor goin' to show up this early unless he's still here this late."

"I'll be all right."

Tom stared at him awhile.

"Sure, you'll be all right. Ever since you were old enough to straddle a horse, I've been tryin' to get you ready for this. Now it's come time, ready or not."

Ed realized his father was not just thinking about Ed's immediate need for nourishment. "Don't you be talkin' thataway. You'll be out of here in a few days if you'll do what they tell you."

"I'm goin' out of here in that long black wagon. We both know that. I could feel old St. Peter breathin' on my neck half the night. But you'll be all right. What you goin' to do about Clay?"

"What's there to do about him?"

"You'll have to talk him into leavin' that piddlin' job at the mill. You'll need his help full-time when I'm gone."

Ed's throat tightened painfully. He did not want to talk about this, but Tom was persistent. He seemed to sense that he did not have a lot of time to get the talking done.

Tom said, "He's a good boy, even if he has got some newfangled ideas. Some of them'll work, and some won't. You'll have to get a feel for how tight to hold the reins, and how loose, same as I did with you and my daddy did with me."

Ed did not know how to reply. It hurt too much to acknowledge what Tom was saying. "You'll come through this all right," he said, though the words were hollow. He knew differently, and so did Tom.

Tom said, "That's the way of the world. It's up to the young ones to keep movin' forward, and up to the older ones to keep the young from runnin' the train off of the track. And it's why the old have to pass out of the picture, so the train won't come to a stop altogether and maybe even slide back down the hill."

"Things wouldn't ever be the same out there without you."

"They ain't meant to be. If my daddy had had his way, we'd still be drivin' cattle afoot to the railroad. If his daddy had had his way, there wouldn't even be no railroad. We don't none of us — old or young — ever have it just the way we'd want it, and that's probably a good thing."

Though some ranchers saw Sunday as just another day for work — it seemed there never were enough days to do it all — Tom Whitley had always accepted Sunday as a day of rest. It was fitting, Ed thought later, that on a Sunday he slipped away into his final rest. Helplessly Ed watched the monitor screen as the line jumped violently up and down, then flattened. The most strenuous efforts of doctor and nurses could not alter the inexorable course of nature.

Frances was with Ed at the end, and so was Clay. It helped, not having to face this dark moment alone.

Ed said quietly, "I don't know how we'll survive without him, son."

"What did he do when his dad died?"

"He picked himself up and went his own way."

Clay gently laid a hand on his father's shoulder. "Then that's what we'll do."

The return to the ranch after the funeral was one of the most trying ordeals of Ed's life. He tried to find comfort in the fact that nothing physical had changed. The entrance gate, the headquarters layout, all looked the same as he drove in. Four horses stood near the barn, waiting for someone to fork hay into the steel rack. Either Tom or Ed customarily did so in the late afternoon. A Jersey milk cow stood outside the milk-pen gate, patiently awaiting the bucket of ground feed that would be poured for her as she took her place in the stanchion. All these things were the same as they had been for years and years. In these, at least, there was constancy.

But Tom's red dog, tail wagging, came out to meet the car. It watched Ed and Frances get out, then looked expectantly for its master. It turned away, its tail drooping in disappointment. It retreated toward the house where Tom had lived since Ed's mother had died, and Tom had turned the larger, newer house over to Ed and Frances. Ed watched the dog and felt anew the pain of loss.

"We'll have to get Red used to comin' to our house for his supper," he said.

Frances nodded. "It'll take him awhile to quit missin' Tom."

Ed winced. "I doubt I ever will."

The dog never did become accustomed to staying around the bigger house. It did not have to. Clay resigned his job at the feed mill, and he and Susan moved into Tom's house. Though it was old and still bore much of Morgan Whitley's imprint, as well as Tom's, it had most of the modern conveniences that a town girl like Susan was used to.

Clay's being around all the time helped Ed's adjustment to the change. Before, Ed had tried to see to it that he and Miguel did the heavier and more menial work, leaving the lighter chores for Tom. Now Clay and Miguel took on most of the heavier lifting, and Ed found himself doing more of the things that Tom had regarded as his own province. Ed resented it a little at first, though he kept his feelings to himself. It seemed they now considered him an old man who had to be sheltered. He was not old, not by a damn sight. But after a time he began to appreciate their deference. His back did not hurt as much as it used to, and he found himself able to spend more time on horseback, riding over the country the way he liked to do.

It warmed Ed's soul, too, to look toward the older house and see Clay's boy Billy riding a stick horse in the front yard. It was high time, Ed thought, to find a pony so the boy could start learning to ride. Billy's cowboy education had been neglected in town. Ed would get him a rope, too, and a plastic steer head to attach to a bale of hay so he could learn to throw a loop around the horns.

Ed sensed that something had begun to nag at Clay. His son became subject to long periods of thoughtful silence, as if he had something on his mind that he was reluctant to voice.

Whatever the problem was, Ed decided the time had come to bring it into the open air. One possibility had occurred to him early. "Is it Susan and that house? I know it's old, and I guess it's got Dad's brand all over it. My granddad's, too. But she's welcome to redo it any way she wants to. It's her house now."

Clay seemed surprised at the thought. "The house is fine. She loves it. We like the idea that we're the fourth generation of Whitleys that's lived in it, and Billy's the fifth. It's like they're all still with us, that nobody's gone."

Ed wished he could see it that way. Tom was gone. The root had been severed. The feeling of continuum was lost.

"Well, if it's not the house, what's the trouble?"

Clay frowned, and he took a while in bringing himself to answer. "I've been workin' on an idea. I've been kind of shy about bringin' it up because I don't know

251

how you'll take it."

"Spill it, and we'll find out."

"You've heard them talk about cell grazin' plans, where they take a pasture and fence it up into twelve or fifteen small paddocks. They throw all their cattle onto one at a time and move them every two or three days. That way most of the ranch is restin', and the grass has a chance to grow. It makes for a healthier range."

Ed could only stare at him. Clay took a sheet of paper from his shirt pocket and unfolded it. Ed recognized a pencil-drawn map of the ranch. Clay placed a finger on the spot that marked the headquarters. "I've figured how we can divide up all our pastures with cheap electric fence and have ourselves four grazin' cells. It's worked on lots of other ranches."

"But this isn't some other ranch." Ed's impatience bubbled to the top. He could imagine Morgan's or Tom's reaction to such a far-fetched idea. "Where did you ever come up with such a radical notion — some Aggie textbook?"

Aggie textbook! Ed wondered for a moment how that expression had popped into his head. Then he remembered. He had heard it from Tom — more times than he wanted to recall.

Looking deflated, Clay studied the paper. "I've had the idea for a long while. I knew better than to try it on Granddad, but I thought you might give it a chance."

"He would've said what I did."

"In the same voice, and the same words, more than likely." Clay managed a wry smile through his disappointment. "You even look like him at a little distance. Funny, you were worried that things could never be the same with Granddad gone. But you've fitted right into his boots."

Ed pondered on what Tom had said about it being the responsibility of the young to originate fresh ideas while the old held the reins, loosening or tightening them as the need came.

Ed compromised, as Tom often had. "Tell you what: we'll try your idea, but we'll go at it slow. We'll take the northeast pasture first and see how it works out. In two or three years, if we like it, we'll talk about doin' the rest of the place. This is a drastic change you're throwin' at me."

"As drastic as Granddad buyin' the first truck, or buildin' the first trailer? Or you startin' artificial insemination and preg-checkin'?"

Ed stared toward the old house. Billy was in the front yard, playing with the red dog.

Red had taken right up with the boy, tagging along with him as he had tagged after Tom. Ed thought about Tom, and about Morgan Whitley. The word came to him from somewhere. "Continuity."

Clay puzzled. "What do you mean, continuity?"

"Just thinkin' about somethin' your granddad said. I'll tell you someday, when it's time for you to think about it."

YELLOW DEVIL

It was already an old kill when Jake Howard's three lion hounds found it. Jake clenched his teeth and futilely doubled a hard fist as he nudged aside with his boot toe the twigs, dead leaves, and bark that covered the carcass. He read the Lazy H brand on the stiffened hide of a two-year-old heifer.

"That yellow devil of a lion again," he muttered. The fore-shoulders of the heifer were all but eaten away. The rest of the carcass had been expertly hidden, the mountain lion's way, and left to spoil.

Old Flop, Jake's lead hound, was eagerly nosing around for tracks. Another hound called Rip followed him. Little Mutt, Jake's pup in training, was sniffing at the carcass.

Jake lifted his stubbled chin and gazed bleakly toward the Carmen Mountains, which lay across the big bend of the Rio Grande. The fall air suddenly carried a chill.

He closed up his old mackinaw, fumbling absently at the place where he had pulled off a button three weeks before and never had gotten around to fixing it.

"Give that old devil a little more time," Jake dismally spoke his thoughts aloud, "and he'll flat ruin me." The lion had already killed the kid crop from Jake's Angora goats, and some of the nannies as well. Now he was cultivating a taste for beef.

Presently Flop opened up and started barking "lion." Little Mutt raised his head, listening, then barreled off to follow the two older dogs.

Jake could tell by the way Flop was picking his way up the side of the canyon that the trail was cold, had probably been there a week. But there was always the chance that by following it the dogs might cut a fresher trail. He swung up into the saddle and pulled the pack mule along behind him.

For hours the dogs struggled along with the trail, sniffing at the tops of rocks, going back and checking when the scent weakened. Finally the trail petered out for good in a heavily timbered header. Flop worked back and forth a long while before Jake reluctantly called him off.

Lions had a knack of doubling back over their own tracks, leaving a pack of confused dogs at what seemed to be the sudden end of a trail. Almost all lions were good at this, and the Yellow Devil was a master.

Desolately Jake shoved his hands deep into the pockets of his worn mackinaw and looked over at the ragged ridge of Big Bend mountains.

"I'd bet my boots he went yonderway, over onto Old Man Budge's ranch," he said to his dogs. "And they tell me the old coot's got a shotgun loaded with stock salt that he saves just to use on hunters."

The sun was edging down to where the trees on the mountains were throwing their shadows all the way across the canyon. The chill was working deeper into Jake's bones. He would have pulled his hounds in and headed back for the lonely old rock house he lived in if Flop hadn't struck a bear trail. It was fresh.

A lingering anger at the lion made Jake eager to catch something — anything — to help work off his frustration. Even if he hadn't wanted to, there wouldn't have been much he could do about it anyhow. His dogs had gone yonder. Their deep-throated belling sent a thrill up his spine as he spurred his horse and jerked the pack mule along. There was music in those voices, and a magic that only a hound-dog man could enjoy to its fullest.

It had been a good fall for Mexican black bears, drifting in from across the river. There were plenty of acorns and piñon nuts and berries. Jake knew this chase would make him lie out in the woods tonight. It would be too late to go back to the house. But the thought of good fresh bear meat instead of dry jerked beef munched along the trail made it seem worth the trouble.

Soon the hounds barked "treed" up ahead of him somewhere. Pulling in, Jake saw the dogs gathered at the bottom of a tree. Up in the top sat a bear, fat and ready for winter hibernation. Jake called the dogs back. He didn't want a wounded bear falling among his hounds and maybe ripping one open with his claws.

One shot was plenty. Skinning the bear, Jake whistled at the fat. Properly rendered, there was no grease in the world could beat good bear oil. Jake thought of Old Man Quincy Budge, and an idea struck him.

"They tell me there's no better way to work on a man than through his women folks," Jake said to inquisitive Little Mutt, who was still sniffing at the carcass. "And I think I got somethin' here that might do the job."

Soon after daylight Jake picked his way up

to the head of a rock-rimmed canyon and the little huddle of adobe buildings that constituted Budge's headquarters. In an ocotillo-stalk corral stood half a dozen fine-looking horses. An old man was currying and brushing a blaze-faced sorrel. As he saw Jake dismount in front of the adobe house, he slipped the rope off the horse's neck, patted the animal, then came walking out to intercept the hunter.

Wood smoke curled out of the rock chimney, and the smell of it was pleasant in the sharp autumn air. Jake untied a canvas-wrapped bundle from the mule's back.

Old Man Quincy Budge stopped between Jake and the house and stood frowning, his feet wide apart. Budge had graying whiskers down to the collar. Jake thought idly that the old stockman would do well to curry his beard once in a while, the way he took care of his horses.

Jake was wary, but he managed a thin smile. "Mornin', Mr. Budge. I'm Jake Howard. I own the Lazy H."

He had met the old man a couple of times before, but Budge had never wasted much time trying to be friendly. He didn't now. He grunted and eyed Jake's dogs with open hostility.

A plump little woman shoved her head

through the door. "Well, don't just stand there, Quincy. Invite the young man in to breakfast."

Budge grunted again and stood aside grudgingly. Moving past him, Jake tried to act as if he didn't notice Budge's animosity. Inside the kitchen, where the warmth clung to him like a wool coat, he laid down the bundle on the raw-topped plank table.

"Killed me a bear yesterday, Miz Budge. I wasn't far from here and thought you-all might enjoy havin' you some bear fat to render out. Can't beat it for good biscuits."

The old lady raised up both hands and chortled happily. She called, "Colleen, come in here and see what we've got."

A girl stepped into the kitchen from another room. Jake caught his breath short. She wore a loose cotton dress that almost swept the floor, and she was lithe and slender. Instinctively he reached up to his stubbled face and wished he had had some way to shave.

"Colleen," said Mrs. Budge, "this is Mr. Howard. Mr. Howard, our daughter."

Jake managed a smile and swallowed hard. Her eyes were big and fresh and brown. They studied him without shyness. Through breakfast Jake could feel the girl's gaze touching him. It made him so nervous, he couldn't eat but twelve flapjacks.

When Budge finished eating, he set his empty cup down in the saucer so hard it rang. He shoved his chair back on the rough board floor.

"Now then, Howard," he said gruffly, "I know you didn't come over here for no social call." He flicked a quick glance at his daughter. "Leastwise I don't think you did. What do you want?"

Jake was caught off guard, but there was no use in mincing words. "That yellow devil lion has been killin' my stock, Mr. Budge. I got a notion he comes over here when my dogs get to crowdin' him. I'd like your permission to hunt for him on your place."

The old man's heavy eyebrows knitted. His dark eyes stared levelly at Jake. "They tell me you're more of a hunter than you are a stockman. They tell me you hunt varmints for pay, and that you furnish dogs and pack outfits to city hunters and guide them around for a fee."

Jake could feel the old man's answer coming. He nodded reluctantly.

Budge went on, his voice flat, "I'm a stockman myself. I like to work with cattle and horses. I got no patience with a man who spends his time out with guns and a pack of dogs when he ought to be home

261

tendin' stock."

Angry warmth started rising in Jake. He could have told the old man why he hunted for pay. He could have told him that he had once owned a ranch bigger than the Lazy H and had it fully stocked with cattle. Then the drouth had come, and low prices, and a man couldn't fight them both. With what he could salvage he came up here to this smaller Lazy H with a handful of cattle, his mohair goats, and a big debt that had to be cleared up.

Hunting for a fee or guiding city hunters were ways of doing that. They paid expenses and left the ranch profit, if there was any, to apply on his debt.

He could have told Quincy Budge that. But stubborn anger was edging up in him, and he didn't say anything.

There was no compromise in Budge's voice. "Next time you come over here, you leave them guns at home. And don't you bring them flop-eared hounds with you no more either, or I'll chase the whole bunch of you back over the hill."

Jake went off vowing he wouldn't come back again. But for the next week or so the memory of a pair of big brown eyes stayed with him. And when he found himself in the vicinity of Budge's one day, he tied up his dogs and spurred off down the crooked trail to the ranch house. A couple of weeks later he did it again. Luckily old Quincy wasn't there. But Colleen was.

Jake was keeping close watch for the Yellow Devil to come back. So far, he and his dogs hadn't found any sign of the lion.

One day Doyle Short, a neighbor, rode into Jake's Lazy H camp with his teenage son Tommy. Doyle swung down from his beat-up saddle and came walking up to Jake's little rock house, his face etched with worry.

"Jake," he said, "there's a bear been killin' my cattle. If you don't get him for me, he's goin' to cost me half my calf crop. What do you say to puttin' your dogs on him? It's worth fifty dollars to me if you get him."

Jake grinned. A man couldn't get rich that way, but fifty dollars would pay a lot of expenses.

Then Doyle sprang the catch. "I thought maybe you might let Tommy here go along and help you. I figure the experience would do him good."

Jake tried to keep from showing his misgivings. He had worked with Tommy on a couple of roundups. The boy was a little wild yet, and given to jumping before he looked to see where he was going to land.

Right now Tommy was sliding a rifle out of his saddle scabbard. He sighted down the barrel, straight toward Jake's horse corral. "You and your dogs jump him out for me, Jake. I'll shoot him right between the eyes."

Jake reached out and pulled down the muzzle of the rifle. "You better shove that back and leave it till you get somethin' to use it on."

He tried to hint to Doyle that he could handle the job better alone, but the hint didn't take. By afternoon he and the boy had the dogs sniffing around the bear's latest kill. It took only a minute for Flop to open up and head out with his nose close to the ground.

A couple of times young Tommy yelled excitedly, "I see him up there," and started hauling out his rifle. But he was mistaken, and Jake would make him put up the rifle. The trail meandered around considerably but was becoming fresher all the time. A little before sundown the dogs were getting excited. Jake figured the bear had heard them and was on the run.

They never came in sight of the killer. Even fat as he likely was, he was too fast for the hounds. When darkness came, Jake took out his old cow horn, called in the winded dogs, and set up camp.

As soon as it was light enough to see again, he turned the hounds loose on the trail. Finally the scent became hot. Once more the bear had heard them and was off in a hard run.

After a couple of hours the bear left Short's range and crossed the deadline claimed by Old Man Quincy Budge. Jake reined up and listened to his dogs going pell-mell along the trail.

"The old man'll have a fit if he finds out we're runnin' bear on his place," Jake said to the hard-breathing boy. "But it'd sure be hard to call the dogs off now."

He spurred on after them. The boy followed, his face flushed with excitement. The bear was looking for rough country.

Finally the sound of the dogs' barking changed.

"They got him treed, Tommy," Jake spoke quickly. "Let's catch up and get this done before Budge finds out we been here."

Flop, Rip, and Little Mutt had put the bear up a big spruce in a canyon not far from a whispering creek. Now the angry bear hunched in the limbs, his wide jaws apart.

Mouth open and eyes wide, the boy

slipped his rifle out and raised it in shaky hands.

Alarmed, Jake said quickly, "Better steady that gun on a tree limb. You've got to make a clean kill."

But the boy didn't heed him. The rifle thundered. With a roar the wounded bear lost his hold. Limbs cracked as he fell. He hit the ground bawling and swinging his big paws. Instantly Little Mutt squatted and ran in at him.

Jake yelled at the dog, but it did no good. A vicious paw barely missed. The second time it sent the pup rolling, angry red claw streaks showing along his ribs. At the pup's sudden yelp of pain, the two older dogs started in.

In his mind Jake could see all three dogs cut to ribbons. He grabbed the rifle from the boy's hand and rushed in closer. For a moment he had to hold his fire to keep from hitting one of the dogs, which were rolling over and over with the bear. Then he got a clean bead. The recoil of the rifle jarred his shoulder.

The bear fell limp, and the dogs soon quieted down. Jake handed the rifle to pale, shaken young Tommy and ran to see about Little Mutt. The pup had some savage claw marks in his hide, but they weren't anything he wouldn't get over.

Jake jerked his head up as he heard Tommy yell shrilly, "It's another bear, Jake. I can see him over yonder."

Jake rose to his feet. "I don't think it's a bear, Tommy. Wait till we —"

He never finished. Steadying the rifle on a limb this time, Tommy fired before Jake could stop him. Jake's heart bobbed as he heard the animal's short scream.

"That's no bear!"

He sprinted as fast as his high-heeled boots would let him in the rocks. Lying in the brush, kicking out its last breath, he found a brown stallion. The Budge B brand was plain on the horse's hip — painfully plain.

Old Man Budge took it about as Jake had expected he would. He stormed like an angry bear. Jake couldn't blame him. The hunter knew he had it coming. Budge wouldn't even listen when Jake offered to pay for the stallion.

The old ranchman fetched a shotgun. "You better not let your shirttail touch you till you're off of my place, Howard. If you ever come back, I'll use this scattergun on you.

"And don't let them dogs come on my

ranch again, neither. First thing I'm goin' to do in the mornin' is put out some strychnine baits. Bring them dogs again and there won't be a one of them git out alive!"

Jake backed away. Colleen tried to speak up for him, but the old man chopped off a few curt words to her and she stopped, her brown eyes full of sympathy for Jake. He gave her a long last glance, knowing that if he ever saw her again, it would have to be in spite of Quincy Budge. Then he got back on his horse and rode off, the hounds at heel.

As if that hadn't been hard luck enough, the Yellow Devil came back. A couple of mornings later the hounds turned up a fresh kill. It was another good heifer, a yearling this time. In less than a week Jake found where the lion had killed a bull calf and covered up its partially eaten carcass.

Always any attempt to track the lion was foiled. The Yellow Devil laid such tangled trails that sooner or later the dogs got balled up. Once Flop led the hounds successfully over a series of the lion's backtracks and kept on the trail. About midday the trail suddenly became hot. The hounds found a spot under a mountainside ledge where the lion apparently had been lying up through the day. Jake guessed the sound of the dogs had scared him into running again.

But the chase was all for nothing. In a couple of hours the trail led over the deadline and onto Budge's ranch. Bitterly Jake pulled up and started calling the dogs. It took a good while, but they reluctantly gave up the hot chase and came back.

Exhausted, Jake threw up his hands in despair and started home.

Winter came, and with it the Yellow Devil seemed hungrier than ever. One after another, Jake turned up fresh kills. Looking at his gradually shrinking herd, he knew he was ruined if he couldn't stop that lion. But he *couldn't* stop him.

So Jake's hatred for the Yellow Devil slowly grew stronger and stronger, until finally he worried no more about taking care of the ranch or the cattle. Only one thought rode in his mind — get that lion — one thought, day and night, week after desperate week.

Then one day it looked as if his luck would change. Following a fresh trail from the carcass of a calf, the hounds scared the Yellow Devil from a ledge so suddenly that the lion was a scant two hundred yards in the lead. As the hounds piled off the ledge,

Jake caught a split-second look at the tawny shape before it disappeared in a tangle of brush across the canyon.

With a yelp of triumph Jake whipped the rifle out of his saddle scabbard and spurred his horse down the easiest way he could find to the canyon floor. By the time he reached bottom the dogs had disappeared into the brush. But their excited barking drifted back to him.

Shortly the trail went up the other side of the canyon. His mountain-trained horse climbed expertly but slowly. The sound of the dogs was farther away now, but maneuvering of the lion and necessary backtracking by the dogs allowed Jake to catch up. Almost before he realized it, he reached Budge's deadline.

He reined up a moment and mulled it over. This was the closest he had ever come to catching the Yellow Devil. If they were let go, the hounds might tree him at any time.

Jake remembered the old man's threat to use strychnine. But the sound of the dogs on a hot trail and the momentary glimpse of the hated killer had whipped him into a frenzied heat. Budge or no Budge, he was going to get that lion.

For an hour the dogs chased their prey across B Ranch land. The big cat was getting more desperate now, Jake knew from the trail. Jake sensed that he had driven the Yellow Devil off his usual range. The killer was on unfamiliar ground.

Suddenly Jake had a vague feeling something was wrong. He didn't know exactly what, but he sensed that one of his dogs had stopped barking. Loping up, he saw the reason.

Little Mutt lay on his side at the fork of a trail, his legs working feverishly, his eyes straining out of their sockets. His teeth were clamped tightly, biting into his tongue.

With a quick catch of breath, Jake exclaimed, "Strychnine!"

He could do nothing except stand there in misery and watch the pup die. He kept blowing the old cow horn until the other two dogs finally came trotting in, their tongues lolling out. Their accusing eyes said they could have treed the lion if only he had let them.

Choking, Jake put leash chains on the two dogs and led them away. Old Flop kept looking up at the dead pup in the saddle and whimpering.

With a deep bitterness creeping through him, Jake turned his back on the Yellow Devil and headed for the shortest trail off the B Ranch. He blinked his stinging eyes.

He berated the lion. He lambasted the ornery old man who would let a killer lion lie up on his range but put out strychnine to poison faithful hounds.

As it turned out, the chase had not been a complete failure. The Yellow Devil did not come back to the Lazy H.

Jake wondered about this. Then reports started coming in. The lion was killing Quincy Budge's horses.

Jake reasoned that the many chases his hounds had given the lion, capped off by the final one that had come so close, had scared the Yellow Devil off his home range. Now the cat had found something he liked better — good, tender, easy-to-kill colts.

Week after week, reports came in. Budge had lost more than half of his last colt crop. The lion seldom returned to old kills now. With horseflesh plentiful, every time he got hungry, he made a new kill.

Time and again Budge had moved the horses, but always the Yellow Devil followed them. The old man had lain out in the biting cold night after bitter night, hoping to get a shot at the killer. The chance never came. But every time he missed a night, another horse would die.

Folks said Quincy Budge had aged ten

years in the two months the Devil had been working on him. Contrary though he was, he loved those horses. But Jake hadn't seen the old rancher. A couple of times he got word Budge was coming over to talk to him. He would leave his ranch then and camp out a night or two, until he figured the old man had come and gone.

But one day Budge caught him unawares. He rode up to the barn while Jake was feeding Flop and Rip and a new pup he was training to take Little Mutt's place. Looking at the old man, Jake felt a bit sorry for him, though he tried not to. The lines in Budge's bearded face were carved deeper than ever. His eyes were like those of a whipped dog.

"Look, Howard," the old man pleaded, "if that lion works on me much longer, I'm through. I ain't done nothin' for two months but hunt for him. I've hired men with dogs to try and track him, but their dogs ain't like yours."

Jake kept his voice flat. "I'm surprised you could get anybody to take dogs in there, seein' as how you've put out strychnine."

The old man flinched. "I knew where I put them baits, Howard. I went out and took them all up."

"All of them?"

Guilt showed in Budge's lined face. "All

but one. I heard about it, Howard. My wife and daughter jumped me good when the word came about your dog. . . . I'm tellin' you, I'm sorry about the pup. It was spite made me do it. I've thought it over aplenty since. I'm askin' you to forgive me, Howard, and help me git that lion."

Jake wanted to. He still hated the Yellow Devil as much as he ever had. But there was a stubbornness about him.

He looked at the sinking sun. "It'll be dark before you get home if you don't get started." He turned his back and walked off.

"Wait, Howard," Budge called desperately, "I'll give you a hundred dollars — two hundred — to catch that cat."

Jake hesitated. Two hundred dollars. That would pay for a good many losses. But no, he wouldn't back down now. He kept walking.

Next day another rider came. Jake recognized Colleen Budge, and his heart quickened. He knew what she wanted. He was determined to turn her down.

But that was not easy to do. "Dad's not a bad man at heart," she pleaded. "It hurt him when he heard about your pup, knowin' it was his fault. You can't imagine what that lion's done to him. It's killin' him. I'm beggin' you to come track down that lion — for me."

He felt his face coloring as he realized he was whipped. "All right. I'll do it."

She kissed him, and the warmth was still with him long after she had gone.

That night Jake took his dogs, horse, and pack mule over to Budge's ranch, to be ready to start the hunt at daylight the next morning. Quincy Budge was pacing the kitchen floor, blowing at his steaming coffee cup and raring to go an hour before pink light began to creep over the great wall of the Carmens to the east. Jake had little to say to him.

Colleen put on a long riding skirt and went along with them. Soon after sunup they were at the site of the latest slaughter. The dogs sniffed around a freshly killed sorrel colt while Budge sat stiffly in his saddle. Jake saw tears in the old man's eyes.

As usual, old Flop was the hound that opened and led out. The trail followed a winding course but continued strong. The colt's blood on the cat's paws was making him easier for the dogs to track.

Finally the trail seemed to come to a dead end along a rimrock. Flop patiently worked the back trail, his nose rubbing raw on the rocks.

Jake looked over the rim and spotted a tall tree not far below. It gave him a hunch. He called Flop and let him sniff around the edge. Surely enough, he picked up the scent just above the tree. The lion had back-tracked, then jumped off into the tree. He wasn't in it now. He must be down there somewhere in the steep-walled canyon.

"I'm takin' the dogs and goin' down afoot," he said. "You-all can keep the horses up here on the rim. Just listen for the dogs and follow them."

Quincy Budge climbed stiffly out of the saddle. "I'm goin' with you."

Jake warned, "It's rough goin' down there afoot. And there's no tellin' how far we might have to run him."

The old man grunted. "It's my horses he's been killin'. Let's go."

It was a tough, dangerous climb down the steep walls. They had to hand the hounds down part of the way. The old man slipped once, bruising his knee against a sharp rock and ripping a hole in his pant leg. But he never seemed to notice it. A grim look had hardened in his eyes.

The hounds picked up the scent at the bottom of the tree and headed out up the canyon again. Jake fell in behind them in a long trot, his rifle balanced in his hand. He wondered how long Budge would be able to keep up.

The old man surprised him. He seldom lagged far behind. Occasionally, where sand had blown into ripples, a lion track was visible. That would bring new life into the old man's steps. But the dogs paid no particular attention to tracks. They kept right on by scent.

The trail led up onto a ledge. There the scent seemed especially hot. The Yellow Devil had been lying up there, Jake figured, until the sound of the dogs had scared him away. He looked off down the canyon as if he hoped for a glimpse of the fleeing lion. But he saw nothing.

Even the pup had the scent now. All three dogs were tearing ahead, fast enough to outrun a good horse and far too fast for men afoot to keep up with them. But Jake did his best. He ran until his heart was like a lead weight in him. He glanced back occasionally. Quincy Budge labored heavily along, falling farther and farther back but not quitting.

Jake's hatred of the cat returned to him now. The tom's trail angled over to the canyon wall again. For a minute it was lost. Then Flop tracked back to where the lion had made a long jump up onto a boulder the size of a small shack. Jake boosted the dog to where he could clamber up on the rock. The scent was there, all right. Jake handed the other dogs up.

The lion had jumped onto another ledge overhead. Again Jake had to lift the dogs up. They seemed heavy as horses now, even the pup, which he put up last. He struggled to pull himself up after them.

The trail led on and on, across jagged rock ledges, back down to the canyon floor, then up again. Jake's mouth and throat were dry. His heart hammered dully. His breath came short and painfully. At times he wanted to call the dogs off. But the sound of them ahead of him kept pulling him on. Still, he knew he could not go much farther. It had to end soon now, or the chase was lost.

The dogs' voices faded thin. Jake stopped and leaned on a tree to regain his breath. His heart bobbed as he recognized the gliding shape creeping up across the rocks. The Yellow Devil had momentarily thrown the dogs again on a double-back. Now he was trying to sneak out of the canyon.

In desperation Jake realized the chase was over if the cat did get out. The hunter didn't have strength left to climb that wall. He raised his rifle and took a long shot. He heard the bullet ricochet off a rock over the lion's head and whine away. The cat whirled back like a whiplash and leaped once more into the canyon.

He disappeared into the brush. Jake heaved on after him. This time, he knew, the hunt would be finished. There was no deadline to worry about, no place beyond which he could not go. He would trail the Yellow Devil into Mexico now, if he had to.

But he wouldn't have to. A new, excited note came into the dogs' voices. They had jumped the lion. Fatigue was a lance shoved through Jake's ribs, but he made himself keep on. He heard the hounds bark "treed."

Flushed with victory, Jake made his weary legs move a little faster. Most of the pain left his chest. He saw the dogs ahead, one after another rearing up onto the trunk of a tall spruce and barking. High in the branches, a tawny form crouched on a limb.

The Yellow Devil.

He was cornered now. He did not stand a chance. But there was a majesty about him as he sat high in the tree, looking down, never taking his eyes off the dogs. His ears were laid back. He spat defiantly at the hounds that had treed him.

But Jake wasn't thinking of the majesty of the beast. He remembered dead cattle — his cattle — and goats he had found where the lion left them. He remembered long, weary chases that led always to disappointment. He remembered a brown pup named Little Mutt.

A choking hatred surged in him, and he raised his rifle. He drew a careful bead on the Yellow Devil. But his hands wavered, and he thought of an old man trudging wearily along the trail back yonder, an old man who had lain out in misery night after night, who had not been able to keep the tears out of his eyes as he looked down at the dead colt.

He remembered Quincy Budge and the hard lines that had edged into his face. In the last two months the tom had become more than a stock-killing cat to Budge. It had been almost a human enemy, an enemy to be hated and hunted, and if possible destroyed, before he destroyed the old man.

For months Jake had dreamed of this moment. Now he had the rifle in his hand and the lion in a tree. He told himself he owed Budge nothing.

But reluctantly he lowered his rifle, the taste of victory sour in his mouth. This shot belonged to Quincy.

Colleen got there before Quincy did. Leading the horses and mule along the rim of the canyon, she had followed the sound of the dogs. When she heard them bark "treed," she spurred ahead to a break in the rimrock and came down.

She found Jake waiting there, rifle in his hands. She was watching when Jake handed Quincy the rifle and turned away.

Jake flinched at the slap of the gunshot. Limbs popped as the dead tom fell. Jake turned and watched the dogs, especially the new pup, wooling the lion's body around at the base of the tree.

Quincy Budge's face slowly relaxed. The lines in it seemed to soften a little. The sag was gone from his shoulders.

Colleen touched Jake's hand. "You wanted to make that shot yourself. Thanks for lettin' Dad do it."

"He's payin' me two hundred dollars," Jake said.

She smiled. "You know that's not it, Jake."

Jake nodded and took the hand she extended toward him. "I reckon it isn't." He looked at the dead lion. "I'm not mad at anybody anymore. Or anything."

He caught the mule and led him up to the Yellow Devil. Time they packed this lion it would be time to get started. It was a long way home.

DRY WINTER

It had been a dry winter all over the Trans-Pecos country, and there wasn't a harder-hit ranch in it than Charlie McDermott's place.

Every day since late in September he had taken his worn-out pickup truck over the dusty pasture roads to pour out cottonseed cake for his cattle and sheep. Now it was March, and there wasn't any end to it. The calf crop had come, and it was lambing time. It was bad business to feed through lambing. Hungry ewes would abandon their lambs and go chasing after the rattling pickup. Lots of them never paired up again.

Pain would lance through Charlie every time he saw a pitiful little body crumpled under a mesquite — but there wasn't any way out. If he didn't feed, the ewes would starve too.

Charlie finished pouring the cubes out of the last sack and onto the ground, then worked back afoot through the hungry sheep. As always, his tired eyes searched the late afternoon skies for any trace of a rain cloud. And as always, he was disappointed. A west wind fanned his face, and the west wind never brought anything but trouble. It carried the pinching smell of dust.

Charlie McDermott was only thirty, but he looked forty. He had had high hopes when he came home from the war in Europe and put the money he had saved into livestock. Now the drought had put a sag in his long back and carved deep lines of worry into his face.

Out on the flat, he saw a young ewe running in toward the feed ground. Far behind her a two-week-old lamb struggled to keep up, its stubby legs wobbling.

Futile anger whipped through Charlie. He hurled a rock toward the ewe. "Damn your worthless hide!" he exploded. "Get back there and act like a mother!"

The hungry ewe kept coming on. Charlie fought down his unreasoning anger. This lamb would catch up, but countless others wouldn't.

A mile from the house he stopped and picked up a weak, flat-ribbed lamb that he found tottering aimlessly along beside the road. The grating anger still worked in him.

He felt better only when he pulled up at the barn and saw the brown curl of smoke from the tin chimney of the tired old house. No matter how bad the day, it was always a pleasure to come home to Mary.

He tossed the empty tow sacks into the barn. They would bring a few cents apiece, if there weren't any holes in them. He saw Mary out in the milk lot. He picked up the lamb and carried it along.

Mary's smile touched Charlie like the warmth of a fireplace on a wintry day.

"I got another dogie lamb for you," he said.

The pretty young woman's smile changed to a frown of pity as she took the lamb out of his hands and cradled it in her arms. "Oh, Charlie," she said, "I'll bet it hasn't had any milk in two days."

Tenderly she took the woolly little animal under the milk shed. There she had been feeding milk to more than a dozen other abandoned lambs.

Charlie watched her, marveling at the patience she showed in trying to get the lamb to take warm milk through a nipple on a soda pop bottle. For the thousandth time he told himself how lucky he had been in marrying her. There in that dusty cowlot, wearing an old, washed-out cotton dress and one of his frayed jackets, she didn't look as if she had been brought up in the biggest house in the country. But if she had ever had a regret in the two years they had spent together, she had never let it be known.

But her father, old Stace Tolliver, did plenty of talking about it. Charlie had walked up behind the big ranchman at Gamlin's wool warehouse one day just in time to overhear Stace remark, "He's making her live like a sharecropper's wife. My own daughter! I warned her before she married him. But she wouldn't listen to me. What's he got? Nothing but a leased starve-out ranch, a handful of cattle, and a mangy flock of sheep he's had to mortgage."

Charlie had let his fiery temper rip loose that day. "It won't be that way forever," he had declared, his flaming face as close to Stace's as he could get it. "Some day we'll have a good ranch of our own, and the best cattle and sheep in the country. We'll build it ourselves, with our own hands, Mary and me. Maybe I'll even start my own bank, and run yours out of business. Mary won't always have to live like a sharecropper's wife. You'll see."

Mary had heard about it later. With her warm hand on his cheek and laughter dancing in her eyes, she had chided him softly.

"Your pride, and your temper! They'll keep getting you in Dutch, Charlie, till you finally learn to boss them instead of letting them boss you."

Charlie rolled and smoked a cigarette as he waited for Mary to finish caring for her family of dogie lambs. He had gotten out of the ready-roll habit these last few months. Walking toward the house, his arm around Mary's slender waist, he said, "Feed's getting low again. I got to go in tomorrow and get some more."

She bit at her pale lips. "We owe an awful lot on feed already, don't we, Charlie?"

He nodded thoughtfully. "More than our next wool clip will bring. And we're starting to feed up the lamb crop too. The way things look right now, I'm afraid we won't raise much of a lamb crop. I don't know how we're going to pay to hold our option on the lease."

On the sagging front porch, she stopped and faced him, her work-roughened hands resting lightly on his arms. "Look, Charlie, you know I have the money my mother left me. Why won't you forget your vow and use it?"

Charlie's face hardened. "You know why. I won't have your dad claiming I bought my way along with your money. We can use it some day to buy us a place. But first I've got to prove to Stace Tolliver and everybody else that I can make good on my own."

She kissed him and smiled. "Sure you can, Charlie. Sure you can."

Charlie pulled his pickup to a stop in front of Archie Gamlin's feed store and wool warehouse. Climbing the concrete steps to the loading ramp, he shoved his hat back. "Morning, Archie."

Gamlin pitched a hundred-pound feed sack onto the back of a truck. "Be with you in a minute, Charlie," he said.

Stace Tolliver stepped out of the wide warehouse door. He saw Charlie, and a frown weighted his face. Mary's father gave Charlie a hostile glance, and then walked off down the ramp.

Stace was a big man with an ample frame that still retained most of the strength of his younger days. But middle age had spread out his beltline and sprinkled gray through his coarse black hair. The flesh was beginning to sag around a powerful jaw that had scared half the men on the Pecos at one time or another.

"Haul that load over to the Gonzales camp," Stace ordered the truck driver. He climbed into his big black car and drove away with his boot heavy on the accelerator.

Watching, Charlie tasted the anger that rode in him and knew it was doing him no good. Stace didn't like him, and probably never would. He hadn't spoken a dozen words to Charlie since Mary had slipped off and married him.

Charlie knew what much of the trouble was. For years Stace had set his heart on seeing his daughter marry the son of his old homesteading partner, Dike Rutledge. It was hard to tell which one had gotten the wealthiest, Stace or Dike. And when Dike had died four years ago, all he had owned had gone to his son Jake. Mary Tolliver and Jake Rutledge. Two family fortunes — a perfect marriage, Stace had thought. And Charlie had sunk the boat.

Presently Archie Gamlin dusted his hands on the legs of his khaki pants and ambled over.

"I need some more feed," Charlie told him. "I have barely enough to run me another four days."

Gamlin frowned and looked down at the scarred concrete floor. "I'm sorry, Charlie. But I got word from the bank that they aren't honoring any more of your drafts."

That was a hard blow. Charlie argued, "But my credit ought to be as good as any other small rancher's around here. I had better than a thousand ewes clear of debt when fall started. I haven't borrowed all they're worth."

Gamlin scratched his head. "Might as well face it, Charlie. If it was anybody but you, the bank'd carry you. But old Stace's the lever that keeps the wheel going around. He passed the word to Fred Purvis and the directors that you weren't to get any more credit."

Weakly Charlie sat down on a row of salt blocks. A thought came to him. "Look, Archie, it's only a month or so till shearing time. If I could get my wool contracted, that'd take care of most of my feed bill."

Gamlin shook his head. "Not much chance, Charlie. Ain't been a wool buyer around here in weeks."

Leaving town, Charlie stopped and looked wistfully at the bank. But he knew it wouldn't do any good to go in and talk it over with Fred Purvis. Like Archie had said, Stace was the lever that made the wheel go around.

Mary saw it in his face the minute he stepped into the old, high-ceilinged living room. He hung his greasy hat on an aged set of deer antlers and told her what Archie had said. Then he turned loose the hold he had held on his anger.

"Stace Tolliver," he gritted bitterly. "The old horned toad's been trying to break me ever since we married. Now he's got me where he wants me. I'd like to take those feed sacks and cram them down his throat."

Color flooded into Mary's face. Her hands trembled with anger for the first time in months. "He's still my father, Charlie," she said, her voice strained.

Suddenly shamed, Charlie managed to force down his bitterness. He caught Mary's hand. "I'm sorry, Mary. I didn't mean to hurt you."

She turned away from him and looked out the window. "Give me the pickup keys," she said. "I'm going to town."

"What for?" he asked worriedly.

"I'm going to talk to Fred Purvis."

"It was your dad's idea, not his."

"I've known him as long as Dad has. I'll talk to him."

Even before Mary returned, Archie Gamlin telephoned Charlie to tell him the feed would be hauled out by late afternoon.

"I got a call from the bank," he said. "They told me to give you whatever you want."

Charlie met Mary as she stepped down out of the pickup and happily swept her into his arms. For a moment he thought she was still angry. But then she smiled with him, and he knew everything was all right.

For weeks Charlie had been looking at the calendar in the kitchen, watching the date he had circled in red. It was almost here now, the specified date by which he had to put down the money for an option if he wanted to renew his lease on the ranch. The five-year lease was expiring this fall. He wanted the place again, but right now he had no forfeit money to pay Ernie Pope, who owned the land.

Mary went with Charlie the day he drove into town to talk to Ernie. It wasn't hard to find him. Charlie made the rounds of the domino halls and located the pudgy man slouched over a game of forty-two with three other loafers.

"I'm busy right now, Charlie," Pope said, shifting a nervous glance at him. The man's eyes gave evidence of a hangover, nothing new to him.

"I drove in just to see you, Ernie," Charlie said.

Irritably Pope pushed his dominoes to the center of the table and stood up. Charlie followed him past the pool tables to the back of the hall. Ernie eased into a wire-braced chair that groaned under his weight.

"It's about the lease, Ernie. I got to have the place again. It's time we were getting some papers signed."

Pope studied the floor and pursed his thick lips nervously. "Contract says you got to show me the money."

Charlie's heart began to sink. "I can't right now, but I will. You could take my note. I've done well by you the last five years."

Ernie Pope took off his hat and wiped the sweat from his brow with a dirty handkerchief. "There's another man wanting the place. He's offered me a year's lease, in advance, to hold the contract. You got a deadline. If you can't pay, I'll have to let him have it. I got creditors too."

Fury strained to break loose in Charlie. "Who's trying to get my lease, Ernie?" But he already knew.

"Stace Tolliver."

Stace didn't really want the place. Charlie had once heard him call it the sorriest ranch in the county. This was just another move in his game of freeze-out.

Choking down a curse, Charlie turned on his heel and made for the front door in long, angry strides.

He met Stace Tolliver a block up the

street. Mary was with him.

"You've pulled some raw deals on me, Stace Tolliver," he exploded, "but this one is the snakiest yet."

Mary stared wide-eyed at him. "Charlie! Have you gone crazy?"

"No," he thundered, "I'm not crazy. But I'm mad, clean through. I've stood for a lot from you, Stace, and I haven't said much. But this is the end of it.

"You're leasing my place out from under me. But any improvements I've put up, I'll take down. I'm keeping the place till my last day, and if you or anybody you send tries to get on it, I'll be waiting with a shotgun."

Tolliver was standing quietly, his thick arms folded. "Are you about through?"

Charlie nodded. "I'm through."

Stace showed a hard, flat grin that had no humor in it. "You're puffed up like a Christmas turkey, McDermott. You think you've gotten by on your own, but you haven't. If it hadn't been for Tolliver money you'd be out begging for a job right now."

Mary McDermott grabbed her father's arm. "Stop it, Dad."

Ice began working through Charlie's veins as he guessed what was coming. "Let him talk, Mary."

Stace narrowed his eyes. "You thought it was the bank that extended your feed credit — that it was strictly business. But it wasn't the bank, McDermott. The only thing that's kept you going has been Mary's money. The money her mother left her."

In bitterness Charlie looked down on his wife. "Is that true, Mary?"

Tears crept into her eyes. "Charlie, it was the only thing I knew to do. It's been terrible, watching what this drought has already done to you. I couldn't let you lose everything."

"You lost your faith in me. You as much as said I'm a failure."

Mary's face was white, her lips trembling. For a moment her stricken eyes dwelt on his. "Charlie, you know that's not —"

She broke off. She whirled away from him and hurried blindly down the street, covering her face. Stace gave Charlie a hard look and went after his daughter.

Dumbly Charlie looked after them, and slowly he realized what he had done. Pride and anger had done this to him. He ached to follow them, to talk to Mary. But even now the pride was still in him. He wouldn't crawl in front of Stace. After an hour or so, he could talk to Mary alone.

But when he went to the Tolliver house,

the Mexican maid met him at the front door. Miss Mary didn't want to see him, the woman said. He argued, but she shook her head.

He drove home alone, a great emptiness tugging within him. The dusty pastures seemed more dismal than ever. The house was vacant and cold. He thought about cooking supper, but he wound up drinking black coffee and smoking cigarettes, sitting in his rawhide chair and listening to the bleak wind rattling the sagging front gate.

The pile of empty feed sacks kept growing in the corner of the barn. Dry day followed dry day. Occasionally a good looking set of clouds would drift over with a promise that set his blood to tingling, but then a strong west wind would drive the rain away. The old West Texas brown clouds would come rolling in, and the surface of the ground would start to move.

Every day he telephoned the Tolliver house, and every day the answer was the same. Miss Mary didn't want to talk to him.

One night the old wall telephone rang, and Charlie knocked over the coffeepot in his haste to get to the phone.

His heart sagged. It wasn't Mary. "Charlie?" came the voice. "This is Archie. Archie

Gamlin. I know it's a little earlier than you like to shear your sheep, but I got a chance to sell a little wool. A wool buyer needs a small clip to finish out a carload of stuff he bought on contract.

"I know you can't shear ewes that have got lambs. But if you could shear your yearling ewes and deliver the wool here inside of two days, I could get you sixty-five cents a pound."

Sixty-five cents. Charlie made a rapid calculation in his head. It wasn't what it had brought last year, but it would be enough to pay Ernie Pope the option on that lease, the way the contract required. He'd stomp Tolliver's toes yet.

"You tell him he's bought him some wool," Charlie said.

An hour later he had pulled his pickup into the Mexican settlement at the south end of town. Leaving the lights burning, he got out and walked up to an old adobe house. After he knocked, he heard the shouting of four or five children. Heavy footsteps tromped toward the door. A big Mexican stood there in trousers, socks and long underwear.

"Evening, Vincente," Charlie said. "Is your shearing outfit in good working shape?"

"*Si,*" the Mexican nodded. During regular

shearing season, which wouldn't start for three or four more weeks, there were always enough transient shearing crews to take care of rush needs. Other times, there was no crew here except that of Vincente Castro.

"I'll give you what I paid you last year, twenty-four cents a head, if you can have a crew at my place day after tomorrow, bright and early."

Castro smiled broadly. "You bet your boots, I'll be there."

Charlie went on about town, hunting up cowboys. He spent the next morning getting the shearing pens patched up and ready. That afternoon he gathered up his supplies and brought the cowboys home. A couple of neighbors promised to come over and help.

There was a strange tang to the air the next morning. Charlie didn't know what it was, but the other cowboys sensed it, too. The wind didn't get up much that morning, and the dust stayed down. It was a welcome thing not to have to fight the sheep along because of wind. They got to the shearing pens with the first bunch of yearling ewes about nine o'clock.

"Where's Vincente, Charlie?" one of the neighbors asked. "Thought he was going to be here, set and ready by this time."

Worry started eating at Charlie. Vincente was usually very prompt. Maybe he'd had a little trouble down the road.

Charlie left the punchers to gather more sheep, and he headed for town. He expected to find Vincente's ancient shearing rig broken down somewhere along the way, but he didn't. At the *capitan's* house Mrs. Castro was sweeping dirt off her pathway.

"Oh, Vincente," she replied to his question, "he's gone to shear for Mr. Stace. He say if you come by, to tell you he get to you tomorrow, maybe."

Anger rose in Charlie. "But Vincente promised to shear for me today. I got the sheep up in the pens."

Surprised, the woman shook her head. "Did Mister Stace not call you? He said he would. He offer more money."

Doubling his fists, Charlie stalked back to his pickup, pausing to kick a rock halfway across the road. Stace again! The old skinflint never sheared anything this early. He had hired Vincente to shear a pasture or two just to balk Charlie.

The neighbor help went home. Charlie intended to keep the cowboys he had hired. Maybe Vincente would show up tomorrow.

But Archie Gamlin telephoned. "Sorry, Charlie. Old Stace's gone and sheared, and that buyer is taking his wool. I'm afraid your sale has fallen through."

There wasn't anything left to do but turn the sheep out and let the cowboys go back to town. Then Charlie loaded up his feed sacks and made his daily circle over the pastures. He moved slowly, hardly seeing what he was doing. This last defeat had taken the heart out of him.

By night that strange feeling in the air was stronger. The sand hadn't blown at all that day. Now there was a trace of dampness in the breeze, and he noticed the unusual playfulness of the horses. Far to the north, lightning flashed occasionally.

Courage crept back into Charlie's heart. By George, it was building up to rain.

Then another thought struck him. He broke out laughing so suddenly that he scared some of the dogie lambs he was feeding.

"Old Stace may have done me a favor today," he said gleefully to one of the lambs. "If I'd sheared today, and it comes a cold rain tonight, I'd have lost half my sheep."

The telephone awakened Charlie a while before daylight. Sleepily lighting his lamp, he shivered in the cold breeze coming through his window. It carried the pleasant smell of rain.

The caller was one of the neighbors who had helped him the day before. "Thought you might be interested to know, Charlie. Old Stace tried to spite you yesterday, and he got his foot caught in a beartrap. He called me a few minutes ago. He's calling everybody else around here.

"Seems he sheared his best yearling ewes. He left before the shearing was finished, and one of his men turned those sheep out in an open pasture. Now it looks like we're in for a cold rain. Stace's got to get them sheep to brush and rough country before the rain starts, or he'll lose them. He's really crying for help."

Charlie hung up the receiver and sat down heavily. He ought to be laughing, he told himself. But he wasn't. He still had his pride.

What better way to show it than to go to Stace's place now, with the rest of the men? He would go there with his head high, and give his help. He would see what it did to Stace's pride, having to accept help from the man he had spited.

Shearing had been done at the Gonzales camp on the Tolliver ranch. The sheep had been turned out into a seven-section open pasture that offered little protection. But

300

west of the Gonzales windmills the broken country and the brush started. If they could get the freshly-shorn young ewes in there, the sheep could find protection from the cold rain. There would be losses, of course, but there would not be so many.

Fifteen or eighteen other men had gathered as dawn neared, and the darkness began slowly to lift. Unloading a saddled horse from his trailer, Charlie turned to find Stace Tolliver looking at him, puzzled and a little guilty.

"You didn't have to come, McDermott," Stace said.

Leisurely Charlie lighted a cigarette. "No, I didn't have to." He swung into the saddle and pulled away from the ranchman.

With Stace in the lead, the men spurred out at a brisk trot. The wind soon knifed its chill through Charlie's worn mackinaw. An occasional drop of rain hit his face, and he would look up at the dark, threatening clouds. Any minute they'd have a drenching, freezing downpour.

The men kept up the stiff trot to the back of the pasture. There wasn't any time to lose. They spread out in a line and started working back toward the Gonzales windmills.

With their wool just gone, the sheep were

cold and hard to manage. The wind was no help. It was a hard fight all the way, keeping the sheep headed west while the chilling north wind howled into their sides. Charlie jumped a number of small bunches of ewes and had little luck in getting them together. He would chouse one bunch, then leave it and go to another. His horse was wearing down, and his own throat was getting raw from shouting so much. But he was doing his job. He was keeping the sheep moving.

At last, through the light mist that began filtering down, Charlie could make out the windmills straight ahead. Many bunches of sheep were coming together there and forming one big band.

The flock filed through the gate, jumping over imaginary obstacles as sheep will. The riders kept pushing; there were a few more miles to the breaks.

It was sprinkling steadily now. They had to make it, had to get those sheep scattered. If the hard rain started there would be no handling that flock — chances were the whole bunch would head straight away from the rough country.

Charlie could feel the raindrops coming faster and harder. He spurred his horse, beat on his chaps, and yelled at the top of his lungs.

At last they reached the breaks. Down in the roughs the sheep could get behind banks to keep the cold wind away from them; they could find brush to stand under to check some of the freezing rain and protect themselves.

"Scatter them," old Stace was yelling.

When the job was done, Charlie reined up and looked around him. Relief washed over Tolliver's formidable old face. As little use as Charlie had for him, he couldn't help feeling a bit happy for Stace.

Presently Stace rode up beside Charlie.

"All right, McDermott," he said grudgingly, "I guess I got to do something to pay you for your help. Supposing I tell Ernie Pope I don't want that lease, after all."

Charlie swallowed a bitter taste. So the old man thought he had just come to blackmail him.

"Forget it," he said testily. "I didn't come over here to whine for mercy." He pulled his horse away — but not before he saw the puzzlement in Stace's eyes.

Through the rain he could see Stace Tolliver's black car drive up. It stopped, and someone got out. It was Mary!

She saw Charlie almost as soon as he saw her. They stood uncertainly a moment, looking at each other. Charlie swung to the ground and ran to meet her.

When at last he turned her loose, she was soaked from the rain, just as he was. But that glistening in her eyes wasn't from raindrops.

"Mary, Mary," he breathed, "I'll never be angry with you again!"

"Oh, Charlie," she cried, "why didn't you call, or come for me?"

"But I did, many times. They always said you didn't want to talk to me."

"Then that was Dad's doing, not mine," she said. "I've been aching for a word from you, just a word." Her lips brushed against his again. "But now I'm glad it turned out this way. It was big of you, Charlie, coming to help Dad after all that's happened."

It wasn't bigness of heart, he knew. It was a matter of pride. Perhaps some day he would be able to tell her about that.

Some day he would be able to tell her something else he had learned here today. A man didn't have to lose his pride just because he was forced to ask for help.

Stace was sitting on his horse in the rain, watching them. Defiantly Charlie turned toward Mary's father.

"Well, we got your sheep to cover. Now if it's all the same to you, I'll be going home. I'm taking Mary home with me. If you got any objections, spill them now."

Tolliver shrugged. "Wouldn't do any good if I did have any, would it?"

Embarrassment and uncertainty showed on Stace's heavy face. "Look, McDermott, I haven't liked you so far. I can't say I like you now. But it looks like I'm stuck with you, and I've got to make the best of it. I always figured that there must be something to a man who wouldn't sell his pride. You wouldn't that day in town, and you wouldn't a while ago, when I offered you that lease.

"Well, I'm going to forget about that lease, just like I said. And the first time you're in town, drop by the bank. I'll tell Fred Purvis that he's changed his mind about your account."

Charlie nodded. "We might be able to talk business."

When Tolliver rode away, Charlie turned back to Mary. The rain was pouring down, and they were both soaking wet. But they didn't care. They had a lot of business to talk about.

THE RELUCTANT SHEPHERD

Hewey Calloway had not been to town in more than eight weeks. Now he had two months' cowboy wages in his pocket and was riding in for a well-earned celebration. Upton City might never be the same again.

Knowing how hung over he would feel by the time he emptied his pockets, he almost dreaded it.

Sister-in-law Eve would have a lot to say afterward, but she had a lot to say about almost everything. He respected her strong opinions about responsibility, sobriety, and thrift, but he did not share them. Now past thirty and proud of maintaining his bachelorhood against contrary advice from almost everybody around him, he felt it was his right to spend his money and his off time in any way he saw fit. Even tight-fisted old rancher C. C. Tarpley understood that his employees had to vent steam occasionally. Otherwise, their work suffered, and C. C.

could not stand for that.

Hewey hoped he might be lucky enough to run into old drinking compadres such as Snort Yarnell or Grady Welch. But if they weren't there, he could holler loudly enough by himself.

He reached deep into memory, reliving rowdy adventures he had enjoyed in times past, recalling the many pleasures and glossing over the pain that inevitably followed. People like Eve kept telling him that at his age he ought to slow down and find a place to settle. But he felt not one bit older than when he had been twenty. He was going to have a good time whether anybody else liked it or not.

He was humming a shady little dancehall ditty when a distant sound first reached him. He listened intently but for a moment or two could not make out what it was. Then it came clearer. He recognized the bleating of sheep.

"Sheep!" he exclaimed, though no one could hear him except his horse. "Biscuit, old C. C.'ll bust a blood vessel."

This was Tarpley land, and C. C. hated sheep like the devil hates holy water. Hewey did not exactly hate them; he just refused to acknowledge their existence.

He rode in the direction of the sound.

Soon he saw a flock moving slowly westward, each sheep pausing to graze, then trotting to catch up. A black and white dog kept pace, its tongue lolling. When an animal paused too long, the dog ran up and nipped at it. The nearby sheep tumbled over each other in their haste to give the dog room.

A tarp-covered wagon, drawn by two mules, rolled along slowly on the upwind side, out of the dust stirred by the flock's tiny hooves. A horseman followed the sheep, not allowing the drags to linger long in one place. The man was hunched over as if half asleep.

I'm fixing to wake him up good, Hewey thought. As a Two Cs hand, it was his job to see after C. C. Tarpley's interests. C. C. was definitely not interested in having sheep cross his cattle range.

Hewey knew this was a tramp sheepman with no land of his own, moving across country and fattening his animals on other men's forage. It was a common enough practice, though it was increasingly frowned upon as more and more Texas state land fell into private ownership.

Hewey had a cowboy way of assessing a man's horse before he made any judgment about the rider. This horse was old, in bad need of being turned out to pasture. The saddle appeared to be just as old, somebody's castoff. The bridle was patched, the reins of cotton rope instead of leather. The only thing not old was the rider. Hewey guessed him to be in his mid to late twenties.

"Hey, you," Hewey said, "don't you know this is private land?"

The man raised his head. Hewey knew at first glance that he was sick. His face had a gray look. The eyes were dull. In a weak voice the man said, "Thank God you've come along. We need help."

"You'll sure need help if C. C. Tarpley finds you here."

The young sheepman pointed toward the wagon. "My little boy, he's awful sick. I'm afraid we'll lose him. My wife's not much better."

"What's the matter with them?"

"I think we got ahold of some bad water."

Hewey said, "I don't know as I can be any help. I ain't no doctor. You need to get your family to town."

"But I can't leave the sheep. They're all we've got. They'd scatter, and the coyotes would get a lot of them."

Hewey did some mental calculation. At the rate the sheep were traveling, it would

309

probably take three, perhaps four days to reach Upton City. He wondered if these people had that much time.

He said, "I'll go take a look at your wife and boy. But like I said, I ain't no doctor." He pushed Biscuit into a lope and overtook the wagon. A young woman held the leather reins. Like her husband, she appeared to be asleep. When she turned her gaze to Hewey, her eyes were dull, her skin sallow.

Hewey said, "He tells me you got a sick boy in that wagon."

"Terrible sick," she said, her voice so quiet that Hewey barely heard it.

Riding alongside, he lifted a loose corner of the tarp. Inside, on blankets, lay a boy with eyes closed. He could have been asleep, or even unconscious.

The man had followed Hewey, but the old horse was slow in catching up. He asked, "What do you think?"

"I think you've got some mighty sick people. You need to leave the sheep and get these folks to Doc Hankins as quick as you can."

"I told you, the sheep are all we've got."

There was a saying in cow country that the only thing dumber than a sheep was the man who owned them. This man was proving the point, Hewey thought.

310

He said, "Well, then, you'd better speed them up."

"You can't hurry sheep."

Hewey shrugged, fresh out of arguments. "Well, when I get to town I'll tell Doc Hankins. Maybe he can ride out in his buggy and meet you."

He moved ahead, coughing from the dust raised by the sheep. It would take at least the first two drinks just to wash his throat clean.

Even after he had traveled half a mile, he could still hear the bleating. He could not understand the thinking of a man willing to gamble three lives on a flock of sheep. If they were his, he could easily ride off and leave them to take their chances with the coyotes. Cattle did not have to be pampered and protected like that. Too bad the family did not have a herd of cows instead of a flock of helpless sheep.

He tried to think ahead to the good time he would have in town, but his mind kept drifting back to the woman and to the boy lying in the bed of the wagon. *Dammit, Hewey Calloway,* he thought, *they're not your responsibility. What if you'd taken a different trail to town? You never would have seen them.*

But he *had* seen them. Now he could not

shake free from the images. Cursing his luck, he turned Biscuit around and put him into a trot, back toward the sheep. The woman hardly looked up as Hewey passed the wagon. The man on horseback had dropped behind the flock again. Hewey rode up to him. "Mr. Whatever-your-name-is, hurry yourself up to that wagon. You're goin' to town."

"But the sheep . . ."

"I'll see after the damned sheep. Just leave me that horse and a little grub to pack on him. And see that you make them mules trot."

"Do you know anything about handling sheep?"

"No, but I learn fast. Get goin' before I change my mind. It's half changed already."

In a short time the wagon was rumbling along the trail toward town, the mules stepping high. Confused, the dog followed it a little way, then turned back toward the flock. It looked at Hewey with evident mistrust.

Hewey said, "Dog, I hope you know what you're doin', because I sure don't." He watched the wagon a minute, then turned to stare at the slowly moving flock. He thought about Upton City waiting in vain to welcome him and his wages. But here he was, stuck with a bunch of snot-nosed wool-lies.

Some days, he thought, *I've got no more sense than a one-eyed jackrabbit.* He reserved some of his frustration for the sheepman, who ought not to be dragging a family across this dry desert in the first place.

Biscuit had been trained to be a cow horse. He seemed bewildered by the sheep, but no more so than his owner. Watching, Hewey gradually came to see that he did not need to do much except follow, and occasionally to help the dog push stragglers along. The sheep moved westward at their own pace, like molasses in January.

From the corner of his eye he caught a furtive movement off to the left of the flock. The dog suddenly snapped to attention, then barreled off in pursuit of a coyote. It came back after a time, panting heavily. Blood was drying around its mouth. Coyote blood, Hewey surmised.

In admiration he said, "I wonder what they're feedin' you. I'd like some of it myself."

Late in the afternoon the dog chased down a jackrabbit and ate it. Hewey realized the animal was not being fed at all. It was making its own living. He told the dog, "You ought to be workin' for C. C. Tarpley. At least he feeds good."

He worried about how he would get the sheep to bed down. To his surprise, they did it on their own at dusk, instinctively pulling into a fairly compact band. The dog circled them a couple of times, chastising a few independent-minded ewes that tried to find a sleeping place a little away from the others.

A while after dark Hewey was reminded why sheep tend to bunch up at night. He heard a coyote howl, answered shortly by another. He had always enjoyed listening to coyotes. He regarded them as a natural element in the landscape, helping give this part of the country its unique character. They had never represented any kind of threat to him before. But tonight was different. These sheep were vulnerable, and like it or not, he was responsible for them. He saw the dog listen intently, then trot off to circle the flock. He had staked Biscuit on a long rope to graze. He saddled the horse and moved off after the dog.

He had no gun. If a coyote showed itself, he could do little except run at it with his rope and chase it away. The dog was a weapon in itself. Somewhere ahead, in the darkness, Hewey heard the yipping and snarling that indicated a fight. In a while the dog appeared, acting proud of itself.

Hewey grinned. "Dog, if I ever get in a fight, I want you on my side."

Next morning, while he fixed a meager breakfast of coffee, bacon, and baking powder biscuits, he wondered how he would go about getting the sheep up and off the bed ground. They took care of the problem themselves, rising to their feet and grazing in the dawn's warm light. They began to drift. The dog moved tirelessly, starting them in the right direction. Hewey had little to do but move a few of the lame and lazy, then follow.

Herding sheep ain't as tough as I thought, he told himself. *The dog does most of the work.*

The flock moved no faster than yesterday. At this rate he figured they might reach town by tomorrow evening, or more likely the day after. A cow herd would have made the distance in half the time, a steer herd even less. A determined turtle could leave these sheep behind.

Toward noon, he saw what he had feared most, three cowboys riding toward him from the east. He had not wanted anyone to see him here. He had swamped out a saloon a few times, but never had he sunk so low as to herd sheep. He could only hope

315

these men were all strangers.

He was not that lucky. A tall, lanky rider grinned, a gold tooth shining as he approached. He exclaimed, "Hewey Calloway! When did old C. C. start runnin' sheep? And why ain't you already quit?"

Reluctantly Hewey reached out his hand and shook with Snort Yarnell. With Snort spreading the word, it would not take two days for everyone within seventy-five miles to know about Hewey's disgrace.

One of the cowboys guffawed. "This can't be the Hewey Calloway you've told us about, Snort. He was supposed to be eight feet tall and a ring-tailed tooter. My, how the mighty have fallen."

Resentfully Hewey said, "I'm tryin' to get these sheep off of C. C.'s range as quick as I can. I don't suppose you fellers would like to help me?"

Snort still grinned. "I don't suppose we would. We got our reputations to think of."

Snort had a reputation as a top hand when he was sober but a hell-for-leather carouser when he wasn't. He asked, "Where's the owner at? Did you shoot him?"

"I don't have a gun with me. Besides, you know I can't hit a barn from the inside. I got these sheep on my hands by tryin' to do some sick folks a favor."

He realized they did not believe him. They probably thought C. C. had fired him and he had to accept whatever job came along. It had happened before, but things never became so serious that he was forced to herd sheep.

The laughing cowboy looked to be about twenty, just old enough to think he knew it all and had nothing more to learn. If he didn't stop laughing, Hewey was of a mind to teach him something new.

Stiffly Hewey said, "I've told you how it is. If that's not good enough, you can go soak your head in a water bucket."

Snort shrugged. "No use gettin' on your high horse, Hewey. If that's the best story you've got, stick with it. Me and the boys are headed for town to do somethin' we'll worry about for a month."

Hewey had never seen Snort worry about much of anything. He said, a little enviously, "You-all have a good time."

Snort said, "We'll drink a toast to you, and to your woolly friends."

They rode away, leaving Hewey thinking about going to Canada or someplace where nobody knew him.

He had hoped no word of this would get back to C. C. That hope was dashed now, for Snort had never kept a secret in his life.

The dog seemed finally to accept Hewey. It trotted along at his side when it was not busy bringing errant sheep back into the flock. *At least not everybody will be lookin' down on me,* Hewey thought.

The dog chased after a coyote late in the day and came back exhausted. It laid down in the scant shade of a greasewood bush and panted while the flock moved on. But its sense of duty soon brought it back to Hewey's side.

Hewey said, "If I could ever find a woman as dependable as you, I might get married."

Eve was dependable, but brother Walter was welcome to her. Along with her many good traits, including being a world-beating cook, she carried a few liabilities such as a tendency to burden him with criticism and unsolicited advice.

Hewey did not sleep much that night. He kept hearing coyotes. He imagined them skulking into camp and dragging off helpless lambs. He had heard that coyotes sometimes ate them alive. He kept Biscuit saddled and made several circles around the bedded flock. That seemed to please the dog.

If I ever get this bunch to town, he thought, *I'll never wear wool underwear again.*

He watered the sheep at a dirt tank which

belonged to C. C. He knew the old man would consider the water hopelessly contaminated and unfit for cattle, but even sheep had to drink. The dog plunged in and swam across the tank. On the opposite bank it shook itself, then jumped back in. Hewey considered doing the same, but the sheep had muddied the water too much.

The sun was almost down on the third day when he caught first sight of the stone courthouse and the tallest windmill in Upton City. He realized he would not be able to get the sheep all the way to town before night. He would have to camp one more time. The realization of being so near, yet so far, chapped him like a wet saddle.

He thought about Snort and the fun he must be having. He wished he could run all these sheep over a cliff, but there was not a decent cliff anywhere this side of the Davis Mountains. Be damned if he would drive them that far.

Approaching town the next morning, Hewey loped ahead to the wagonyard to open the gate into a large corral. He saw the stableman walking toward him from the barn and shouted, "Sheep comin' in."

"Been expectin' you," the stableman answered back.

So much for secrecy. *Damn Snort Yarnell,*

he thought.

He knew how to pen difficult cattle, but he had no idea how to go about penning sheep. They approached the open gate with suspicion, a few ewes almost starting in, then running back into the flock. The stableman grabbed a ewe and dragged her through the gate despite her stiff-legged resistance. Several ewes made a tentative move to follow, then the flock surged through like water from a broken dam. Some in their haste bumped heavily against the gate posts. The dog finished the job by pushing a last few reluctant sheep through the opening.

Hewey tied Biscuit to the fence while the stableman closed the gate. He said, "You were lookin' for me?"

The stableman replied, "When those sick folks hit town, they said some cowboy was bringin' in their sheep. They didn't know your name. Then Snort came in, and we all knew Hewey Calloway had turned sheepherder."

"I owe Snort a good cussin' out."

"You won't have any trouble findin' him. He's over yonder under the shed with the two punchers he brought along."

When cowboys came to town they usually slept on cots or on the ground at the wagonyard rather than pay for a room at the boarding house. No one as yet had built a hotel in Upton City.

Hewey asked, "What about the sick folks?"

"Doc Hankins fixed them up pretty good. Says they ought to be able to travel in three or four days."

Hewey walked with the stableman to the open shed where the cots were. The smart-talking young cowboy was leaning against a post, bent over and holding his stomach. The other squatted on the ground, moaning, his eyes glazed. Snort Yarnell sat on the edge of a steel cot, holding his head in both hands. His face was pale as milk.

The stableman said, "They haven't drawn a sober breath since they hit town. Now they're payin' the fiddler."

Hewey found it in himself to feel sorry for Snort, a little.

The stableman said, "If you hadn't got yourself saddled with those sheep, you'd be in the same shape now that Snort is. You're lucky."

"Awful lucky," Hewey said sarcastically, thinking of the good time Snort must have had.

A wizened little man in slouchy clothes and a battered felt hat came walking down from the boarding house. Hewey groaned as he recognized C. C. Tarpley. He said, "I was hopin' he wouldn't hear about these sheep. I reckon I'm fixin' to get fired."

A scowl twisted C. C.'s wrinkled face. He declared, "I thought you were workin' for *me.* What's this I hear about you bringin' those sheep to town?"

Hewey had been trying to decide how best to tell him. He said, "Wasn't nothin' else I could do, C. C. Sick as them folks was, and as slow as they were movin', there's no tellin' how long they might've had their sheep on your land. I was tryin' to get them off of it as fast as I could."

This implied that Hewey was just trying to do the boss a favor. C. C. would appreciate that more than the thought of doing a favor for a sick family. The old man was not often given to doing favors for anybody.

C. C.'s scowl slowly faded as he thought it over. "I never looked at it that way. You done right, Hewey."

Relieved, Hewey said, "All in the line of duty, C. C."

The old rancher started to turn away but paused. "By the way, how long have you been gone from the ranch?"

Hewey counted on his fingers. "This is the fourth day."

"Looks to me like you've had enough

holiday for now. You'd better be gettin' back to work."

Hewey's disappointment went all the way down to his toes. "Yep, reckon I had."

He stood with hands shoved deeply into his pockets as C. C. walked away. The stableman said sympathetically, "There'll be a next time."

Hewey felt the roll of bills he had intended to spend on celebration. He drew them from his pocket and extended them to the stableman, holding back one to buy his dinner. He said, "Those sheep are goin' to need some hay, and that dog deserves a good chunk of beef to chew on. With what's left of this, I wish you'd make sure those folks' wagon has plenty of groceries in it when they leave."

Smiling, the stableman placed a hand on Hewey's shoulder. He said, "You're a better man than you know, Hewey Calloway. Even for a sheepherder."

Hewey grunted. "Don't blab it around. I've got my reputation to think of."

He untied Biscuit and swung into the saddle. "See you in a couple of months. I'll throw a real party next time."

He was already dreading it.

THAT 7X BULL

That old motley-faced bull bellowing his arrogant way up and down the caprock country was about all that was left to show for the sprawling 7X outfit. The 7X had been burned onto his roan-colored hip in the last fall branding before the receivers took over. They sold the rest of the cattle and scattered them all over hell and half of Texas. But nobody ever smeared a loop on old 7X again. His horns were mossy now from age, and his red-flecked hide was scarred from scores of fights which had all ended the same way.

Old 7X was a holdout of the longhorn strain. True, his sire had been a white-faced Hereford brought in to deepen the bodies and shorten the legs of the rangy Texas cattle. But 7X had taken after his mammy, a waspy old outlaw long of horn and leg, short of patience and temper.

I said the bull was *about* all there was left.

Dodge Willingham was still around too. He was on the off side of sixty, spare and dried as a strip of jerked beef. He'd been with the 7X outfit ever since they'd trailed their first longhorn cattle up from the South Texas brush country. There hadn't been any barbed wire then, and a man whose luck played out could still lose his scalp under a bloody Comanche moon.

After the bust-up, Dodge had stayed on with the new Bar J, which had bought out the headquarters division of the 7X.

Dodge and the big bull had a right smart in common. They were both throwbacks to a time that was gone. And they were fighters, the both of them. Every so often an old restlessness got to riding Dodge, like the time in Midland he decided a saloon was too quiet for his taste. He hollered disgustedly, "What is this, a church?" and tipped a table full of cards and poker chips into the players' laps. They beat the whey out of him. Dodge had a wonderful time.

He was an old hand when I first knew him. I was just a raw young kid who wanted to walk in his footsteps, but mostly he acted like he didn't know I was there.

I'll never forget the spring day the Bar J foreman dropped in at our dugout line camp. Ellison Finch was Old Man Johnson's son-in-law. Finch never wanted you to forget who the boss was. He jerked his thumb at Dodge's .30-.30 rifle on its pegs over the door.

"Dodge," he said, "I've took all I'm goin' to from that old red roan bull. He's killed a dozen of my . . . of the ranch's good bulls, and he's chased off plenty of others. He's sired more scrawny wild calves than me and you could both count. Now I want you to take that gun and go find him. Spend a week if you got to, but find him. And make almighty sure he's dead before you ride away."

Dodge's pale gray eyes seemed to glisten as he looked up at the gun. His horny fist knotted up hard as a live-oak stump.

"Looky here, Finch," he spoke after a long minute, "old 7X has been around a long time. He ain't got much longer to go. Why don't you just leave him be?"

When he had been an ordinary thirty-a-month cowboy like the rest of us, Finch had stood in awe of Dodge. Now he had married into the order-giving class. He glared a hole through the aging cowpuncher.

"That old bull has outlived his time," Finch said. "He's a nuisance, even a hazard. If you won't kill him, I'll get me somebody that will."

After Finch left, Dodge walked out to the barn to sit and brood. He stayed there till dark, and I knew better than to go bother him. In my own mind I was already grown. But to Dodge Willingham I was still just a button and supposed to keep quiet. Next morning he took the .30-.30 and rode out. About suppertime he was back, his mouth a straight, hard line. He barely spoke a word for a week.

Old 7X was never mentioned again until the fall roundup. The wagon was camped at Comanche Wells on the caprock the day Dodge failed to come in on drive. We went on with the branding and cutting out of long-age cattle to push to the railroad. But all the time we kept looking over our shoulders. Late in the afternoon we saddled fresh horses and started out to search.

We met Dodge walking in, a mile from camp. His clothes were torn and smeared with blood. The side of his face was skinned like he'd slid down a mountain on his ear.

"That old dun stumbled on a slope and broke his neck," he told Finch. "Taken me an hour to work my saddle off of him. I carried it a good ways and left it where I could find it again."

I noticed that Dodge looked at the ground as he talked. He had always been able to stare the devil straight in the eye and spit on him. Something in his voice didn't ring true. I knew. But Finch took Dodge at his word. That is, till we got the old puncher back to the wagon and stretched him out on his tarp-covered bedroll. We took the blood-smeared shirt off of him. Finch stared in wonder at Dodge's wound. Anger boiled into his sun-blistered face.

"That gash you've got there . . . I know a horn tip when I see one. Did you shoot that 7X bull like I told you to?"

Dodge knew he was caught. You could tell by the sick look that wiped across his stubbled face.

Finch bent over him, his fingers stuck out stiff as wagon spokes. "I ought to fire you, Dodge. I would, if I didn't know the old man'd raise hell. Now that bull's sired him another crop of mean, scrubby calves. You ought to've shot him. We'll bring him in now. We'll tie a clog to his foot and drag him in if we have to. He'll go to market with the steers and wind up as sausage. Before it's over, you'll wish you'd killed him."

Anybody else would just send another cowboy out to kill the bull and say nothing more. But Finch wanted Dodge to know who the boss was.

Dodge didn't seem to be worried much. I

guess he knew the old outlaw too well. "I jumped 7X up there close to the bluffs," he told us later. "I thought I'd run him off away from the drive so nobody would see him. But before I could hardly move, he'd rammed a horn right through that dun. I like to've not got away from there myself."

Even then you could hear the pride in Dodge's voice. "What I mean, boys, he's a fighter. Ain't many of us left."

For the next few days Finch would detail a few punchers to go and try to bring old 7X in. The results were always the same. Some of the hands never got close enough to see anything of the bull except his south end going north. Others caught up with him and wished they hadn't. The rest of us went on with the regular roundup work. Finch had taken Dodge out of the saddle and put him to swamping for the wagon cook — washing up the utensils, shagging in the wood.

One day two cowboys came walking in from the bluffs, leading their half-crippled horses. Finch blew up and left camp, talking to himself. When he came back two days later he brought two mean-looking dogs with him.

"Cow dogs," he said, his gloating eyes resting on Dodge.

Dodge snickered. "Old 7X'll tear up them pups like a lobo wolf does a jackrabbit."

Finch shook his head. "You're goin' with us tomorrow, Dodge. I want you to see this."

I felt sorry for Dodge as I watched Finch walk out toward the remuda. Dodge had never seen cow dogs work. I had. I'd repped for the Bar J one time when the Rafter D's had used them to jump outlaw cattle down out of the rough country.

We quartered north from camp next morning and came upon a wild steer we had missed somehow.

"Watch him, Dodge," Finch said. He spoke to the trailing dogs. They went bounding after the steer, faster than a horse could run. It went so quick we hardly saw how it happened. The biggest dog darted in and grabbed the steer's nose with his teeth. Somehow he swung his body between the animal's forelegs. The steer went crashing to the grass-matted ground. He got up and ran again, only to be thrown once more.

For the first time, the confidence began to drain out of Dodge's face. Worry settled into his smoke-gray eyes.

The bluffs and the rough, broken country around them had been old 7X's favorite running grounds ever since his snaky mammy had first stood over him, licking him clean and giving him his first bellyful of warm milk to steady those wobbly legs. There, except for the year he had been a calf, he had showed his heels to cowboys every time they went after him.

Strange tales about him had grown by the dozen. And a bright light always flickered in the eyes of old cowboys like Dodge Willingham as they told those tales around crackling mesquite campfires, or by dancing yellow lamplight in a smoky bunkhouse. Old 7X represented a time when they had been young like us, when a man could still glory in the wildness of the country and all the creatures on it.

We found where the big roan bull had been watering in a low swale which always caught the runoff from the rains. Tracks showed there might be a couple of cows with him. Excitement began to flush Finch's heavy face. His hands kept rubbing his leather chaps as we worked along the edge of the bluffs.

We rode up on one of the cows first. She was a rangy, high-tailed old sister that showed her Hereford blood only in her markings. Her long legs carried her clattering down a slope with the speed of an antelope. One of the cowboys spurred after her. Finch called him back.

"Let her go. It's the bull we want."

Old 7X spotted us first. We saw him break from a small clump of mesquite and take out in a high lope for the broken ground that lay to the south. Whatever else his age might have done, it hadn't slowed his speed.

Finch hollered like a half-grown kid and socked spurs to the sorrel horse he rode. We fell in behind him. Even Dodge, reluctant as he was, stayed right up with the bunch. We didn't get within shouting distance of old 7X till he went sliding down the steep side of a hill, taking a shower of small rocks with him.

Down past the crest of the next hill waited the bluffs. It wasn't but a minute or two till we had old 7X ringed in. The only way out for him was down the face of a cliff. He stood looking at us in anger and contempt, his long tail arched, his horned head proud and high, jerking from one of us to the other. He decided the foolishness had gone on long enough. He lowered that great head and came charging like the locomotive on a Santa Fe freight. Every one of us except Dodge had our ropes down and our cinches hauled up tight. But the sight of that snorting old bull bearing down on us made us forget everything except to get out of his way. We could hear Finch shouting at us, but he didn't sound nearly so mean as that bull.

Old 7X roared through the line and kept going. I wouldn't have given a plugged nickel for anybody's chance of catching him.

But Finch didn't quit. He sicced the dogs after the old roan. They must have run a quarter of a mile before they finally caught up. He slid to a stop and turned to face them, those sharp horns down. He made a quick pass at the smaller of the dogs. I heard the dog yelp as a horn glanced off his lanky rump.

The older dog knew his business. He jumped in and clamped his sharp teeth on 7X's long ear. The bull roared and shook his head violently. The dog had to let go. The bull lunged at him, but the dog scooted out of the way. The younger dog leaped in and tried at 7X's other ear but missed. Then the big dog got hold of the bull's nose. The smaller dog tried again, and this time he grabbed the ear.

Old 7X pitched and bellowed, the dogs staying with him. The two were trying to pull him down, but he was too heavy.

We reined up and watched, hardly knowing whether to believe it or not. Even as 7X fought his hardest, we knew he was licked.

Old Dodge was licked too. Never had I

seen the hopelessness that had sunk into his wind-carved face. I wished I could help him. But what was there a button could say?

Cruel pleasure glowed in Finch's face. His eyes fairly glittered with the pride of doing something nobody else had done.

"For God's sake, Finch," Dodge pleaded, "call them dogs off of him. Ain't you got a drop of human blood left in you?"

"We'll call off the dogs when we get our ropes on that old hellion."

Finch rode in close and dropped a small loop over the outlaw's horns. "Somebody else tie on," he said. "We don't want him bustin' our ropes loose."

Johnny Tisdale dabbed another loop over 7X's horns. A third rider worked around and heeled the bull. They rode off in opposite directions. Stretched out, the old roan fought for balance, then heaved over onto his side with the solid thump of a boulder smacking into mud. The dogs let go. They moved off and faced around to watch, their lank sides heaving, their tongues lolling out.

Finch turned his horse over to another cowboy to keep the rope tight. He swung down, his big Chihuahua spurs jingling. He cut his grinning eyes toward Dodge, then away again. He was taking his time, letting

Dodge get the full benefit of this. Finch walked to a mesquite tree and whittled off a limb to about three feet in length. Notching one end, he tied it to the bull's huge right forefoot with a pigging string.

"Now, old bull," he said, "let's see how you run with this clog on you."

Finch trotted back to his horse. The moment the bull felt the ropes slacken he jumped to his feet, head down in challenge. He tried to paw dirt and felt the clog drag. He shook the foot, but the long stick still hung there.

With a bellow he charged at one of the horses. The first long step shook the heel rope off his hind feet, but two ropes were still fastened around his horns. He tripped on the clog and plunged to the ground. He got up again, shaking his head. It was then that I noticed for the first time that his left eye was gone. He had probably lost it in some bruising battle here among these bluffs.

Old 7X tried to charge again, but the same thing happened to him. Time and again he would get up, hind feet first, and once more the clog would send him crashing down. Finch would let the dogs rush in and grab him to add to the bull's misery.

Feeling humiliated myself, I knew how

this must be affecting Dodge. "Come on, Dodge," I said, pulling my horse around. "What say we go back to the wagon?"

He shook his head, anger building in his eyes.

Old 7X gave up at last, his muscles quivering from fatigue. I expected him to sull, to refuse to move. But that in itself would have been a form of surrender.

Finch said, "All right, boys, let's take him in."

Ropes still on his horns, they started the bull toward the wagon. Every time he faltered, the dogs grabbed at his heels. Every time he tried to run, the clog stopped him. Finch had won.

As we rode in we found the rest of the hands working the day's gather in the plank corrals. The roan bull began to bellow at the sight and sound of the other cattle. Finch and Johnny led him through a gate. Finch pulled up and grinned.

"Here you are, you old scorpion. Next stop's a sausage grinder."

They had to heel him and throw him down again to get the ropes off. Then Finch left him in a tiny pen with a bunch of long-age steers and gave us all plenty to do. The last I saw of old 7X for a while, he was hooking irritably at the unlucky steers that had to share the small space with him. If it weren't for the clog, he would go over that fence like it wasn't there and be back in the bluffs before the dust was well settled.

After we ate supper, we went to the corrals to brand the calves dropped since the last roundup. Catching my breath while waiting for a heeler to drag up another calf, I sighted Dodge slipping around behind the corral where old 7X was. The bull had quieted down and stood beside the plank fence. I saw Dodge look around quickly, then take a knife out of his pocket, kneel down and reach under the bottom plank. In a moment he came bowlegging it back, satisfaction in his grizzled face.

After the branding, Finch sent most of the hands out to push the herd far back on to the south end of the ranch. That way the freshly worked cattle weren't so apt to get caught again in the next few days' gather. Most of the outfit gone, Finch walked to the small corral where 7X was. "Turn him out in the trap with the steers," he said. "He ain't a-goin' to do much with that clog on him."

Johnny Tisdale opened the gate to let the steers out of the little pen into a bigger one. Old 7X waited until the rest of the cattle were out before he budged. Then, with resignation, he moved slowly toward the gate.

Suddenly he stopped and shook his right forefoot. The clog was gone. He stood there as if he was trying to puzzle the thing out. Then he shook that great head, lowered it, and came on the run.

Finch just had time to let out a startled yelp and hit the fence. He climbed it three planks at a time. The rest of us weren't far behind him. I glimpsed Dodge standing off to one side, laughing fit to bust. The bull made a beeline for the outside gate. He tried to jump it but splintered the top two planks like matchsticks.

Our horses were tied outside, up and down the fence. At the sight of that monster of a bull bearing down on them they snorted in panic and popped bridle reins right and left. In seconds every horse was loose, and every one of us was left afoot. Unable to move, we just stood there and watched while old 7X headed for the bluff country in a high lope.

A mule skinner would have blushed if he could have seen Finch tear the hat from his head and stomp on it and could have heard the things Finch said. When he finally ran out of cusswords in English and had used up the few Spanish ones he knew, Finch walked over and picked up the clog. Anybody could tell it had been cut. He stomped out of the pen, his raging eyes fixed on Dodge. His fists were knotted, his jaws bulging out.

"You damned old reprobate, you'll wish you'd left this country ten years ago!"

Dodge didn't back away. When I saw Finch was going to hit him, I stepped between them. I was getting mad myself. "Better take a dally on that temper, Finch," I said. "Lay a hand on Dodge and you'll have to whip me too."

Dodge caught my shoulder and roughly pushed me aside. "Keep out of it, button!"

My feelings were hurt by the old man's rebuff. Finch's eyes brimmed with fury. "You're fired, the both of you, and I don't care what Old Man Johnson says about it. Either I'm the boss here or I ain't."

Dodge just shrugged. "I'd done decided to quit anyhow. This is no place for a *man* to work."

We stayed there that night because it was too late to leave the wagon. All Dodge would say to me was, "You sure ripped your britches, boy."

Next morning we watched the hands rope their horses out of the remuda. Finch was taking about half the crew to the bluffs. He swore he was going to get that bull today and get him alive. He stopped for one last dig at Dodge.

"He won't get away this time. We'll use the dogs again. And once we catch him, he'll tame down quick. I'm goin' to take the pride out of him." He pulled out his knife, holding it up for Dodge to see.

Dodge brought up his gnarled fist and drove it into Finch's face. A trickle of blood worked down from Finch's nose. Dodge crouched to do it again, but I caught his arm. Finch brought up his fists, looking first at Dodge and then at me. He turned around, climbed into the saddle, and led out in a stiff trot, his back arrow straight.

We watched the riders move away as daylight fanned out across the rolling short-grass country. Dodge saddled his horse, jerking at the cinch harder than was necessary. Finished, he led him toward the chuckwagon. Grim purpose came into his face as he wrapped the reins around a mesquite limb a proper distance from the cookfire. He reached up into the wagonbed and pulled out a rifle that the cook kept there.

The cook's jaw sagged. "Good God, Dodge, they'll hang you!"

The same thought had hit me, and the pit of my stomach was like ice.

340

Dodge shook his head. "I ain't after Finch. He ain't worth what it'd cost me." Sadness settled over him. "Looks like old 7X has finally got to go. But he deserves better than what Finch'll give him. At least he ought to be allowed to die respectable." He turned to me. "Comin', boy?"

Dodge swung into the saddle and spurred out in the lead, rifle across his lap. We skirted east a ways, to be out of sight of Finch and the other punchers. Then we moved into an easy lope and held it. After a while we knew we were ahead, for even in anger Finch would keep his horses in a sensible trot to save their strength.

When we got to the bluffs we climbed up high and looked behind us. We saw no sign of Finch. That gave us a little time to find old 7X first. We needed it. It took us the better part of an hour before we finally saw the old patriarch trying to hide himself in a clump of mesquite brush. We eased down toward him, our horses alert, their ears poking forward like pointing fingers. Seeing that we had spotted him, 7X bolted out of the thicket, popping brush like a buffalo stampede. But there was a bad limp to his right forefoot.

"Damned clog done that to him," Dodge muttered. He spurred up. The bull saw he

341

couldn't outrun us, and he faced around. He tossed his head.

Dodge's Adam's apple worked up and down as he levered a cartridge into the chamber. He raised the rifle to his shoulder, held it there a moment, then slowly let it down. His hands trembled.

"I can't do it. I'd sooner put a bullet in Finch."

Right then old 7X decided to fight his way out. He charged. Dodge whipped the rifle up, but panic had grabbed his horse. The big gray boogered to one side, and Dodge tumbled out of the saddle. The rifle roared. The bullet exploded a brown puff of dust from the ground.

My heart was in my mouth; 7X was almost upon Dodge, and there wasn't any place for the old puncher to jump. I spurred up beside Dodge and grabbed at his shoulders. In desperation he dug his fingers into my leg, trying to pull up beside me. I managed to swing my horse around to protect Dodge. But 7X's huge head plowed into my dun's haunches. The horse fell.

I landed on top of Dodge. We both jumped to our feet, but we were too late to grab the bridle reins. My horse ran away. We stood there with our backs to the steep bluff. Not a solitary thing could we see to grab onto or a place to climb.

As old 7X whirled around to fasten his good eye upon us, I saw Dodge's rifle lying in the dust. So scared I could hardly breathe, I grabbed it. Somehow I managed to lever another cartridge into place as the great roan bull bellowed and came at us.

There wasn't time to aim. I jammed the rifle butt to my shoulder and squeezed the trigger, my teeth biting halfway through my lip. Old 7X went down on his knees. The bullet had glanced off just above the right eye. He staggered to his feet again. He stood shaking that huge head in pain. Blood trickled down from the wound.

Dodge saw the trouble as soon as I did. "By George, that blood has blinded him."

Hearing Dodge's voice, the bull stopped shaking his head. In one last wild charge, he lunged blindly at the sound of the man he hated. We jumped out of his way, and he kept running.

At the edge it seemed he stopped dead still for a second. Then he was gone, plunging down off the sheer face of the bluff. I heard Dodge gasp. From below came the crashing sound of impact.

It took us a while to catch our boogered horses and work our way down to the base of the bluff. We found the mossy-horned old bull lying there just as he had landed. Life was gone from the battle-scarred body. I saw the glistening in Dodge's gray eyes. The old puncher knelt and traced with his finger the dim outline of an ancient 7X brand on the roan hip.

"I put that brand there myself, a long time ago." He was silent a while, remembering. "But times change, and things that won't change have got to go. Old 7X and me, we stayed beyond our day." He straightened and gazed a long while across the rolling short-grass country to the south of us, the old 7X range. "He went out in a way that was fittin' to him. He fought every last step of it."

I held my silence as long as I could. "We better be movin' on, Dodge. Finch'll be along directly."

Dodge squatted stiffly on his spurred heels and began rolling a cigarette, making it plain he was going to wait. "Old 7X left here a-fightin'. So will I."

"But you don't really think you can whip Finch, do you?"

Dodge shrugged. "I'll never know till I try." He turned up his tough old face and glanced at me with that brimstone look in his eyes. "If it turns out *I* can't whip him, I expect *you're* man enough to."

I knew then that I wasn't just a button anymore.

MAN ON THE WAGON TONGUE

One of the first things Hall Jernigan did after he joined the West Texas wagon crew of old Major Steward's M Bar outfit was to develop a strong dislike for Coley Dawes.

The reason? Well, it wasn't anything a man would be proud to admit, but the dislike was real, chafing like chapped skin rubbing against a saddle. Maybe the main thing was just that Coley Dawes was there, and his presence was an affront to a man of Hall's upbringing. Besides, Coley was just too blamed good at everything.

In the six weeks Hall had been with the wagon crew, he had seen Coley ride any number of pitching broncs, and he hadn't seen him thrown but once.

What really got Hall's hackles up was the morning when a bronc in his own string threw him off twice. Old Major March Steward rode up scowling as Hall swayed gasping to his feet the second time.

"Coley," the major said crisply, "you get up there and top off that bronc for the boy, will you?"

The word *boy* had done it, for Hall was a grown man and proud to say so. But the breath was gone from him, and the only protest he could make was a wild waving of his arms. Coley rode that bronc and made it look easy. When Coley got down from the saddle, the fight was out of the horse. It was *Hall* who wanted to fight. But there was the old major, sitting yonder on his horse and looking fierce as an eagle perched over a baby lamb. A glance at those sharp eyes and that graying beard made Hall choke down whatever he had started to say. It wasn't fittin' for a boss to put somebody else on a man's bronc that way and shame him. But the major was running a cow outfit, not a school in range etiquette. The roundup wouldn't wait for some cowpuncher who couldn't stay on. Some of those old mossyhorns like Major Steward were a lot more interested in getting cattle worked than in sparing some cowboy's wounded pride. Cowboys came cheap.

Coley handed Hall the reins and stepped back without a word. But try as he might, Coley couldn't keep the smile out of his eyes. He had been proud to do something the white man couldn't.

For Coley's skin was as black as a moonless night in May.

Maybe one reason Hall had held his silence so long was that the other cowboys accepted Coley and rode alongside him as if he were the same as the rest of them. The only time you could tell his color meant anything was around the wagon at night, and at mealtime. Coley always toted his bedroll out to the edge of camp, a little apart from the others. Come mealtime, he waited till last to take his plate, and he always sat on the wagon tongue, to himself. Nobody had ever told him he had to, and likely no one would have said anything to him if he hadn't. But he had spent his boyhood in slavery. He would carry the mark of that, even to the grave. He remembered, and he presumed little.

The way the other cowboys told it to Hall, Coley had been a lanky, half-starved kid of maybe fifteen when the war ended. The Yankees had told him he was free, but they must have meant just free to starve. Nobody wanted him. Nobody had a home for him, or any work. One day Major Steward had come across the ragged, pathetic button and had felt compassion. Steward was a little lank himself in those days, just beginning to build what was later to become a huge herd of cattle. But he picked up the boy and found something for him to do. With the major's coaching and his own natural ability, Coley had made himself a first-class cowboy. Many Negroes did, in those days.

When you came right down to it, maybe that was what rankled Hall Jernigan the most. Hall had learned his cowboying the hard way. His diploma had been several scars, a couple of knocked-down knuckles and a broken leg that had almost but not quite healed back straight. All this, before he was twenty-three. And here was Coley Dawes, several years older with no visible scars of the trade. Coley could ride, and he could rope. Up to now Hall hadn't found a thing he could do that Coley couldn't do just a little better.

It wasn't fittin'. Broke though he was, Hall made up his mind he was going to ask for his time and leave this haywire outfit.

He caught the old major by the branding-iron fire, watching the irons turn a searing red. Scowling, Steward drew his thick fingers down through his ragged, dusty beard. "It's on account of Coley Dawes, I reckon. I been seein' it come on. Coley don't mean you any harm."

"Mean it or not, he's done it."

349

"Leave now and you're admittin' he's the better man."

Hotly Hall said, "I'm admittin' no such-of-a-thing."

"Aren't you?" The major's eyebrows drew down, and his eyes seemed to burn a hole through Hall. When Steward stared like that, most men started looking for something to get behind. "The only thing you've got against Coley is his color, ain't that right? If he was white like the rest of us, you'd pass it over and not get the ringtail just because he's better than you."

Hall clenched his fist. "I ain't said he's better . . ." He broke off, knowing that indirectly he had. The major had a way of cutting through the foliage and getting right to the trunk.

Hall shrugged, somehow wanting to explain. "I reckon it's just that I never did have no use for his kind. I growed up in Georgia. The rich plantation people called us 'poor white trash.' We never owned no slaves, never hoped to. War came, mostly on account of the slaves. Rich landowners up the road had a hundred of them, and my pa had to go to war to try and keep them from losin' their darkeys. Them rich plantation folks sat at home while Pa went and got hisself killed. There was seven of us kids, me

350

the oldest, and just Ma to try and feed us. We like to've starved. Them rich folks up the road, they never gave us so much as a fat shoat. Just sat there and held those slaves till the end, till old Sherman come. All that misery on account of them slaves. That's why I never had no use for a black man. They've caused too much misery. When I see one, I remember Pa, and all them hungry days."

Major Steward nodded. "Looks to me like you misplaced your hatred. Those slaves, they were caught in the middle same as you."

Hall shrugged. "If it hadn't been for them, there wouldn't of been no war. I can't help how I feel. I'd be obliged if you'd just pay me and let me ride on."

The major shook his head. "If you'll remember, I got you out of jail. I paid your fine and loaned you money to buy a new outfit. You haven't worked here long enough yet to pay out."

Hall swore. It hadn't been fair, that deal in town. They'd been cheating him at poker, and he had called their hand at it. Seemed like the law sided the gamblers, though, especially the one who had lost three teeth to Hall's hard fist.

"All right," Hall said reluctantly, "I'll stay

long enough to get even. Till then, Major, I'll thank you to keep that Coley out of my way."

So Hall stayed on, and Coley Dawes gave him plenty of room. It bothered Hall sometimes, the way most of the cowboys associated freely with Coley, talking, joshing, acting almost as if he were white. But there was always that color mark: when mealtime came, Coley sat alone on the wagon tongue.

Bye and bye the outfit had put a steer herd together, something like fifteen hundred of them. From somewhere east came a pair of buyers with a whole trail outfit of cowboys, ready to push the steers up the trail to Kansas. Hall Jernigan was at the wagon the day the final tally had been finished and the buyers paid off the major in cold cash. They had brought it with them in a canvas bag. With the bunch of cowboys they had along, nobody would have dared try to take it. Hall got to wondering what the major was going to do with all that cash.

He didn't have to wonder long. That night the major called him over to the cook's fire. Steward was sipping a cup of coffee, and he made silent sign for Hall to do likewise.

"Hall," he said, "I got a special job for you. From what I heard in town about that fight that put you in jail, you're a right peart scrapper. And the boys tell me you're a crack shot."

Hall shrugged. "I can shoot some," he admitted.

"Most of these cowhands I got couldn't hit a barn from the inside. Dangerous, them even carryin' a gun around."

Hall sipped the steaming coffee and nodded agreement. Cowboys and loaded guns had always bothered him.

The major said, "I got a lot of cash on hand, and I need to get it to the bank in Fort Worth. Generally I take it myself, and nobody's ever had the nerve to try and steal it from me. But this time I got so much cow work left that I can't go. Got to send it with somebody I can trust."

Hall felt a glow of pride. "Thanks for the compliment."

"Don't thank me till I tell you about the rest of the job. I always take a man with me on my money trips. Even send him by himself when there's not much of it and I figure there's no risk. He knows all the ropes, but I wouldn't call him a fighter."

"I'll take care of him for you."

Major Steward brought his gaze down level with Hall's eyes. "You'd better. I'm talkin about Coley Dawes."

"Coley?" Hall stiffened. "You mean you'd

353

ask me to ride with that darkey all the way to Fort Worth?" He threw out his coffee and stomped around the fire a couple of times, face clouded as if the major had asked him to spit on the Confederate flag. "Hell no! Git yourself somebody else!"

"Got nobody else I'd send. I'll cancel out whatever you still owe me, Hall. Even give you fifty dollars extra bonus to fetch that money clear through to Fort Worth."

Fifty dollars! Hall paused to reflect. For that much he would almost shake hands with General Sherman.

Sharply he said, "Seems to me you're puttin' a heap of trust in Coley. How do you know he won't take your money someday and just run off with it?"

"First place, he's too simple and honest. The thought probably never would enter his head. Second place, what could he do with it? Anybody would know he had no business with that kind of money. He couldn't spend it."

"How do you know I won't take your money and run with it?"

A twinkle of humor flickered in the rancher's eyes, one of the few Hall had seen in all the weeks he had worked here. "Same reason. You've got too much of a cowhand look about you. Anybody could tell you

354

couldn't have come by that much money honest."

Hall flinched. He had asked for that, and he had gotten it.

Hall hadn't accepted, but the major plowed right on as if assuming there was no doubt about it. "One more thing: Coley knows his way around, so he's boss on this trip. You do what he says."

"Me, take orders from Coley?" It was unheard of, a thing like that.

"You'll do what he says or you'll answer to me."

Hall stalked off talking under his breath. The things a man would submit to, just to get out of debt.

The stars were still out crystal-sharp when Hall Jernigan and Coley Dawes finished breakfast and headed eastward away from the chuckwagon. Old Major Steward had taken Hall off to one side and had spoken quietly. "Coley would die before he'd let anybody get hold of them saddlebags. It's your job to see he don't have to."

From the beginning Hall had made it clear he didn't care to do any jawing with Coley's kind, so Coley quietly hung back and didn't say a word. Hall thought perhaps the Negro was riding along asleep, but when he looked back he saw the man's eyes thoughtfully appraising him. It wasn't hard to guess what was running through Coley's mind, for a quiet resentment showed plain and open.

Hall turned back, shrugging. Didn't make any difference, he told himself, what the likes of Coley thought of him.

They rode along silently hour after hour, and the quiet began to get on Hall's nerves. He had thought, before they started, that Coley would probably wear a man's ear down to a nub with useless talk. But the only time Coley opened his mouth was to spit out a little dust. Time came when Hall wanted to loosen up and talk a little. He would turn in the saddle and try to start a conversation. All he got was a coldly polite "Yes, sir," or "No, sir," to his questions.

Patience wearing thin, Hall finally growled, "Well, don't just hang back there behind me. We're not a couple of Indians that we got to go single file."

Coley's teeth flashed in a momentary smile, then he caught himself and forced the smile away. The smile somehow brought up fresh anger in Hall. Suddenly he lost his wish for talk. Coley had won again. He always did, seemed like.

They jogged along in a steady trot all that day. A while before sundown they stopped to cook a little supper. That done, they moved on and didn't stop till dark. Hall had kept a good watch all day and hadn't seen sign of anybody or anything suspicious. But when you carried enough money to start a new bank with, it didn't pay to advertise.

They didn't see anything notable the second day, either. In the afternoon they turned into a well-worn wagon road that meandered in a more or less easterly direction. "This here trail," Coley volunteered, "will take us to Fort Worth bye and bye."

That was almost the only thing the Negro had said, the whole two days. Hall had given up trying to lure him into conversation. Hall came to realize that Coley had a strong pride, and Hall had injured it.

What does he think he is, Hall thought angrily, *a white man?*

Late in the afternoon Coley reined his horse off the trail. "Settlement up yonder a little ways," he said. "The major and me, we always cuts out around it when we got money with us. Major says most folks down there is honest, and he don't want to be givin' them no temptation that might cause them to stray."

Hall pulled his horse to a stop and eyed the trail speculatively. "Settlement, you say? Bound to have some drinkin' whisky there,

357

ain't they?" When Coley nodded, Hall rubbed his hand across his mouth. "By George, I got a thirst that would kill a mule."

"Mister Hall, we can't do that. We got to go on."

"It's comin' night. We go to stop some place. We ain't seen no signs of trouble and I don't think we're goin' to. I'm thirsty."

Worry was in Coley's eyes. "Mister Hall, I know how you feels about me and all, and I know you don't favor my complexion none. But the Major he done give us a job. We got to go to Fort Worth." Coley's argument only firmed Hall's intentions.

"You can go to Fort Worth . . . even to hell if it suits you. I'm goin' to the settlement."

He touched spurs to his horse and rode on down the trail toward the settlement. He didn't look back to see what Coley was doing, but in a minute or two he heard the sound of Coley's horse, following.

It wasn't much of a settlement, just a rude scattering of log and picket houses and a few small frame buildings. Whole place probably couldn't roust out seventy-five people. Hall picked what was plainly a small saloon and stepped down in front of it. Looking back, he caught the sharp disapproval in Coley's eyes. It only strengthened his own resolve.

"You comin' in, Coley?"

"Them folks don't want me in there."

"Then I'll bring you a bottle. They won't mind you sittin' here on the front porch."

Coley's back was stiff. "I don't want no bottle. I reckon I'll just sit here and wait till you're ready to go."

It was a typical small-settlement saloon, one kerosene lamp giving it what little light it had. There obviously wasn't a broom on the premises, and the rough pine bar would leave splinters in a man if he dragged his arm across it. The whisky was made to match. It tasted bad as kerosene, but it had a jolt like the shod hoof of a Missouri mule. Hall paid twice what the bottle was worth and took it back to sit down at a table that rocked unevenly when he touched it. Each drink seemed to taste better than the one before it. Under the whisky's rough glow he began losing the sense of degradation that had pressed down on him ever since he had left the major's chuckwagon. This would show them, he told himself defiantly. They might make him ride with a Negro, but they couldn't make him take orders from one.

He had been in the place an hour or more

when he became aware of rough voices out front.

"Turn around here to the light so we can see you, boy," someone was saying. Then, "You was right, Hob, it *is* the major's old pet Coley. What you doin' here, Coley? The old man must be around someplace, ain't he?"

Coley's voice was strained. "Mister Good, I ain't wantin' no trouble."

"We ain't fixin' to give you none, Coley. But seein' you reminds us that a couple of cattle buyers was through here a few days ago with a bunch of cowboys on their way to get some stock off the major. And it strikes us that the only time you're ever away from the ranch is when you and the old man are a-carryin' money to the bank. So you tell us where he's at, Coley. Us boys want to pay him our respects."

"The major ain't here, and there ain't no money," Coley lied. "I done quit workin' for the major."

"Quit? A pet dog don't quit its master. And that's all you are — just a pet dog. Quit lyin' and tell us where the major's at. Tell us or we'll take the double of a rope to you."

Hall was suddenly cold sober. He pushed to his feet, knocking the bottle over. It rolled off the table, and whisky gurgled out into the sawdust at his feet. Pistol in his hand, he pushed through the door and shoved the muzzle against the back of the nearest man's neck.

A startled gust of breath went out of the man at the touch of cold metal. Hall said, "You boys lookin' for trouble, you better come talk to me. Take your hands off of Coley before I do somethin' my conscience will plague me for."

The two men jerked away from Coley as if he had suddenly turned hot. Hall said, "Coley, you get on your horse."

Coley wasted no time. Hall's voice was brittle as he faced the pair. "Now, was there anything else you-all wanted to say?"

Neither man spoke. Hall said, "Next time you-all go to jump somebody, see if you've got the guts to take on a white man. Now git!"

They got. Hall swung into the saddle. "Coley, I think it's time we moseyed."

Coley nodded. "Yes, sir, Mister Hall. High time."

They left town in a walk, for Hall didn't want to appear in a hurry. Out of sight, they spurred into a lope and held it awhile. When he felt his horse tiring, Hall pulled him down to a trot.

"Who were they, Coley?"

"They ain't no friends of the major, I'll guarantee you that. They're the Good brothers, and there sure ain't much good about them. Used to work for the major till he found out they was stealin' every maverick they could get a rope on. Major ran them off — said they was lucky he didn't just go and hang them." His face twisted in worry. "They'll be trailin' after us, I reckon. They smell a skunk in the woodpile, sure as sin."

Hall looked at Coley's bulging saddlebags, and shame came galling him. "My fault, Coley. I oughtn't to've gone to the settlement. Mostly I just did it to show I wasn't takin' no orders from you."

Coley shrugged. "Ain't no use shuttin' the barn door after the milk's spilt. If it's all the same to you, I think we better keep a-ridin'."

Hall said, "You're the boss."

They rode until at least midnight. They didn't even build a fire for coffee, for neither man doubted that the Good brothers were somewhere behind them. Knowing as much as they already did, the Goods would have to be stupid not to figure out the rest.

Hall and Coley were up and riding again by daylight. With luck, Hall figured, they might reach Fort Worth by night. Maybe with the long night's ride they had gotten a strong lead on the Goods anyway. He and

Coley kept a sharp eye on the trail, both behind them and ahead. Once Coley, turning in the saddle, pulled up and said, "Mister Hall, behind us!"

Hall stopped and looked. "Nothin' back there, Coley."

"I'd of swore, Mister Hall . . ."

They waited a little but saw nothing. There wasn't even enough breeze to wave the grass. Coley admitted, "I could've been wrong. I reckon. I'm still a mite skittish." Hall nodded, somehow satisfied. This, then, was *his* department. This was one place, at least, where the Negro couldn't outshine him.

Riding, Hall could see tension wearing on Coley. The dark man's eyes were wide, the whites showing more than Hall had ever seen. Again Coley called out, "Mister Hall . . ."

But when Hall turned, Coley was looking uphill and shaking his head. "Nothin'. Guess I didn't see nothin'. For a minute I'd of swore . . ."

A bullet snarled past Hall's face and thudded into the grass. A second later he heard the sharp slap of a rifleshot and saw powdersmoke rise from behind a bush up the hill. Automatically he brought his pistol up and fired an answering wild shot that didn't hit within twenty feet of target.

"Ride, Coley!" he shouted.

Spurring, he dropped the six-shooter back into its holster and pulled his saddlegun out of its scabbard beneath his leg. Ahead of him, Coley Dawes was leaning well forward and putting heels to his horse. Scared to death, Hall thought. The ground seemed to fly by beneath. Looking back over his shoulder, Hall could see a rider come out from behind the brush and spur into pursuit.

There were two of them, Hall thought. *Where's the other one at?*

Ahead of him he saw a dead tree. He slid his horse to a stop, jumped down, leaned the rifle barrel over the fork of the tree and took aim. As the rifle roared, the pursuing horse went head over heels, and its rider rolled in the grass.

Afoot, Hall thought, he can't hurt us much.

Coley had slowed up and was waiting for him. Hall re-mounted and caught up. "Real peart shootin'," Coley said.

"You just have to know your business, is all," Hall said as they rode on. "But we got no time to be a-pattin' ourselves on the back. There's still another one someplace."

No sooner had he spoken than he felt his

own horse jerk under the impact of a bullet. Instinctively Hall kicked his feet out of the stirrups. He felt himself hurled forward, rifle in his hands. He slid on rough ground, his clothes ripping, the dead limb of a mesquite gashing his hide. But he was up again instantly, crouching, his anxious gaze sweeping the skyline. He saw smoke in a thicket ahead. He raised the saddlegun and triggered a shot in that direction. An answering bullet whined by him.

At least now I know where he's at. And he can't get out of that thicket without me gettin' a lick at him.

"Coley," Hall shouted, "you take that money and get the hell out of here!"

Coley had pulled his horse up behind a big mesquite and was bending low, watching the thicket. "I can't just ride off and leave you here alone, Mister Hall, with two of them white trash a-shootin' at you."

"I got one afoot and one bottled up. Long's I'm here they can't go after you. Now git yourself gone."

"But Mister Hall . . ."

"Damn it, Coley, I got you into this, and I'm gettin' you out. Ride now before I nail your hide to the fence!"

Reluctantly Coley rode away. To cover him, Hall kept firing into the thicket. Coley got away clean.

Well, Hall thought, *Coley won't stop now till he's got clear to Fort Worth.*

For the first time, he looked back to where the first robber's horse had fallen. He could see the dead horse, but not the man.

Slippin' up on me. Hall knew he had to shift himself to a more advantageous position. Here he had a cutbank to protect him against fire from the man in the thicket, but his back was exposed. He looked toward his dead horse and wished he had the extra cartridges that were in his saddlebags. But to get them he would have to go out into the open, and maybe roll that horse over as well. No matter, he had another two or three shots left in the rifle. After that, there was still the six-shooter.

All he had to do was stall the pair around till dark. By then Coley should reach Fort Worth. And in the darkness Hall could steal away unseen.

The only thing he dreaded was the long walk. Ahead of him he could see a gully, where hillside runoff water had cut into the grass and soil and eroded an outlet. In that gully he could have protection from both front and rear. Moreover, weeds had grown up on either side, which would help hide him from view without keeping him from watching what the two robbers were up to.

He lay still, studying the ground a minute, estimating how long it would take him to run to the gully. A few seconds should do it. He took a firm grip on the saddlegun, steadied himself, then broke into the open.

He almost made it to the gully. Then a bullet cut through his leg, and he went sprawling. He tried desperately to push himself to his feet, but the leg wouldn't hold him. Another bullet thumped into the grass ahead of him. Suddenly his mouth was dry and his heart was racing.

He hadn't seriously thought they could hit him while he was running. But they had. Behind him he could hear a man afoot, moving fast. The robber whose horse he had killed was closing in on him. Just ahead of him was a mesquite tree. Water had cut around the base of it, leaving a pile of drift on the offside which might give him some protection from the man behind him. The tree itself would shield him from the man in the thicket. Hall turned and fired a quick shot at the man who was trying to close with him. The man dove into the protection that Hall had abandoned only seconds before. That gave Hall time to crawl to the tree.

He quickly found the protection here was not so good as it had appeared. The drift was deep enough to protect him only so long as he kept his head down. The moment he raised his head to take a shot, he was exposed to the man behind him. This way he had lost any advantage he might once have had over the man in the thicket.

Despair swept over him now as he realized he was boxed. All the man behind him had to do was fire to keep Hall's head down while the outlaw in the thicket calmly took his time and came out. He would be able to come up and put a bullet in Hall while Hall lay helpless, waiting for it.

It didn't take the two robbers long to figure this out, either. The one behind began firing sporadically at Hall's hiding place. The slugs thudded into the soft earth and showered Hall with dirt. Hall would raise up slightly and answer occasionally with a shot of his own, but he knew all the advantage was with the outlaws.

It wouldn't be long before they decided to close in and kill him, for they knew Coley was getting away.

The man behind waved his hat. That, Hall knew, was a signal. In a moment Hall heard hoofbeats. A horse was coming out of the thicket and running toward him. Hall carefully brought up the rifle. They might get him, but they wouldn't do it cheap. . . .

A bullet smacked into the earth at Hall's face, showering him with sand, half blinding him. He snapped a shot at the man behind him and realized with sick heart that he had missed.

He knew he had just a moment left to live, but that moment was long enough for him to know the sick feeling of desperation and the cold hand of remorse. If he hadn't been so all-fired resentful of Coley . . . If he hadn't gone to that settlement . . .

The man behind him jumped up and came running, firing as he moved. Hall heard the hoofs pounding harder, coming from the thicket. He blinked the sand from his eyes and pushed up on one leg, knowing this would give the horseman a chance at him but knowing too that it was the only way he could get a clear shot at the man afoot.

He heard a man scream, and almost at the same time he heard a rifle shot from somewhere uphill. Then he had his bead, and he squeezed the trigger. He saw the outlaw in his sights drop to his knees. The man braced himself on one hand and tried to level the pistol he held. Hall levered another cartridge into the breech and fired again. The man went down hard that time, down to stay.

Hall spun around, hearing the horse almost upon him.

The horse was there, all right. It passed him and kept running, its saddle empty. The rider from the thicket lay out there in the grass, his legs twitching, one arm twisted crazily beneath him. Down the hill came another rider, rifle in hand.

Coley Dawes.

Coley caught the outlaw's horse and took Hall to a ranch house he knew of. He left him there while he rode on to Fort Worth with the major's money. He stopped by briefly again on his way back to the Steward ranch, but Hall didn't get to talk to him. Right about then, Hall's fever was at its highest, and there wasn't any talk in him. A couple of weeks later Hall rode up to the major's chuckwagon just at dinnertime and unsaddled. He limped over to the wagon and took a plate. He glimpsed Coley Dawes. As always, Coley sat alone, on the wagon tongue.

Hall got himself some beef and beans and stopped in front of Coley. Coley looked up with a grin. "Welcome back, Mister Hall. How's the leg?"

"Mendin' fair to middlin'. Ain't goin' to lose it." He frowned. "Coley, you never did say why you came back that day. You was

370

supposed to keep runnin'."

"I couldn't just go off and leave you in that kind of a fix. I hid the money and went back to see could I help."

"I'm sure tickled you did. But you never did tell me you could shoot like that."

"I don't recollect as you ever asked me. You didn't like it 'cause I could ride and rope. Figured you'd sure disappreciate it if you was to find out I could shoot, too."

"Coley, from now on I won't care what you beat me at."

Humor sparkled in Coley's eyes. "Care to try me some evenin' on a little hand of poker?"

Hall chuckled. He looked at the long wagon tongue and at the Negro who sat on it, all alone.

"Move over, Coley," he said, "and make a little room for me."

ABOUT THE AUTHOR

Elmer Kelton (1926–2009) was the seven-time Spur Award-winning author of more than forty novels, including the Texas Rangers series, the Hewey Calloway series, and the Buckalew Family series. He was also the recipient of the Owen Wister Lifetime Achievement award. In addition to his novels, Kelton worked as an agricultural journalist for forty-two years, and served in the infantry in World War II. He passed away in 2009.

The employees of Thorndike Press hope you have enjoyed this Large Print book. All our Thorndike, Wheeler, and Kennebec Large Print titles are designed for easy reading, and all our books are made to last. Other Thorndike Press Large Print books are available at your library, through selected bookstores, or directly from us.

For information about titles, please call:
(800) 223-1244

or visit our website at:
gale.com/thorndike

To share your comments, please write:
Publisher
Thorndike Press
10 Water St., Suite 310
Waterville, ME 04901